LOVE AND VENGEANCE

Love and Literature
Book 2

Aviva Orr

ARE YOU SIGNED UP FOR DRAGONBLADE'S BLOG?

You'll get the latest news and information on exclusive giveaways, exclusive excerpts, coming releases, sales, free books, cover reveals and more.

Check out our complete list of authors, too!

No spam, no junk. That's a promise!

Sign Up Here

www.dragonbladepublishing.com

Dearest Reader;

Thank you for your support of a small press. At Dragonblade Publishing, we strive to bring you the highest quality Historical Romance from some of the best authors in the business. Without your support, there is no 'us', so we sincerely hope you adore these stories and find some new favorite authors along the way.

Happy Reading!

CEO, Dragonblade Publishing

Additional Dragonblade books by Author Aviva Orr

Love and Literature Series
Love and Literature (Book 1)
Love and Vengeance (Book 2)

Epigraph

You remember, I suppose,
How the August sun arose,
And how his face
Woke to trill and carolette
All the cages that were set
About the place.
In the tender morning light
All around lay strange and bright
And still and sweet,
And the gray doves unafraid
Went their morning promenade
Along the street.

—Robert Louis Stevenson, "To Ottilie"

PROLOGUE

Here is the ancient floor,
Footworn and hollowed and thin,
Here was the former door
Where the dead feet walked in.

—Thomas Hardy, "The Self Unseeing"

Dartmoor, Devonshire
Autumn 1866

J ACK BASTIN SAT atop his chestnut mare and peered into the hazy darkness as if searching for a sign of life.

"Dang!" his companion Owen Brandt said. "We've faced some dangerous terrain before, but ain't nothing I ever seen compares to these fogged up, pitch-black wetlands. We'd be better off cast out at sea."

"You've got nothing to worry about," Jack said as they navigated through the white mist that covered the night like an ethereal shroud. "I grew up on this moor."

Brandt leaned forward and patted his steed's muscular neck. "Wouldn't be the first time I relied on you to keep me alive."

"Ain't that the truth." Jack mirrored his partner's accent.

"Now you're sounding more like the cowboy I know." Brandt chuckled. "But I guess I'll have to get used to you talkin' pretty all the time seein' we're on your territory."

Jack smiled to himself. He'd been born an Englishman, but ten turbulent years in Texas and the American West had taught him to develop a chameleon's skin. He'd learned to play the part of cowboy, vigilante, gambler, businessman, and gentleman to perfection.

"I see something up ahead." Jack straightened his back and pointed at a flicker of orange. "See that light? It belongs to *Ye Olde Ash Tree Inn*. All we need do is ride toward it."

"What light?" Brandt strained his body forward. "That spark yonder? Looks like a firefly. Are you sure we ain't chasing insects?"

Jack chuckled. "Trust me. Follow the light, and you'll have a fiery whiskey in your belly in no time."

"What are we waitin' for then?" Brandt spurred his horse to a trot.

Within minutes, a whitewashed, granite longhouse emerged out of the mist like some ghostly apparition. A warm glow flickered in two of its mullioned windows, and thin whips of smoke spiraled out chimneys on either side of its thatched roof. In front of the tavern, a row of horses waited for their masters, their reins knotted over a makeshift wood fence, and their feet stamping against the cold. They whinnied and flicked their tails as if to welcome the newcomers that approached.

"I'll be damned!" Brandt said. "This looks mighty inviting."

Jack halted his mare and gazed at the building. "Never thought I'd see the likes of this place again."

"Let's get inside." Brandt dismounted his horse. "It's too dang cold out here."

A swing of light brought forth a scruffy stable boy carrying a lantern.

Jack handed over the reins. "Fill up a bucket of water for these critters and give them some hay too."

"Aye, sir." The boy held out his grubby palm, and Jack pressed a coin into it. He glanced at the row of horses. "Make sure none of them go without water or food, you hear?" He dropped another coin into the boy's hand.

The child nodded.

"Come on." Jack slapped Brandt on the back. "Let's get you that whiskey."

Voices merry with drink filled the fire-lit tavern, and a swift glance across the room told Jack time had stood still. The building and its occupants were as he remembered them ten years earlier. Two fireplaces carved into the granite walls at both ends of the room provided a shadowy light, and local farmers seated on small wooden stools around roughly carved tables basked in their warmth. A hush fell over the room as Jack and Brandt strode to the bar. Jack knew the locals weren't used to strangers and certainly not a couple of Americans dressed like cowboys. They'd be suspicious and wary, but Jack didn't care. As long as nobody recognized him as the lad who'd run from this moor years ago.

"Howdy." Jack tipped his cowboy hat at the publican—a stout, bristly-haired man he recognized as Amos Adamson, who'd owned the tavern since Jack's boyhood. He tossed a silver coin on the table. "Two whiskeys."

Adamson nodded, placed two glasses down, and filled them. "Where be ye to this time of night? T'ain't safe out on the moor after dark."

Jack shrugged and took a long swallow of his drink. "We're both good horsemen."

The publican nodded. "Still, plenty good riders fall afoul of bogs. There be rooms upstairs. Ye'd best keep safe an' stay the night."

Jack doffed his hat at the publican. "Appreciate the advice."

"Ye be a long way from home." Adamson looked from Jack to Brandt. "What be ye wantin' in these parts?"

"We're lookin' for someone," Brandt said.

"Maybe I can help. Lived here all me life."

"A vicar. Goes by the name Greyson."

"Reverend Greyson?" Adamson's shaggy brows rose in surprise. "Why, ee's been dead six years back."

Jack's stomach lurched. He'd expected as much, but it still felt like a knife in his gut.

"Why be ye wantin' him?"

"A friend asked us to deliver him a message," Brandt said.

Adamson cocked his head. "What friend be that?"

Jack ignored the man's query. "How did he die?" he asked flatly.

"Of a broken heart, to be sure." The publican's plump wife looked up from wiping a spill on the counter. "Poor man suffered some black times—lost ee's missus an' little girl in days of each other." She rested a hand on her hip and stared above Jack's head as if seeing the past play out behind him. "Still, the good vicar never missed a service. Then one day ee's boy ran off, an' later, he got word the lad drowned at sea." She shook her head. "He never recovered from that sorrow. Ee's boy was trouble, but the vicar cherished him all the same."

Jack's throat closed. He took another swallow of whiskey.

"Be thee well?" Mrs. Adamson leaned forward and peered at Jack.

"Just tired from the long journey. Another drink will do me right. Brandy this time—double."

"I'll stick with whiskey," Brandt said.

The publican poured the drinks, and Jack tossed another coin on the table.

Mrs. Adamson scooped it up. "Been in these parts 'afore, 'ave ye?" She eyed Jack.

"Don't be daft woman," the publican grunted. "They be Americans."

Jack swallowed his brandy and motioned for another round. "Did the poor vicar die alone?"

"No, thank the good Lord. Had ee's daughter to care for him until the end, he did. Poor maid! Her was alone after the reverend died. But the new vicar, bless his soul, took pity, an' put her to work."

"Doing what?" Hope quickened Jack's pulse.

"Governess to ee's young uns. Her was a quiet, learned young thing. Always sitting atop some tor with her nose deep in a book."

Jack leaned forward on the bar. "Why do you speak of her in the past tense? Did she go somewhere?"

"The new vicar only served us a year afore the fire. He was a young man, Reverend Paddon, with a young family. Full of energy and love for the parish, he was. An' us was glad to have him. But a year after he come—*poof!*" She mimicked an explosion with her arms.

"I don't understand. Did the Greyson girl die in a fire?" Jack struggled to keep the urgency from his voice.

"Some folks swear her was gone from the vicar's afore the fire, but I knowed different."

"What do you mean?" Jack asked.

"That same week, I heard the vicar's wife in the apothecary cryin' up a storm. Her young uns was taken ill with the fever, see, an' the new governess was delayed. Mrs. Paddon didn't know how her was to cope alone with two young uns sick. So, I said to ask Miss Greyson to stay 'til the new governess come." Mrs. Adamson sniffed and blinked as if to stay tears. "I promised to send our Betty round to help if Miss Greyson wouldn't stay." The woman's chin trembled. "I almost sent our girl to her grave."

Jack closed his eyes. "But you didn't, because of course, Miss Greyson agreed to stay and nurse the children."

"Thank the good Lord." She shook her head. "I'm sorry fer Miss Greyson, I am. But I thank the Lord fer sparing our Betty."

A bitter taste crept into Jack's throat. "What caused the fire?"

"Fallen candle. It happened late at night when all was asleep." She twisted her cleaning rag. "I only hope them good folks didn't suffer. They never will rebuild the parsonage. The land is cursed, folks say."

"Don't talk rubbish, woman!" Adamson interjected.

"T'ain't the land that's cursed. 'Tis them Greysons." An emaciated, stringy-haired man slid into the seat next to Jack.

"What?" Jack said through gritted teeth.

"Them Greysons. Part devil if ye ask me."

"Shut yourn trap, Jeb Fowler," Adamson said. "Ye got no business talkin' ill of the good vicar. He were a God-fearin' man."

"I ain't speakin' ill of the vicar." Jeb smirked, revealing a row of stained teeth. "I'm talkin' about ee's spawn, sprung from tha' Londoner he wed."

Black anger rose in Jack's chest. He squeezed the empty glass in his hand.

"Ye be drunk. 'Tis time to git thee home," Adamson growled.

"I tell ye," Jeb said, ignoring the publican's warning, "the good Reverend Paddon was mistaken when he took pity on that Greyson witch. But he were saintly, so he let the Greyson curse inside."

"Stop yourn evil talk!" Mrs. Adamson said. "I remember the vicar's young uns. Lambs, they was."

"Devils!" Jeb snarled. "Specially tha' no-good boy. Broke me uncle's nose unprovoked an' stole ee's horse, he did."

"T'was well-deserved as I remember it," Adamson said. "Yourn uncle, God rest ee's soul, were a brute, an' the Greyson boy did right tryin' to stop him from beatin' that poor pony 'alf dead."

Jack smiled. He'd knocked that damn fool flat on his back and set the pony free. The poor thing couldn't get away fast enough.

"The vicar's missus let them young uns run wild," Jeb muttered. "Never took proper care like a good mother should. Unnatural, I tell ye."

Jack's hand moved instinctively to his holster hidden beneath his jacket. But Brandt caught hold of his wrist.

"The vicar tried to set his boy straight, but he were always gettin' into scrapes an' causin' the vicar grief," Jeb continued his tirade.

Jack's hand moved from his holster and closed around the base of his glass. The urge to beat the self-satisfied and smug expression off Jeb's face threatened to swallow him.

"It be a blessing them Greysons be dead an' buried."

"Now, don't ye talk ill of the dead in me tavern. I'm warnin' thee, Jeb Fowler." Mr. Adamson waggled a finger at Jeb.

"Good riddance to them Greysons, I say." Jeb spat on the floor.

Fury blinded Jack as he lifted the glass in his hand and brought it down on Jeb's head. The man fell off his barstool and dropped to the ground, but his lips continued to move as he shouted for help. Jack pounced on him and slammed his fist into Jeb's face. But Jeb's mouth kept moving. Determined to shut him up, he brought his fist down again and again. Voices shouted in the distance, but Jack could not stop. Brandt's voice grew louder, and someone tried to pull him back, but rage blinded and deafened him. He kept hitting until blackness overcame him.

CHAPTER ONE

And sometimes ladies hit exceeding hard,
And fans turn into falchions in fair hands,
And why and wherefore no one understands.

—Byron, "Don Juan", Canto 1

Ten months later
London, July 1867

OTTILIE HAMILTON STIFLED a yawn and forced herself to smile at the elderly gentleman standing before her. "I am terribly sorry, Lord Towne, but I seem to have overstrained my feet tonight. I will be retiring early. Lady Hudsyn and I were about to ask Lord Hudsyn to escort us home."

"I'm sorry to hear it, Miss Hamilton. I hoped to have the pleasure of dancing with you. Your aunt has sung your praises, and this is the first ball I have seen you attend this year."

"I'm afraid I only arrived in London from Canterbury a few days ago, and I am still exhausted from my journey. But I am certain we will get a chance to dance together in the near future," Ottilie lied. She did not intend to frequent society balls during her holiday or participate in her aunt's scheme to marry her off to someone old enough to be her grandfather.

"I do hope so, Miss Hamilton." Lord Towne bowed and

exchanged a glance with Lady Hudsyn before retreating as if she possessed the power of divine intervention and could force Ottilie to acquiesce.

As soon as the gentleman strolled out of earshot, Lady Hudsyn turned to admonish her niece. "Your behavior was uncivil. Society has certain expectations of a lady, and tired feet do not provide sufficient reason for rebuffing a gentleman. It's unacceptable."

"I know, Aunt, and that is why I am grateful not to be part of society. To think a lady must dance whether she feels like it not just to spare a gentleman's feelings strikes me as absurd."

Lady Hudsyn glared at Ottilie. "I do wish you would consider your age, dear. At six-and-twenty, your beauty will not last forever."

"I *do* consider it, which is why I claimed my independence long ago and have little interest in dancing with Lord Towne, who is nearing fifty."

"Lord Towne is a baron with an estate and a fortune to his name."

Ottilie sighed. "I don't need a fortune, Aunt. As I have told you, I am happy with the life I have chosen for myself."

Lady Hudsyn compressed her lips as she often did to express her grave disapproval. "Well, you'd best find my son. We must leave posthaste, or Lord Towne will realize what a little liar you are."

"Good idea," Ottilie said, ignoring her aunt's dig. "I haven't seen Henry since he escorted us here, and he promised to introduce me to the notorious Mr. Bastin. It's the only reason I agreed to attend this ball—and the delicious food, of course."

"The writer?" Lady Hudsyn spat out the word *writer* as if it left an acrid taste in her mouth.

"Yes." Ottilie craned her neck in search of her cousin.

"How did my son come to know such a man? And what is he doing here?" Lady Hudsyn frowned. "I am not sure I approve. Mr. Bastin has the reputation of being a rapscallion."

"And a rather handsome one at that," Ottilie said as she caught sight of her cousin standing next to a well-built gentleman who she recognized to be Jack Bastin. Fame had made the writer easily identifiable. Since bursting onto the literary scene with the publication of his controversial novel, *The Renegade*, it seemed nothing was written about him without making mention of his dangerously handsome and brooding countenance. And now Ottilie could see the depictions weren't exaggerated. His angular face sported sculpted cheekbones, a Roman nose, and full lips. These delectable features were complemented by a head of tousled dark hair, which rested on his shirt collar and grew into long sideburns on his jawline.

Mr. Bastin appeared to be in deep conversation with a middle-aged woman who looked fetching in a dark-green silk gown. And Henry conversed with a distinguished silver-haired gentleman standing beside her.

"Do you see him?" Lady Hudsyn asked.

"He's over there."

Lady Hudsyn turned her head to follow Ottilie's gaze. Her height allowed her a clear view of her son without the need to crane her neck.

"Who is he talking to?" Ottilie asked.

"Lord Enwick," her aunt said with a hint of approval. "Lady Enwick is next to him in the green dress, talking to that handsome young man. Who is he, I wonder?"

"That is Mr. Bastin. I recognize him from his likeness printed in the newspapers."

"Oh." Lady Hudsyn curled her lip.

"Shall we go?" Ottilie stepped forward, but her aunt caught hold of her arm. "I do hate to disrupt Henry's evening. Are you certain you won't change your mind and take a turn on the dance floor with Lord Towne, Ottilie dear?" Lady Hudsyn raised her eyebrows in a questioning manner.

"Don't judge me, Aunt. It is not you who has been pestered to death and expected to dance all night without having a moment to yourself."

"If only the privilege were mine again." She frowned at Ottilie. "What a strange creature you are! Any girl would be grateful to have a full dance card. Stubborn, just like your mother."

"I know, Aunt." Ottilie smiled. "Now, do come along. I am anxious to meet the infamous Mr. Bastin."

"I don't like this one bit," Lady Hudsyn said as she followed Ottilie.

Ottilie ignored her aunt's protests and continued to move toward her cousin. As they neared him, Lady Hudsyn stopped her once again.

"Wait until there is a break in his conversation. That is the polite thing to do."

"I know, Aunt. I wasn't planning to—" Ottilie's words were cut short when someone bumped Lady Hudsyn from behind and sent her reeling forward.

"By Jove!" Ottilie caught hold of her aunt, preventing her fall.

"Wench!" A shrill scream ripped through the air.

Ottilie and Lady Hudsyn froze simultaneously, and a hush fell over the room. The guests turned and gaped at the hostess, Madame Baudelaire, as she roared like an injured lioness and hurled a glass in the direction of Lady Enwick.

EVERY FIBER IN Jack Bastin's body sprang to attention as he focused on the object flying toward his companion. Energy surged through his veins, and he dove into action, grabbing Lady Enwick by the arm and dragging her to safety. The crystal bounced once on the parquetry floor before it shattered, sending splinters of glass and blood-red port up onto Lord Enwick's expensive trousers. A collective gasp rippled through the ballroom. The orchestra skidded to a stop, and dancers froze mid-step.

"What in the devil?" Lord Enwick jiggled each of his legs as if he could fling off the offending stains as he would clinging beetles.

Jack looked up from the mess on the floor and Lord Enwick's spoiled trousers to see his lover glaring at Lady Enwick. He inhaled sharply, recognizing the wrath of jealousy in Madame Baudelaire's countenance as she manifested two vicious claws out of her hands and flew at Lady Enwick, who cringed and squealed like a trapped mouse.

Jack moved to stop the harpy, but Lord Enwick must have had the same idea because he stepped into Jack's path. "Get a hold of yourself, Madame!"

"Villain!" Madame Baudelaire sunk her nails into Lord Enwick's fleshy jowls.

Jack watched in stunned silence as Lord Enwick stumbled back in a bewildered daze, his cheeks a mess of red streaks.

"George!" Lady Enwick flew to her husband's side.

"M-my word!" Lord Enwick stammered. "The woman is completely mad!"

Jack's temper flared. She'd been drinking again, dammit! The situation called for drastic measures. He had to stop her before she killed someone. He stepped forward; Madame Baudelaire took the bait and lunged for him. With one expert flick of his wrist, Jack lightly cuffed his opponent's neck, and she dropped like a dead man into his arms. Another collective cry ripped through the crowd, and Jack prayed that no one in the audience recognized the defensive strike he'd used to incapacitate a lady of high society.

"Don't be alarmed," Jack told the bystanders as he laid Madame Baudelaire on the floor. "She has merely fainted and will soon recover." He took off his jacket, folded it, and placed it under her head. Looking at his lover's now-peaceful face, he seethed inwardly.

What is wrong with you, Madame?

He'd witnessed prostitutes using their fingernails to inflict injury and engage in brawls, but he'd never expected a woman of high society to behave in such a manner. She knew the rules. Hadn't he been clear from the beginning? He didn't want a wife or a relationship of any kind. Moreover, she'd sought him out, characterized her husband as an overweight bore, and declared she wanted some fun.

"Smelling salts!" someone shouted. "Fetch the smelling salts."

Jack glanced up to see the squat figure of Monsieur Baudelaire wading through the crowd, followed by his mother-in-law and a host of servants.

Hurry up, Monsieur! Jack muttered to himself and hoped the puffing steam engine running toward him wouldn't have heart failure before reaching his wife.

When the family approached, Jack stepped back, eager to distance himself from the scene. The servants fluttered around their mistress like a flock of confused birds until someone placed a sack of smelling salts under Madame Baudelaire's nose. Seconds later, she opened her eyes and clutched her chest with both hands, coughing and sputtering as though she'd been strangled. Jack exhaled, releasing the tension from his body.

Thank heavens, she's not hurt.

Whispers filled the ballroom as Madame Baudelaire recovered her breath and fell sobbing into her mother's arms.

"No need to worry. She's quite well now," Monsieur Baudelaire reassured his guests. while dabbing the sweat from his brow.

"Look here, sir! What are you all about?" Lord Enwick stepped forward, blotting the blood from his cheeks with his handkerchief. "That woman is plain as day mad! If she hadn't fainted from hysteria, she would have cleaved Mr. Bastin in half with her claws."

Jack eased back two steps, hoping to disappear into the crowd unnoticed, but Lord Enwick turned to him.

"Am I right, sir?"

Jack shrugged. "She seemed a little unbalanced."

"Unbalanced!" Lord Enwick bellowed. "She is gripped by

hysteria. She belongs in the likes of Bedlam!"

"I am terribly sorry." Monsieur Baudelaire shifted his focus from Lord Enwick to Jack. "She has not been herself since we left France." He gave a helpless shrug. "It is as though a demon has taken possession of her in this country. I must remove her from England at once and take her back to her homeland."

Excellent idea, Jack thought.

"I should think so!" Lord Enwick barked. "If I so much as encounter your wife across the street, I will see to it she is locked away."

"No need for extreme measures!" Monsieur Baudelaire held up his fleshy hands in a defensive gesture. "We have excellent doctors in Paris."

Lord Enwick snorted his disapproval and turned back to comfort his wife.

Monsieur Baudelaire turned to his guests with a forced smile. "Please, continue. I am sorry for the interruption." He looked toward the band. "Play on!" He gestured wildly with his hands. "Play on!"

The band resumed its playing, but the onlookers failed to dissipate.

Jack inched back, hoping to finally make his escape. Instead, hands rested on each of his shoulders and a voice murmured in his ear, "What would Monsieur Baudelaire say if he knew the name of his wife's demon?"

Jack smiled. He didn't have to turn around to know the voice belonged to his friend, Lord Hudsyn.

"You are slipping, Bastin," Hudsyn said, stepping forward to face Jack. "This little liaison has gotten out of control. And now it seems you have your very own Lady Caroline Lamb to contend with. Gentlemen will start keeping a sharp eye on their wives when you're about."

"I can see that." Jack glanced around the room, now a wall of bent heads and low whispers, punctuated only by furtive glances in his direction. "I think it is time for me to leave."

"Let's give it a few minutes, so it doesn't look like you're a guilty man slinking away to hide. Then, at the risk of my reputation, I'll walk you out," Hudsyn offered.

CHAPTER TWO

My days of love are over; me no more
The charms of maid, wife, and still less of widow,
Can make the fool of which they made before—
In short, I must not lead the life I did do

—Byron, "Don Juan", Canto 1

"**S**HAMEFUL!" LADY HUDSYN repeated the sentiment for the tenth time as if shock had stripped her of her vocabulary. She, like the rest of the spectators, seemed rooted to the spot, unable to carry on with the evening's festivities despite the drama ending and the music resuming.

"I quite agree," Lady Witley chimed as she scooted in next to Lady Hudsyn. "It is disgraceful, indeed. Never in all my life have I seen such a despicable public display of emotions. An English Lady would die before engaging in such antics."

"I feel sorry for her." Miss Clara Witley popped up next to Ottilie and interrupted her mother's tirade. "It is rumored that Mr. Bastin—" she paused and lowered her voice before continuing—"seduced Madame Baudelaire and made her fall in love with him."

Lady Hudsyn inhaled sharply.

"Do not speak of such sordid things. I forbid it!" Lady Witley admonished her daughter.

"Everyone is talking about it, Mama!"

"They certainly are not! And neither shall you." Lady Witley opened her pocket fan and cooled her beet-red face.

"It's true!" Miss Witley turned to Ottilie for support. "You've heard the talk, haven't you, Miss Hamilton?"

"I don't know what you mean." Ottilie played ignorant.

"The rumors about Mr. Bastin and how he—you know," Miss Witley urged.

"I'm sorry to disappoint you, but I haven't heard any such thing. I only arrived in London a few days ago."

"But your cousin is his friend, so you must know something—more than I, at least," she pressed.

"Lord Hudsyn and Mr. Bastin are not friends," Lady Hudsyn snapped. "They are merely acquaintances."

Ottilie peered across the way to where her cousin stood. Mr. Bastin and Henry were huddled together, and the two appeared to be engaged in deep.

"They look to be very close acquaintances," Miss Witley murmured under her breath. "I am certain you can learn all sorts of interesting details from your cousin," she continued to whisper so only Ottilie could hear her.

She smiled. Only seventeen, Miss Witley was the same age as many of Ottilie's students; while she understood the girl's curiosity and desire for excitement, she knew better than to indulge her whims. "Sorry to disappoint you again, but Lord Hudsyn doesn't engage in gossip, and you will do well not to, either."

"I only seek your opinion on the matter." Miss Witley's voice was laced with dejection.

Ottilie glanced at the girl's downcast face and flushed cheeks. The poor child needed to escape her mother's clutches and socialize with young ladies her own age. But she'd likely be bargained off into a marriage arranged by her mama before she'd even had a chance to grow into herself.

"I don't mind sharing my opinion with you," Ottilie relented.

"Oh?" Miss Witley's countenance brightened. "Tell me." She inched closer to Ottilie as if the two were best friends, and Ottilie's heart went out to her again. Young ladies her age belonged in school, not on the marriage market.

Ottilie linked arms with Miss Witley and whispered. "I think it probably wouldn't take much for a man like Mr. Bastin to make a woman fall in love with him."

"I agree." Miss Witley's voice grew wistful. "Look at him. He's as beautiful as Adonis."

She makes a good point. Ottilie peered at Mr. Bastin. *The man does look like a Greek god. No doubt he had the power to seduce Madame Baudelaire and many other women besides.*

As though he felt her stare, Mr. Bastin looked up and met Ottilie's gaze. His dark eyes traveled from her face down the length of her body and slowly up again.

Ottilie's skin tingled with pleasure, and she stiffened in an attempt to control the sensation.

"I do believe he is staring at you," Miss Witley said.

"Who?" Ottilie played ignorant and attempted to suppress the quiver in her voice.

"Mr. Bastin."

A nervous laugh escaped Ottilie's throat. "Nonsense! Why would he be looking at me?"

"Perhaps he thinks you're beautiful." Miss Witley sighed. "I don't know. But I do wish he'd fix those lovely eyes on me."

"My dear." Lady Hudsyn came up behind Ottilie and clutched her elbow. "Will you fetch your cousin? I should like to go home now."

"Of course, Aunt. Do you need to sit down?"

"Yes, I think I will. No need to accompany me." She waved Ottilie away like one would a pestering fly. "Just go and fetch Lord Hudsyn. I'll be waiting in the sitting room."

"May I accompany you, Miss Hamilton?" Miss Witley pleaded. "I would so love an introduction to Mr. Bastin."

"You most certainly may not accompany her!" Lady Witley

snapped before Ottilie could reply.

"Why not, Mama? He is a famous writer. I only want to meet him."

"Come along, dear," Lady Witley said. "I do believe you have some dances left on your card."

"But Mama—"

"At once!" Lady Witley arched her eyebrows at her daughter.

Miss Witley pushed her lips into a pout and followed her mother.

Ottilie spun around and made her way toward Henry, only to discover both he and Mr. Bastin had disappeared. She scanned the ballroom but saw no sign of either man. Henry would not leave without her and her aunt, but perhaps he'd accompanied Mr. Bastin to his carriage. No doubt, Mr. Bastin would want to make his escape as soon as possible. But should she follow them or wait for Henry to return? Violet, her dearest friend and the founder of Canterbury Ladies' College, would never forgive her if she let the great Jack Bastin slip away without at least a mention of the college. Yet, it seemed ridiculous to ask the writer for a favor now. He might mistake her for one of those obsessed female admirers of his—and that was the last impression she wished to give of herself.

"Go home and get some rest." Hudsyn patted Jack on the back. "That was not a scene which wants repeating. The gossips and papers will be full of it tomorrow."

Jack breathed in the crisp night air. He could not deny that the incident with Madame Baudelaire had left him shaken. *Attacking Lady Enwick in a jealous rage? Sheer madness.*

He massaged his forehead. "I need to take a short walk to clear my mind," he told Hudsyn. "Then I think I'll go to my club. I don't have calm enough for sleep."

"Have you gone mad, Bastin? You'd best get in your carriage

and ride away, or the she-devil might come after you again." Hudsyn glanced over his shoulder as if he expected Madam Baudelaire to come hurtling out the front door like a wild cat.

Jack tugged at his cravat, loosening its grip on his throat. "I don't think so. She's in the care of her family now, and they won't risk letting her out of their sight."

"Let us hope not." Hudsyn shuddered. "I need to rush back inside and find my mother. She'll be shaken to the core by the events."

"I imagine so," Jack said.

"Stay out of trouble, old fellow. I'll check in on you tomorrow." Hudsyn slapped Jack on the back before dashing up the stairs and disappearing inside the townhome.

Jack set off down Grosvenor Street, deep in thought. Hudsyn spoke the truth. He'd grown careless, and it would not do to further his cause. He slipped his gloved hands into the pockets of his overcoat. His formula for choosing women had always worked in the past, so what went wrong this time? He turned the rules he lived by over in his mind and tried to spot his error:

1. *Choose beautiful women married to wealthy gentlemen whose pride and losses would be too great to prompt a scandal after a liaison ended.*
2. *Choose a woman above the age of six-and-twenty who should have sense and maturity enough not to romanticize a liaison.*
3. *Never say, "I love you."*
4. *Make no promises.*

He'd followed all the rules with Madame Baudelaire. A thirty-year-old, high-born lady, wife to a wealthy French merchant, and the mother of four children, she fit all the requirements. They'd begun their liaison with a clear understanding of each other's situations and intentions. What went wrong? Had he done something to encourage her to fall in love with him? He didn't think so.

Jack crossed Audley Street and continued along Upper Brook Street. He stopped across from a stately townhome that stood dark and uninhabited amidst its lively neighbors. Narrowing his eyes, he blocked his peripheral vision and focused solely on the house. The old scar on his back ached, and he cursed under his breath. He'd allowed Lydia Baudelaire and her incessant need for attention to distract him from his purpose. He hadn't come to London to engage in love affairs—those could be enjoyed anywhere. He'd come for Sir Richard's head.

Where are you hiding, uncle?

The blackguard would return. And when he did, Jack would be waiting. It was time to swear off women and solidify his plans for revenge. Recompense was long overdue.

He turned on his heels and strode back toward Grosvenor, where his carriage waited in front of Madame Baudelaire's rented mansion. He was relieved to be free of her, but how would he ease his restlessness and calm his thoughts without the distraction of a woman? Perhaps he should try writing something new? He ran a hand through his hair. He hadn't written anything of merit since his first novel. The book had catapulted him into instant notoriety and continued to win great acclaim from critics.

"Mr. Bastin spins a dark and oftentimes disturbing tale of human suffering," one critic wrote.

"His work is brutally honest and forces the reader to face man's inherent hypocrisy, immorality, and cruelty," lauded another. Yet another had claimed, *"Bastin's fictional world is not without hope. Friendship, loyalty, and love exist, and they blossom in the darkest of gardens."*

Such were the accolades he'd received, yet he could not understand how he'd managed such an achievement.

Jack rounded the square back to where his carriage stood. "St. James's Street," he instructed the driver before climbing inside.

The coachman flicked the reins, stirring the slow-to-move horses. The animals pawed the ground with their hooves as though waking their legs from a long sleep. Jack leaned back in his seat and returned to his thoughts as he gazed out the window. Light emanating from the street's gas lamps bathed the night in an orange glow.

He hadn't planned to write a novel, nor had he ever fancied himself a writer. Yet, after the shock of discovering that both his father and older sister were dead, he'd been seized with the strongest desire to put quill to paper, and once he started, he could not stop. He'd spent four months holed up in a house in Bristol, writing day and night, often foregoing food and sleep. The words poured from his soul like a great purge, and when he finished, it left him depleted.

At seven-and-twenty, he had nothing left to say.

Jack sighed and rapped on the carriage roof with his walking stick.

Why hadn't the blasted driver departed yet?

He reached for the door, ready to step out and investigate what kept them, when he caught sight of a young woman on the Baudelaires' raised portico, peering into the night as if in search of someone. She wore a red ball gown with a sloping neckline, which exposed her creamy skin and accentuated her voluptuous cleavage. Jack leaned closer to the window. Flaxen ringlets hung in tendrils around her face, and although he could not see the color of her eyes, he knew them to be a brilliant blue. She was the girl he'd seen and enjoyed looking over in the ballroom earlier.

The carriage lurched, and the young lady stepped forward as though she intended to approach the vessel, but it rolled onto the street. Jack pressed his face close to the window, not wanting to lose sight of the beauty. She, too, appeared to be straining so as not to lose sight of him. The horses found their stride, broke into a trot, and pulled the carriage farther away. Jack itched to jump out of the carriage and run back to the square but feared the young lady would disappear if he took his eyes off her. He twisted his body and strained to see out of the rear window, keeping the beauty in sight until she transformed into a hazy red speck in the distance.

"Stop!" he shouted suddenly, but the coach rolled on.

He banged his cane on the rooftop. "Stop!"

The horses came to a sudden halt, and Jack flung open the carriage door.

"Is something the matter, sir?" The driver called as Jack raced down the street on foot.

He didn't stop running until he reached the Baudelaires' townhome. But he arrived too late. No sign of the young lady remained. Perhaps she'd gone inside. Or perhaps she'd never been there at all. Maybe he'd drunk too much port, and she'd been no more than a mirage—a vision of one of Artemis's virgins—a temptation of the mind after he'd sworn off women.

CHAPTER THREE

Her glossy hair was cluster'd o'er a brow
Bright with intelligence, and fair, and smooth.
Her eyebrow's shape was like the aerial bow,
Her cheek all purple with the beam of youth,
Mounting at times to a transparent glow…

—Byron, "Don Juan", Canto 1

A BRINY SMELL filled Jack's nostrils and seeped into his lungs. He opened his eyes and blinked to clear his sight, still hazy with sleep, then widened his gaze to greet an inky river that journeyed across the writing desk on which his head rested.

"Dash it!" He sat up in one swift motion and followed the trail of ink, which ended in a slow, dripping waterfall at his desk's edge. "Dammit!" He jumped out of his seat. Ink soaked the sleeve of his white shirt and stained his forearm and fingers. He unbuttoned his shirt, pulled it off, and threw it over the spill on the floor. Then he remembered what he'd been doing the night before. He surveyed his desk in one frantic swoop and fell on a row of neatly scripted papers set out to dry. They were unscathed by the ink. He allowed himself a single sigh of relief before cursing his stupidity.

Bloody fool! You could have ruined your best work yet.

He wiped his hands with a stained rag kept next to his inkwell and poured himself a glass of whiskey. Swallowing the liquid in one long gulp, he took a moment to embrace its warmth before pouring himself a second drink. Then he gathered his freshly written pages, made himself comfortable on one of the buttoned-leather armchairs in his study, and began to read. Several minutes later, Jack finished reading and smiled. It seemed the daughters of Zeus had favored him again, and now he held the beginnings of a masterpiece in his hands.

Jack sipped his whiskey thoughtfully. It was all thanks to the young lady who'd appeared on the Baudelaires' portico like one of Artemis's virgins. Something about her had awakened his lost urge to put quill to paper and brought forth the words he'd been unable to grasp. After seeing her, they'd pounded on his skull like forgotten inmates of the Bastille. It was no surprise she'd become the subject of his poem—a doomed romance between a goddess protected by Artemis and a mortal poet. Jack clutched the pages, brought them to his mouth, and kissed them.

Not a temptation, but a muse. Whoever she is, she's my muse, and I need to find her. But where to start?

He pushed himself halfway out of his chair and then sat down again. No, he would not go in search of her. He'd sworn off women, and for the first time in months, he felt alive, clear-headed, and energized. He picked at the dried ink on his arm. He smelled like a distillery and itched from the stains on his skin. What he needed was a long soak in a hot tub. Jack sprang out of his chair and trotted down two flights of stairs to the basement. He strode into the kitchen and narrowly missed colliding with Mrs. Wilson, the widowed housekeeper he'd inherited when he'd purchased the townhome.

"Heavens!" she exclaimed, coming to a dead stop in front of Jack's bare chest.

Before he had a chance to explain, the housekeeper scuttled to a far corner of the kitchen, turning every which way and bumping into things as if she'd suddenly lost her sight.

"Slow down, Mrs. Wilson. It is only me," Jack spoke in a

gentle voice. "I am sorry if I gave you a fright."

"Yes." She put her hand on her chest and breathed. "I did not expect you to be—" She blinked and busied herself with moving objects around the kitchen. "Is it breakfast you're wanting?" she asked, still not looking at him. "Cook went to the market, but I can fix something for you if you like."

"No, thank you, Mrs. Wilson. I spilled some ink in my study, and I wondered if you would take care of cleaning it for me. I also need a jug of warm water and a bar of strong soap brought upstairs," Jack said, deciding to spare the woman and forgo the bath.

"Certainly, sir. But you need only ring for me. No need to come all the way down to the kitchen."

"I don't like to send you up and down the stairs unnecessarily."

"Much obliged, sir." The housekeeper gave a little curtsey and scurried to fetch the copper water jug, seemingly grateful to have something to keep her occupied and out the way of Jack's nakedness.

He turned to leave the flustered woman to her business, then stopped and said, "I used my shirt to soak up some of the spilled ink, and I don't think it's salvageable."

"Do you mean to say I should discard your shirt, sir?"

"Yes, that's precisely what I mean." Jack exited the kitchen and trotted up the stairs to the ground floor. As he stepped into the hallway, the knocker sounded at his front door. He hesitated.

"Mrs. Wilson!" He turned to look for the housekeeper.

The knocker sounded again.

"Bugger!" He strode toward the door. "You'd better not be from one of those gossipy newspapers!" He yelled as he yanked open the door.

Then he froze.

It was her—his muse.

⇒⟫⟩⟨⟨⇐

FACING JACK BASTIN'S bare chest, Ottilie inhaled sharply.

"Have you lost all sense of reason, Bastin?" Henry placed his hand over his cousin's eyes. "Where is your shirt?"

"On the floor of my study, stained with ink."

"And your valet?"

"He is away conducting some business for me."

"So, you thought you'd open your front door whilst half-naked? After last night's events, that is not what I would call discreet."

"I had no choice. Mrs. Wilson is otherwise occupied."

Ottilie pulled her cousin's hand from her face. "Really, Henry! I hardly think the sight of Mr. Bastin's chest will turn me to stone." She tried to appear nonchalant, even as heat spread across her cheeks, and her gaze unwittingly traveled from Mr. Bastin's face to his tanned, muscled torso, so different from her own soft curves that it looked as if it had been carved from steel. She marveled at the similarity between this real-life display of masculinity and the sculpted one depicted on the towering statue of Achilles in Hyde Park.

"I apologize for my naked state, but I didn't know you intended to surprise me by bringing a beautiful young lady to my door."

Ottilie dragged her gaze from Mr. Bastin's abdomen to see that a slight grin played on the writer's lips.

"For heaven's sake, Bastin! Step aside and let us in before someone sees you." Henry glanced over his shoulder before placing a hand on Ottilie's elbow and steering her past his friend's nakedness. "You really ought to stop letting your valet come and go as he pleases," Henry said, sounding like the baron he was. "I am starting to get the impression he is the master of this house, not you. At the very least, get him to hire you more staff."

"You know me," Mr. Bastin said, closing the door behind

them. "I don't like the idea of too many servants snooping around and disrupting my peace. Besides, I like my independence. I don't need a servant to help bathe and dress me like a child," he teased. "Speaking of what's proper"—his gaze shifted back to Ottilie— "aren't you going to introduce me to this lovely lady so we may converse freely with one another?"

Henry cleared his throat. "Of course, allow me to introduce my cousin, Miss Ottilie Hamilton."

"Your cousin?" Mr. Bastin said without taking his eyes off Ottilie. "I am honored to meet you, Miss Hamilton."

"The honor is all mine, sir." Ottilie felt as though she had to force the words from her mouth. Up close, the man's beauty was striking and had the effect of rendering one speechless. The only flaw on his face was a short, deep scar near his left eye. But even this, somehow, added rather than detracted from his charm.

Mr. Bastin grinned at Ottilie, and her cheeks heated with the realization she'd let her eyes linger too long on his face. She turned to the house's interior and pretended to be intensely interested in its decor. An elegant swirl of gray and white marble paved the hallway and staircase. Mahogany banisters and matching wall trimmings complemented the marble and added warmth to the room. Identical statues of a bare-chested Aphrodite in a swan-like pose framed the staircase entrance.

"What a charming home you have, Mr. Bastin."

"Thank you, but I cannot take credit for the decor. It is exactly as the previous owner left it. The books and statues are my only contributions."

Ottilie glanced at the two disrobed statues of Aphrodite and suppressed a smile.

A creak sounded on the stairs behind her, and an elderly maid carrying a water jug stepped onto the landing.

"I'll take the water, Mrs. Wilson. You can go up and see to the ink in the study."

The maid gave Jack the copper jug and fished a bar of soap from her apron pocket that she handed to him before continuing up the stairs unencumbered.

Henry cleared his throat. "Shall we wait for you in the parlor, Bastin?"

"Yes, do. Make yourselves comfortable while I rid myself of this ink and put on a fresh shirt."

As he turned and made for the stairs, Ottilie caught sight of a raised scar, running from his right shoulder to his left flank, marring his otherwise perfectly sculpted, muscular back.

"How did he get such an awful scar?" she whispered to Henry as they made their way down the hallway toward the parlor.

"I don't know. He never talks about his past. Whenever I ask, he changes the subject. All I know is he spent several years in America."

"Yes, I read as much in the newspapers. Although, he doesn't have much of an American accent."

"No, he speaks like an English gentleman. He was born and raised here, and I think he puts a great deal of effort into retaining his Englishness because I have heard him utter the odd American-ism here and there."

"Do you think he involved himself in dangerous activities over there?"

Henry showed Ottilie into the parlor. "I doubt it. He is more of a romantic than a rabble-rouser. If you ask me, the wound came from a jealous husband."

Ottilie raised her eyebrows. "What do you mean? Are you saying Mr. Bastin makes a habit of chasing married women?"

"Of course not," Henry said quickly. "But women have a tendency to become obsessed with him—married or not—and those who are married have husbands who don't take kindly to their wives' admiration for another man, even if it is through no fault of his own."

"I imagine so," Ottilie said dryly, thinking that her cousin protested too much to be telling the whole truth. She scanned the masculine room, admiring its tall mahogany bookshelves, well-stocked bar cabinet, and whiskey-colored leather seating.

Henry flopped onto one of the buttoned-leather chairs, and Ottilie strolled to the bookshelves lining the rear wall.

"Is that what happened last night?" She kept her eyes on the books. "Did Madame Baudelaire attack Lady Enwick because she'd become obsessed with Mr. Bastin?"

"Precisely. Madame Baudelaire has been stalking Bastin for months."

"And he never encouraged her?" She glanced at her cousin.

Henry shrugged. "Who knows what Madam Baudelaire views as encouragement? The French have a different way of conducting themselves, as you well know."

"Maybe," Ottilie said. "Although, I suppose I can see how any woman might easily become obsessed with Mr. Bastin. He is devilishly handsome and rather charming."

"Hello again." A smooth, deep voice sounded behind Ottilie, causing goosebumps to rise on her flesh. "I'm pleased to see you've made yourselves comfortable."

She turned to see Mr. Bastin standing in the doorway of the parlor, wearing a clean white shirt, open at the neck and rolled up at the sleeves. He met Ottilie's gaze and flashed her a smile. Her cheeks burned. Had he heard what she'd said?

"Say, Bastin, when you mentioned you had a bit of a run-in with a bottle of ink last night, did you mean you've started writing again?" Henry asked.

Ottilie forgot her embarrassment and rejoined the conversation. "What do you mean by started again? Had you stopped writing?"

"I've been navigating a bit of a dark patch recently, but I had a sudden burst of inspiration last night. And this morning, I awoke at my desk to find the beginnings of a poem written out and a bottle of ink soaking my shirt."

Henry leaned forward in his chair. "Did you say a poem?"

"Not merely a poem, the start of an epic work."

"What came over you last night to bring that on?"

"I can't say exactly." Mr. Bastin glanced at Ottilie, and his eyes twinkled as though they held a delightful secret. "But I think I found a new muse."

A smile tugged at Ottilie's lips, and she turned casually to the bookshelf. Mr. Bastin's charm made it impossible for a person not to feel flattered by his attention. But she didn't want to give the impression of a gushing female admirer. She'd come to secure his services for the ladies' college and needed him to take her seriously.

"Where are these magical pages you composed last night?" Henry asked. "May I see them?"

"All in good time," Mr. Bastin said. "I am not yet finished with them. New inspiration has hit me today."

Ottilie felt his eyes on her back and worked to quash the quivering in her stomach. Inhaling deeply, she squared her shoulders and strolled to the settee. "I hope we aren't keeping you from your work," she said, taking a seat opposite the two gentlemen.

"Not at all. I only wish you'd come sooner. Hudsyn never told me he had such a charming cousin. Where has he been hiding you?"

Ottilie ignored the flirtatious comment. "I live in Canterbury, but I'll be in London for the duration of the summer holidays."

"Summer holidays?" Mr. Bastin cocked his head. "From what?"

"From school."

He laughed. "You look far too grown up to be a schoolgirl and not nearly dowdy enough to be a schoolmistress."

"As a matter of fact, I *am* a teacher at Canterbury Ladies' College." She lifted her chin.

"A ladies' college?" Mr. Bastin raised his eyebrows. "And what do you teach there? Sewing? Piano? Dance? French, perhaps?"

"Mathematics, mostly." She suppressed a smile, secretly delighting in her ability to surprise him.

"Mathematics?" he repeated as if to confirm he'd heard her correctly.

"Our college is an academic institution that provides quality secondary education for women. We don't teach sewing, manners, piano, or dance. But we do have an excellent science and mathematics department. In addition, we have a classics department where our young ladies learn Latin, Greek, and classical literature."

"I'm impressed." Mr. Bastin leaned forward as though genuinely interested. "And does this ladies' college of yours have many students?"

"We had twenty borders and sixty-day students last year. The school has grown steadily since it opened in 1862."

"Fascinating!"

"Why do you sound so surprised? Many women have a strong desire to learn and are interested in a host of subjects. Is it fair that only men should have the pleasure of knowledge?"

"I knew a girl once who sounded exactly like you." Mr. Bastin smiled, but Ottilie detected a hint of sadness in his eyes.

"Did you?" She waited for him to volunteer additional information, but when none came, she broke the silence, saying, "She sounds like someone I would have loved to meet."

"It was a long time ago." He brushed away Ottilie's comment but retained his wistful look.

"It might impress you even more to know that fifteen of our students took local examinations at Cambridge last year." Ottilie steered the conversation back to the college.

"Truly?" Mr. Bastin folded his hands together. "Are women permitted to attend Cambridge nowadays?"

"Of course not!" Henry interjected.

"Unfortunately, Henry is correct," Ottilie said. "Although, we won't stop fighting until women are permitted to earn degrees from Cambridge, Oxford, and every other university open to men."

"A lofty goal indeed."

"It is, but not because women aren't capable. We've already proven that when given the chance, ladies do as well as gentlemen academically."

"How did you manage that?"

"We worked hard to convince Cambridge to allow our students and those from other ladies' colleges to take their local examinations—and they eventually agreed."

"Other ladies' colleges, did you say?"

"Indeed, there are several and the number grows every year. All of which are run and funded by dedicated women."

"And what is the point of these examinations when women cannot attend Cambridge?"

"To prove our capabilities and our worth—as women must, Mr. Bastin."

"And you've managed to do so?"

"Year after year," Ottilie said. "Yet, despite passing their examinations, universities continue to deny women the chance to earn a degree. So, we must persevere. The longer women demonstrate their abilities, the harder it will be for men to lock them out of the universities."

Mr. Bastin leaned back in his chair. "I must say, I'm impressed with what you have told me. Times have changed. It seems I've been absent from England for too long."

"I am glad you approve." Hope rose in Ottilie's chest. *Perhaps Mr. Bastin is impressed enough to agree to lecture at the college.*

"I most certainly approve." He locked his dark eyes on her face, making her heart flutter. "I've always admired educated women."

Ottilie cleared her throat, determined not to become distracted from her purpose. "I am pleased to hear that, Mr. Bastin, because I came here today to ask if you would consider—"

"Bastin!" A man's voice bellowed from within the bowels of the house, ending Ottlie's request mid-sentence.

"Excuse me a moment." Mr. Bastin sprang out of his seat and rushed to the parlor door.

"Bastin! Where the heck are you?"

Ottilie turned to her cousin, utterly bewildered.

Henry folded his arms and shook his head. A wry smirk played on his lips.

"Who is that?" Ottilie mouthed.

"The valet," Henry replied, his voice heavy with scorn.

JACK STUCK HIS head out the door and shouted into the hallway. "Up here, Brandt. I'm in the parlor."

"Do you mean to say your valet is making that racket?" Hudsyn asked.

"He's American. You know as much." Jack turned his attention back to his guests.

"He's a cowboy," Hudsyn clarified, leaning toward his cousin.

"That's right, and a fine one too." Jack checked the irritation that had crept into his voice. He valued his friendship with Hudsyn. The man was an excellent companion and provided him with a solid connection to society, but he was young, and insecurity had made him resentful of Brandt. Hudsyn didn't know the truth about Brandt, but he must have sensed the brotherly bond Jack and the cowboy shared, and it no doubt stung him.

Jack returned to his seat just as Brandt skidded to a halt in the doorway. He'd freed himself of his jacket, vest, and cravat, which Jack knew he hated wearing, and stood before them in a white shirt, open at the neck, with his sandy hair sitting messily on his forehead. Jack took careful note of his friend's appearance, which gave the impression the man had been up all night, and this, together with the urgency in his tone, suggested he'd made strides in his investigation regarding Sir Richard.

Brandt eyed Hudsyn and Ottilie, clearly surprised to see them. "I didn't realize you were entertaining." He straightened his stance and cleared his throat before greeting them with a curt nod and a cautious, "Howdy."

Hudsyn and his cousin returned the greeting with bewildered

smiles.

"Mrs. Wilson should have informed you I had guests when you passed through the kitchen."

"I didn't pass through the kitchen; I came through the front door," Brandt said, and Jack glimpsed Hudsyn and his cousin exchange a look.

"Right, well, no doubt Mrs. Wilson is upstairs mopping up my ink spill."

Brandt's gaze shifted from Jack to Ottilie and then back to Jack. The cowboy grinned.

"I assume you have news for me?" Jack said, irritated Brandt seemed to have guessed his attraction to Ottilie.

"I sure do." An infuriating grin remained on Brandt's lips. "But we can talk later." He flicked his eyes back to Ottilie.

"Certainly, I will oblige you as soon as my guests leave." Jack continued to play the part of master to his valet though his stomach knotted with anticipation to learn Brandt's news. His friend had been entertaining a potential lead privy to vital information about his uncle.

"Take your time," Brandt said before retreating.

"Actually, Bastin, we're leaving right now." Hudsyn stood up abruptly. "I must get my cousin back before my mother returns from her excursion into town. She'll be furious if she finds out we left the house without a chaperone. She insists on holding onto her belief Miss Hamilton will acquiesce and marry before she is relegated a permanent spinster by society."

"Stop it, Henry!" Miss Hamilton sprang to her feet and flicked her cousin lightly on the shoulder.

"Why don't you marry her, Hudsyn?" Jack teased. "It will solve the problem, won't it?"

"I can assure you, Mr. Bastin, my aunt has bigger plans for Lord Hudsyn than his wayward cousin. Besides, I'd have to fight off legions of women." She cupped Henry's jaw in her gloved hand. "Look at those crystal blue eyes, sculpted cheekbones, and that gorgeous cleft chin. Simply divine."

Henry laughed and twisted his chin out of Ottilie's grasp. "All true. But don't forget the most important point—I am only three-and-twenty and intend to remain a bachelor for at least ten more years."

"Wise choice, young man." Jack slapped Hudsyn on the shoulder and turned to address Ottilie. "Miss Hamilton, I am certain your aunt will be successful on your behalf. I have no doubt your beauty will capture many hearts."

She grimaced. "Rest assured, Mr. Bastin, I have no intention of giving up a life of independence for marriage, no matter what my aunt desires."

"You are a woman who knows what she wants. And that is admirable," Jack said.

"Do you know, cousin—" Hudsyn stepped closer to Miss Hamilton—"after the fiasco last night, Mr. Bastin swore to devote himself to his writing and nothing else?"

"Now that is something to be admired," Ottilie said.

Jack heeded the warning in Hudsyn's voice and took a step back. "It's true." He held up his hands, feigning an innocence he did not feel. "I plan to devote myself to my writing—for at least the next—" He paused to think.

"Three months," Hudsyn interjected.

Jack cocked his head. "Do I hear a challenge, Hudsyn? Shall we see which one of us breaks first?"

"Certainly." Hudsyn extended his hand, and Jack shook it firmly.

Miss Hamilton lowered her lashes and directed her smile to the floor.

Jack caught a glimpse of the dimples in each of her cheeks and thought how much he'd like to kiss them.

CHAPTER FOUR

O Pleasure! you are indeed a pleasant thing,
Although one must be damn'd for you, no doubt:

—*Byron, "Don Juan", Canto 1*

"THAT CERTAINLY PROVED interesting," Ottilie said as she and Henry walked home to Berkeley Square from Mr. Bastin's residence on Half Moon Street. "Is that Brandt fellow truly Mr. Bastin's valet?"

Henry shrugged. "Bastin claims he is, but I believe Brandt is more a friend than a valet. I don't know. Perhaps it's the way they do things in America."

"Fascinating," Ottilie said. "I can see why you've chosen Mr. Bastin as your friend. He is an odd combination of talent, charm, and intrigue."

"Don't be sucked in by Bastin's charms," her cousin warned. "He is a wonderful friend, but he would make a terrible husband."

"Really, Henry! Do you take me for a silly little girl? It might do you good to remember I'm three years your senior."

"It's only that I've witnessed first-hand the effect Bastin has on women, and you are wearing the look."

"What look?"

"The dreamy look of a woman smitten."

Ottilie scoffed. "I admit finding the man interesting, but I am far from smitten." Warmth spread across her cheeks, and she turned her face to prevent Henry from seeing her embarrassment. She didn't want him to guess her thoughts—to know her mind had been intermittently wandering to the image of Mr. Bastin's defined, muscular torso. Or that, when she closed her eyes, she traced and retraced his scar in her mind, wondering at its history. Her cheeks grew warm again, and she feigned interest in the pedestrians on Curzon Street.

"Why have you grown quiet?" Henry asked. "Did I say something to upset you? I'm sorry if I did."

"You haven't upset me." Ottilie took a breath and collected herself. "I was thinking"—she turned to face her cousin—"did you notice Mr. Bastin's valet also bears a terrible scar? It runs from the tip of his jaw and curves around his neck."

"Of course, one can hardly ignore a wound of such magnitude on a person's face. Although, I hadn't realized the extent of it until today. The man usually wears a cravat with his collared shirt, so the full scar isn't entirely visible. I wonder how far down his back it goes."

Ottilie frowned. "Don't you find it odd they both carry similar marks on their bodies? These are not the childhood scars one gets from scraping one's knee. They looked more like knife wounds or something even more sinister."

Henry shrugged. "Bastin hardly talks about his life in America. But he lived there during the war, so I imagine life had its difficulties."

"Do you suppose he took part in the American Civil War?"

"An Englishman like Bastin fight in an American war? Never!"

"You're being territorial, cousin. He may have been born an Englishman, and he plays the part well, but he spent a significant portion of his life in America. Surely, he would have been expected to fight. Weren't all able-bodied men forced to join?"

"I believe many paid their way out of service. Bastin must have done. He is too much of a free spirit to be a soldier. He wouldn't do well following orders."

"I think you're right about that."

"It doesn't matter, does it? He's a born Englishman, so he is back where he belongs now."

"Where was he born?"

"Kent, maybe? I'm not sure. I only met the man six months ago. And he doesn't talk about himself much."

"So, you hardly know him?"

"I know he's a brilliant writer and an excellent friend. He has charmed society. Everyone wants him to attend their dinner parties and balls. Now, I am not saying society sees him as an eligible bachelor or would condone him marrying one of their daughters, but he does liven a party."

Ottilie frowned, remembering the cuff to the neck she'd seen Mr. Bastin give Madame Baudelaire. But it happened so fast, she couldn't be sure he'd actually touched the woman. And he'd treated her with such care after she'd fainted, laying her down and cradling her head until her family arrived to administer the smelling salts. Either way, Madame Baudelaire had been unharmed, so whatever he did—if anything—it only served to prevent her from injuring herself or others. Still, it was curious. "It does seem odd the gossips in high society aren't more interested in his background."

"They are, believe me. And I think he keeps his past a secret on purpose. It's part of his mysterious persona. I get the impression he didn't come from money and that his family moved to America for a better life. It must have worked because he has a fortune now. But it's not why I value his friendship so dearly." Henry stopped walking and Ottilie turned to give him her full attention. "Jack Bastin is the only person, aside from you, to encourage me in my poetic pursuits. He doesn't think I am wasting my time, nor does he try to humor me as though I am a child who needs to outgrow a silly dream. He takes me seriously as a poet. And he has helped a great deal with my writing. He has been an inspiration to me."

"Then he is indeed a worthy friend, cousin. And I am glad you found someone you can trust."

"Oh, I do trust him, but no woman should." He eyed Ottilie.

"You might be surprised to learn I agree with you there." She had enjoyed Mr. Bastin's company. He had flattered her with his attention and made her feel special. She could see how one could become lost, basking in the glow of his charm. It would be easy to lose sight of one's purpose, priorities, and propriety while under his spell. And when he decided to withdraw his affections—breaking the spell—well, one only needed to look at Madame Baudelaire to understand what a crushing blow that could be.

"NO, NO, NO!" Jack leaned his forehead against the closed door. What was happening to him? He was losing control and heading in the wrong direction. He'd sworn off women and vowed to make a clean start. So how had Miss Hamilton managed to crawl inside his head, nestle in his brain, and derail him in the space of a few hours?

She didn't fit his code. He'd lived by a set of rules for years, and bedding Miss Hamilton would mean breaking all of them and spell disaster for him. She was young, unattached, and no doubt a virgin. But worst of all, she was his friend's cousin. He groaned. He could have any woman he wanted, so why fixate on this one? Yet, he desired her. And even worse, he feared he could not write without her. He had been floundering for months, unable to write anything worthwhile, until last night.

Stop! Jack reprimanded himself. *A pretty face has inspired many a poet. There is nothing unusual about it. I'm turning this gift into a problem and using it to doubt my talent. Let the memory of her face be my muse; I do not need to bed her. Whatever thoughts I may have are private and cannot hurt Hudsyn. I've done terrible things in my life, but I will not stoop so low as to betray a friend. Loyalty is everything. My survival has depended on it.*

"What the heck are you doing?"

Jack lifted his head and spun around to see Brandt frowning down at him from his place on the stairs. "Nothing. I was just on my way up."

"Have they left?"

Jack nodded. "On second thought, why don't you come down? Let's talk in the dining room. I haven't eaten yet."

Brandt trotted down the stairs. "Who's the girl? Hudsyn getting married or something?"

"No, nothing like that. She is his cousin. Came to ask a favor of me. But never mind her, what was all the urgency about earlier? I hope it means you have good news for me."

"I do." Brandt's face took on the same satisfied look as a well-fed cat's.

They entered the dining room, handsomely furnished with a rich mahogany table and chairs upholstered in tufted red velvet. Jack reached for a small bell sitting on a silver tray in the middle of the table and rang for Mrs. Wilson. Then he picked up a crystal decanter of whiskey from the same tray and poured two glasses. He slid one of the glasses across to Brandt and sat down.

"Tell me." Jack lifted the whiskey to his lips and then paused, thinking better of it. He'd already consumed two drinks without a morsel of food in his stomach.

Brandt dropped into his chair and stretched his legs across the table. "Percival Jebkin of Jebkin and Jebkin. He's the weak link."

"Do you own him yet?"

"Sure do. All it took was a few glasses of brandy and a little encouragement." Brandt reached into his pocket and withdrew a small knife. Closing one eye, he aimed at a pile of fresh fruit arranged on a silver pedestal bowl that stood on the table. Finding his target, he threw the knife. It landed in the center of an orange, splitting the flesh with a clean cut and releasing a faint burst of citrus fragrance into the air. Brandt pushed himself up and grabbed the knife's handle, pulling the weapon and catch toward him. "Darn fool. Thirty years old and still works as a law clerk for his pa."

"He's not a solicitor yet? What do the two Jebkins stand for then?"

"His older brother was a partner in the firm until he broke his neck riding at his country estate four months ago."

"Damn!" Jack rubbed the back of his neck. "Now, the pressure is on Percival, I presume."

"That's right." Brandt yanked the knife from the orange and put the fruit to his lips.

"Did you ring for me, sir?" Mrs. Wilson stood in the doorway, eyeing Brandt, who drained the juice from the orange like a ravenous vampire.

"Yes, could you bring us some ale and a bit of luncheon? Nothing fancy. A couple of boiled eggs, some bacon, and a few slices of bread and butter will do."

"Right away, sir." She nodded and retreated with one last terrified glance at Brandt.

"You frighten her," Jack said.

"Who? Wilson?"

"Yes, Wilson. Try to remember we're no longer in the American West. This is Mayfair, and we have to act the part."

Brandt wiped his dripping chin on his sleeve, and Jack winced. "Don't worry." He smirked. "I know how to be a gentleman when the situation calls for it. How else do you think I accomplished all I did this week?"

"Tell me more." Jack leaned forward.

"So far, Percival's been nothing but a disappointment to his daddy, so it's real important for him to prove himself now. If he doesn't, his pa will sell up when he's ready to retire, and Percival will have to go on working as a law clerk in someone else's firm."

"He told you that?"

Brandt nodded and picked up his whiskey glass. "He's hoppin' mad, and it makes him partial to drink. Thinks his pa unfairly favored his brother."

"Where does he do his gambling?"

"He favors Boise's Gentlemen's Club because it's easy on credit. The place is full of the entitled, wayward sons and nephews of wealthy merchants and Lords. The club owner knows their families will pay up when they owe."

"But not Mr. Jebkin?"

"That's the impression I got. Seems his pa has warned him to lay off the gambling more than once. Percival was shakin' in his boots, thinking how to scare up the money to pay his debt."

"Sounds like he's easily intimidated and will give us what we want."

"He's as yellow as a baby chick."

"How much did he lose?"

"Fifteen hundred pounds."

Jack whistled. "What's his game of choice?"

"A little poker and a lot of faro ever since I convinced him it's an easy win."

Jack mirrored his friend's grin. They'd both become skilled at faro during their time in the American West.

"I got him started on a winning streak—advising him what cards to bet on and all. He did the predictable, got excited, an' started playing reckless. I'm guessing a law clerk don't get paid much, even if it is your pa's firm. All I had to do was leave him in charge of his own destruction."

"Works every time." Jack chuckled. "And you purchased his debt from the club?"

"I did." Brandt pulled two slips of paper from his pocket and handed them to Jack. One contained a bill of sale from the club, and the other an IOU made out to Owen Brandt and signed by Percival Jebkin along with two witnesses from the club's management.

Jack kissed the paper. "We got him."

"We sure did. He was grateful, too. Thinks I'm his best pal."

"When do we make our next move?" Jack asked.

"Tonight, at seven. He'll be at the club trying to win back his losses." Brandt raised his whiskey glass.

"Tonight, at seven!" Jack lifted his glass and clinked it against Brandt's. He took a long, satisfying sip of whiskey.

Brandt leaned back in his chair and eyed his friend. "So, what was the favor?"

"What favor?" Jack asked, momentarily forgetting what he'd told Brandt earlier about Miss Hamilton.

"Hudsyn's cousin. You said she wanted a favor from you."

"She never said. You interrupted the conversation, and she never got round to asking."

"I reckon that means she'll be back," Brandt said.

"I expect it does." Jack leaned back in his chair and attempted to ignore the pleasurable warmth that flooded through him.

CHAPTER FIVE

You write so of the poets, and not laugh?
Those virtuous liars, dreamers after dark,
Exaggerators of the sun and moon,
And soothsayers in a teacup?

—Elizabeth Barrett Browning, "Aurora Leigh"

"I DO HOPE we're in time for tea." Ottilie climbed the stairs to her cousin's elegant townhome. "I'm absolutely starving."

"You are always starving," Henry said with a laugh.

"Good afternoon, my lord, Miss Hamilton," Benson greeted them upon opening the door.

"Afternoon, Benson." Henry took off his hat and gloves and handed them to the butler.

Ottilie's stomach rumbled as she slipped off her shawl. She glanced at the butler and giggled. "Sorry, Benson, but my stomach demands its tea."

Benson kept his face expressionless and bowed in acknowledgment of Ottilie's request.

"Arrange for tea to be sent to the dining room before Miss Hamilton faints. Thank you, Benson." Henry said as he strode toward the dining room.

"Yes, my lord—" Benson looked as though he wanted to say more, but Henry wandered out of earshot.

"Is there something you wish me to relay to His Lordship?" Ottilie asked.

"Yes, Miss. Tea has already been served in the dining room, and Her Ladyship is there awaiting your arrival."

"Oh dear—thank you, Benson," Ottilie said and scurried after her cousin.

"Henry," Ottilie whispered urgently, coming up behind him.

"Be sure and remember *not* to mention our visit to Bastin when Mama returns." Henry marched into the dining room without turning to look at Ottilie. He stopped abruptly.

Ottilie came up behind him. Lady Hudsyn sat with a cup of tea in her hand and glowered at them with an expression frightening enough to make Medusa whimper.

"How could you, Henry?" Lady Hudsyn put down her teacup.

"How could I what, Mama?" Hudsyn sauntered to the tea tray and picked up a biscuit.

"You took your cousin, unchaperoned, to see that rapscallion?"

"Rapscallion?" Hudsyn frowned. "I know no rapscallions." He lifted the teapot. "Is this tea fresh?"

"It's a half-hour old. You are late."

"Well, I suppose it will have to do." He poured two cups of tea. "And to be clear, Ottilie wasn't unchaperoned. She was under my protection."

"A man is not an appropriate chaperone for an unmarried lady."

Ottilie groaned inwardly. Why did her aunt insist on treating her like some nubile debutante instead of the independent, grown woman she was?

"I'm not *just* a man. I am her cousin. Don't you trust me to protect Ottilie?"

"Of course, I trust you. But if you refuse to take a chaperone, people will talk."

"I don't *need* a chaperone, Aunt," Ottilie said. "I am not interested in—"

"She didn't need a chaperone," Henry interrupted loudly, "because Mr. Bastin employs a respectable widow called Mrs. Wilson who remained present during our entire visit." He handed Ottilie a cup of tea and a plate heaped with an assortment of biscuits.

Ottilie accepted the plate and peered at the dark liquid in the teacup. "I drink mine with two lumps of sugar and cream, remember?"

"Sorry, I got distracted." Henry swept the cup back to the tea tray.

"And what of your reputation and your responsibilities to your title?" Lady Hudsyn's voice grew shrill. "I assume you still intend to marry well and do your part to increase the wealth and status of this family."

Henry laughed and dropped two lumps of sugar into Ottilie's teacup. "I am a man with a title and a fortune." He stirred cream into Ottilie's tea. "It does not matter what I do."

"I hardly think socializing with a rogue will do you any good."

"There is no need to be so dramatic, Mama." Henry glanced at his mother's sour face. "Jack Bastin is a famous author and has as much chance of being shunned by society as the king himself. No one will blame him for last night's fiasco. Certainly, they will gossip and fuss for a few days, but in the end, society will blame Madame Baudelaire for cuckolding her husband."

Lady Hudsyn sucked in her breath sharply.

"And—" Henry continued—"for making a spectacle of herself in public. She is French, after all—so not one of us."

"And Mr. Bastin is an American!" Lady Hudsyn trilled.

"He is not an American. He is an Englishman who spent a few years in America. I spent the first ten years of my life on the continent, and you spent over twenty. Does it make us no longer English?" Henry handed Ottilie her tea and went to retrieve his cup.

Lady Hudsyn clicked her tongue. "And what did he accomplish in America?"

"I don't know. Getting rich, it seems." Henry settled his seat and took a sip of tea. "Now, he has returned to England and charmed society, despite your disapproval."

"That may be so, but he should not get too comfortable," Lady Hudsyn said with an air of smugness. "Society shunned Lord Byron, and he was both a successful writer and an English baron!"

"Lord Byron bedded his sister. And as far as I know, Mr. Bastin has no sister, so you need not concern yourself."

Ottilie stifled a laugh.

"Don't be vulgar, Henry." Lady Hudsyn took up her fan and sniffed.

"You needn't worry, Mama. As Ottilie is my cousin, I can assure you that Mr. Bastin will not compromise her in any way whatsoever. You have my solemn promise on that count."

Ottilie picked up a biscuit and took a bite to mask her smile.

"You really must try and cut your sugar consumption, Ottilie," Lady Hudsyn snapped. "A young lady must show constraint while eating. A small appetite and dainty portions are admirable qualities."

"Yet another sacrifice women are expected to make in order to please a gentleman and secure a husband in this society you so admire, Aunt. The perfect lady will be idle and half-faint with hunger so as to appear pale, weak, and helpless. All to make a man feel like a man."

Ottilie saw Henry give her a slight shake of his head just as Lady Hudsyn turned her tightly pursed face to him. "Do you see what you are encouraging, Henry? How could you take your cousin to see that rogue when you know her own father was…" Lady Hudsyn flapped her mouth as if searching for the appropriate term.

"A poet," Ottilie offered when Lady Hudsyn seemed unable to find the word.

"Of bad blood." Lady Hudsyn smoothed the ruffles of her blue taffeta skirt and turned her face as though she could not bear to look at the living proof of her words.

An awkward silence fell over the room.

"Not all poets are drunken rakes, Mama." Henry's face steeled with fury. Ottilie knew he'd kept his love for writing poetry a secret from his mother because of her father—the man who'd brought her mother low and stained the family name with his debauchery. Ottilie wished she could take her words back. Why did she provoke her aunt when she knew the woman placed so much importance on the past?

"Perhaps if you read Mr. Bastin's book, you would change your mind, Aunt," Ottilie said, determined to break the tension. "It's quite marvelous. Mr. Bastin has great talent, and his novel is an outstanding study of humanity and its extraordinary capacity to endure. Which is why I am so eager to secure him as a guest lecturer for the college—" She paused, suddenly realizing she'd forgotten to ask the favor of Mr. Bastin after being interrupted by his valet.

Her aunt stood up. "I feel a headache coming on. I need to lie down. Henry, ring for my lady's maid."

"Let me help you." Ottilie stood up.

"No need. Sit down and finish your tea."

"Don't be silly, Mama. I'll take you upstairs." Henry put down his cup and stood up. "Ottilie, ring for Mama's maid, please."

"Thank you, dear." Lady Hudsyn said icily, "I can manage on my own. I think you have done quite enough for one day."

"As you wish, Mama." Henry clenched his jaw and sat down again.

Lady Hudsyn swept out of the room like a martyr on her way to the gallows.

Ottilie sipped her tea and decided it would be better not to enlist Henry's help in speaking with Mr. Bastin again. It wouldn't do to drag him into another disagreement with his mother. She would have to solve the problem on her own.

JACK STOOD OUTSIDE Boise's Gentlemen's Club in St. James's and slipped his gloved hands into his navy sack coat.

"You're certain he'll be here?" he murmured.

"I'd bet my life on it," Brandt replied. "A gambler always believes he can dig himself out of his own grave. You've buried enough of them to know as much."

"True." Jack maneuvered his neck, cracking it to release his pent-up tension. "I'm ready," he said.

They entered the building and ascended the carpeted stairs leading to the gambling hall. Cigar smoke clouded the room, already weighed down with an air of entitlement and frivolity. Well-dressed gentlemen plied with an abundance of drink and coins clustered around various card tables in accordance with their game of choice.

"Ain't it a sight for sore eyes," Brandt said. "Spoilt dandies throwing fistfuls of money away, thinking they know how to play cards. I could fleece them all in one night."

"But we're not here for that," Jack said.

"Don't worry, partner, I know we ain't. Still, it's tempting."

"It certainly is." Jack surveyed the room. "'A foole and his monie be soone at debate, which after with sorrow repents him too late.'"

"Shakespeare?"

"Thomas Tusser."

"Never heard of him. But it sounds like he figured out how to fleece some rich fools in his day."

"Not exactly. Tusser cared more about hard work and frugality."

Brandt scoffed. "Seems like he could've put his brain to better use."

"Speaking of fools," Jack said, "let's go find our man."

"I bet my life he'll be at the faro tables," Brandt said.

They moved through the room, weaving past crowded tables and navigating a haze of smoke.

"There he is." Brandt stopped several feet from a conglomerate of tables, where men gathered around playing faro. "Left side, back row. He's the tall, ginger fella."

Jack studied his target. The man stood with a drink in one hand and fiddled with a stack of coins with the other. He appeared disheveled as though he'd lost several nights' sleep, and he'd clearly neglected to shave or change his clothing.

Oh man! You're in deep trouble, aren't you?

"Get a drink and wait for me in the gentlemen's sitting room," Jack instructed Brandt. "I don't want him to see us together yet."

Brandt made his way out of the gambling room, and Jack strode to the faro table. He stood behind Percival Jebkin, pretending to be a casual observer. The man smelled of fear—Jack knew the smell well. He'd encountered it many times and in many different situations, but whenever he smelled it on wealthy men who'd gambled away their money, businesses, and estates, he felt nothing short of contempt.

He'd won a substantial portion of his wealth from such careless men. But the money hadn't come easily. He'd depended on his wits to survive, and he'd used his brains and cunning to become the best. Only those handed money for doing nothing were stupid enough to gamble it away while their brains marinated in spirits. When he gambled, he stayed sharp and only gave the impression he'd been drinking.

The dealer turned over the cards—two of diamonds first and queen of diamonds second. Percival's face crumbled as the dealer reached for his coins, which lay on the losing two of diamonds. Jack grinned inwardly. The fool picked up the remainder of his coins to bet again. This time, his hand hovered over the queen.

Jack leaned forward and whispered, "Not the queen! Put your

money on the ace."

Percival turned and peered at Jack through puffy, red-rimmed eyes. "Who are you?" he slurred.

"No one in particular." Jack restrained himself from stepping back to escape the stench of the man's alcohol-drenched breath. "Only an observer."

Percival shrugged and turned back to the table. His hand hovered over the queen of diamonds before jerking to the ace of diamonds. He plunked down his coins and drained his glass.

Jack smirked.

Once all the players had placed their bets, the dealer extracted two cards from the faro box. First, he turned over a five of spades, and then he turned over an ace. Percival whooped in the air. He'd doubled his money.

Jack clapped Percival on the back. The fool didn't even question why a stranger had decided to help him. Such was the smell of desperation. After a few wins, the clerk trusted him completely and bet all his money on the high card. When the dealer turned over a king first, Percival dropped his head in his hands and stumbled backward.

"I'm ruined," he moaned.

"It can't be all bad," Jack said. "You only played a few coins. You didn't lose much at all."

"It's all I had! I was trying to regain some of my losses from yesterday."

"Yesterday?" Jack feigned innocence. "How much did you lose yesterday?"

"Fifteen hundred pounds, and I borrowed another two hundred from the club today."

"You owe the club fifteen hundred pounds, and they let you borrow more?"

"An American purchased my debt yesterday, so I only need to pay him and not the club."

"But you still owe it?"

"Yes."

"Well then, you'd better let me buy you a drink." He led Percival toward the gentlemen's sitting room.

"I suppose it's not so terrible. My father won't find out about my losses as long as I don't owe the club money, which gives me sufficient time to win it back. I am a rather good player, you see. I'm simply having some rotten luck, that's all."

"Of course, you are." Jack stopped beside Brandt's chair and put his arm around Percival. "Is this the man who purchased your debt?"

"Howdy, partner." Brandt smiled brightly. "You're back at it, I see."

"Mr. Brandt, I didn't realize you'd be here tonight."

"It seems I have to head back to America earlier than I thought, so I'll be needing my fifteen hundred pounds by Friday next."

"*What?*" Percival rasped.

"It ain't so bad, fella. This way, you'll only be paying one week's interest."

"Interest?" Percival swayed on his feet. Jack put his hand on the man's shoulder and guided him into a leather armchair.

"Ten percent, as agreed," Brandt said.

Percival shrunk in his seat. "I don't remember—"

Jack sat down next to Percival. "Do you have a loan agreement?"

"Sure do." Brandt extracted the loan papers from his pocket and handed them over.

Jack pretended to study the papers and whistled softly to himself.

"What is it?" Percival's face turned a sickly white.

"It's true; you agreed to pay ten percent interest."

"I don't remember signing it." He looked wildly from Jack to Brandt.

Brandt leaned back in his chair and laced his fingers together. "Are you telling me you can't get my money? Because that ain't the song you sang last night."

"I'll pay you back; I swear it. But I need more time. Please, I cannot go to Debtors' Prison," Percival babbled. "I'm the son of a respected solicitor. It will kill my father. He'll disown me."

Brandt crossed his legs and eyed the jabbering fool.

Percival licked his thin, cracked lips. "If you advance me a little more tonight, I will double your money." His face brightened a shade as though warming up to the idea. "Luck is on my side. I can feel it."

"Advance you money when you already owe me fifteen hundred pounds? Sounds like suicide. Only a chronic gambler would suggest that." Brandt smirked. "I can feel your desperation, Mr. Jebkin, and I don't like it. Desperation makes a man dangerous. So, I must insist you pay up immediately. Otherwise, you will beg the money off someone else, lose it, and owe them as well as me. I'll never see my money in that case."

"But I don't have the money to give you at present."

"You own some valuables, maybe?"

Percival pulled at the skin on his throat. "My father has all the valuables under lock and key. But I earn a salary. Perhaps you will accept payments?"

"What, for the next ten years? Are you mad? You're a mere law clerk and a hopeless gambler. I'd be a fool to take payments from the likes of you."

Sweat dotted Percival's brow. "I need more time."

"I'll give you a day extra. If you can't scare up the money, I'll have to pay your father a visit. He owns the law firm Jebkin and Jebkin on Fleet Street, am I right?"

Percival swallowed. "No. I mean—yes, he does, but do not speak to him, please. There must be another way."

"I think there might be," Jack interjected. He'd kept deliberately quiet up to this point. He needed the man to be desperate. "How about I agree to buy your debt from Mr. Brandt in exchange for a small service?"

"Anything! What do you want me to do?"

Jack leaned back in his chair and smiled. "Well, it so happens,

I'm in need of some information."

"What sort of information?"

"The sort you keep stored in the offices of Jebkin and Jebkin."

"Impossible," Percival said. "I am only a clerk. I don't have the authority."

"You don't need authority, only access."

"What do you want access to?"

"The will of a dead man."

Percival blinked. "Who is the man?"

"One Edward Knoll. A wealthy merchant banker who died in a carriage accident a year before my birth, in 1839."

"1839? I would need to dig through the archives."

"Is that a problem?"

Percival shifted in his seat. "I don't know. If my father ever discovered that I betrayed his trust—"

"I think you've already done as much, don't you?" Jack kept his voice icy. He wanted Percival to understand he meant to show him no mercy.

Percival tugged at his cravat as if it choked him. "It will have to be before my father returns from Nottinghamshire."

"The sooner the better. I'll need to view the original will, and I'll want a copy made for myself. Have it ready for me on Monday morning at dawn; that should give us sufficient time before the other clerks arrive, I presume?"

"And you'll forgive my debt?" Percival asked.

"Forgive? No, but I will allow you significant leeway in how or when you pay what you owe."

Percival nodded and shrank back in his seat.

"Excellent!" Jack turned to Brandt and raised his whiskey glass. "Then, I believe we have a deal."

"We sure do," Brandt said and raised his glass to toast Jack.

CHAPTER SIX

Yet ofttimes in his maddest mirthful mood,
Strange pangs would flash along Childe Harold's brow,
As if the memory of some deadly feud
Or disappointed passion lurked below:

—Byron, "Childe Harold's Pilgrimage"

FLEET STREET LAY in the shadow of St. Paul's as dawn broke through the darkness. Jack took a moment to admire the emerging glow that inched across the horizon, illuminating the London skyline and bathing St. Paul's magnificent dome in a pink hue.

"Do you see it?" Jack asked.

"What?" Brandt mumbled, sounding half asleep.

"St. Paul's Cathedral. You'll never see a building that splendid in America."

"I miss the mountains and the deserts," Brandt grunted without bothering to look up.

"London is too cramped and wet for my taste."

"It's different. That much is certain." Jack stepped into the arched frame of the sandstone building affixed with a gold plate on the outer door that read, *Jebkin & Jebkin, Solicitors.* He rapped on the door with his walking stick and then leaned on it as he waited for a response. When none came, he lifted it again and rapped with more force.

Hurried footsteps sounded from within, and seconds later, the door creaked open.

Percival screwed up his face as though pained by the emerging daylight. His red-rimmed eyes told Jack the clerk had lost yet another night's sleep.

"Come in." He uttered. "I spent all night making a copy of Mr. Knoll's will for you, sir," he said as he worked to re-bolt the door.

"I'll need to check it against the original," Jack warned.

Percival blinked as though surprised to find himself doubted.

Jack raised his eyebrows. "Do you object?"

"Of course not. But we must make haste. There's but one hour before the other clerks arrive." They followed him up a twisted stone staircase, which led to a maze of book-filled rooms and spacious offices.

"Not bad," Brandt murmured as he and Jack followed Percival to a large office furnished with enormous bookshelves crammed with law books, a hefty mahogany desk, and a buttoned-leather settee with a set of matching chairs.

Jack smirked. "Your father's office, I presume?"

Percival walked to the desk and put a shaky hand between two documents. "The one to my right is the original will and testament of Mr. Knoll. And here on my left is the copy I made. The ink may still be a little wet."

"I'll start with the original." Jack strode forward but stopped short of picking up his grandfather's will. Instead, his hand hovered above the document. Had his grandfather truly given up on his daughter? Had he resented her enough to leave her with nothing and overlook the welfare of his grandchildren? Jack didn't want to believe it, but the chance to discover the truth about his past had arrived. Even if his mother had been disinherited, he needed to find out what happened to his grandfather's estate. If his uncle had gotten his hands on it, he'd rest at nothing to get it back.

"Careful," Percival squeaked, "you'll tear it."

Jack blinked to see his hand closed around his grandfather's will, creasing the delicate paper. He relaxed his grip.

"Give us some privacy," Brandt barked. "We'll let you know when we need you."

Percival darted his eyes from Brandt to Jack and back again.

"Out." Brandt took a menacing step toward Percival. The clerk backed out of the room as if afraid to lose sight of the man.

Jack scanned the document in his hand until he located the relevant passage:

I, Edward John Knoll, leave my lodgings in London, the furnishings and valuables contained therein, and the sum of 50,000 pounds to Mr. and Mrs. Richard Neville Astyr. The Knoll family estate in Kent, including all furnishings and valuables contained therein, shall pass to my eldest living grandson. The estate, together with the sum of 65,000 pounds to be used for the estate's maintenance and upkeep, is to be kept in trust by Richard Neville Astyr for such child until he comes of age. If both my daughters fail to produce a male heir, the Knoll country estate and the sum of 65,000 pounds shall pass to my third cousin and son-in-law, Richard Neville Astyr.

"Blackguard!" Jack slapped the document onto the mahogany desk.

"What does it say?" Brandt asked.

"That my grandfather was a cold-blooded wretch who cared nothing for my mother or my sisters. The fool left his country estate and 65,000 pounds to his eldest living grandson, who hadn't even been born yet."

"That's you! Ain't it?"

"It is, but I'm not legally his grandson anymore. I'm Jack Bastin, and I have no way to prove my true identity."

"So, what happened to your inheritance?"

"It went to the trustee. My uncle."

"That infernal son-of-a..." Brandt picked up the will and

scanned its contents.

"He stole my inheritance." Jack clenched his fists. "I am certain my parents never saw my grandfather's will. Sir Richard must have used his influence and power to keep it from them, and he did the same to make sure I was as good as dead before I came of age to claim anything."

Brandt dropped the will onto the desk. "But your grandfather wanted you to have his estate. That's something, ain't it?"

"He didn't want me to have it. He didn't even know me. No doubt he thought Lady Astyr would give birth to a son long before my mother, who'd already birthed a daughter—a child he doesn't even acknowledge in his will. All he cared about was passing his estate onto a male heir. He left nothing to his wife, daughters, or granddaughters. In the absence of a grandson, he settled everything on his cousin. The estate wasn't entailed, so he could have left it to my sister, but he clearly didn't want his money or land falling into the hands of a woman. It seems he was willing to absolve me of my mother's sins, but not my sisters. What a cad he must have been. No wonder my mother wanted to escape his clutches."

"It don't matter why your grandfather left you his estate. What matters is he did, so it's yours, and your uncle knows as much."

Jack ran his hand through his hair. "My father and sister are both dead. It would be his word against mine. It's my fault for trusting my uncle in the first place," he said, hating himself.

"Why did you?"

"I was a troubled lad desperate to escape my pain. I thought if I changed my name and left England, I would leave the hurt behind. So, I didn't stop to ask why Sir Richard agreed to help me, and I trusted him when he said he'd found a rich American to take me on as his apprentice. I had no idea he'd indentured me to a monster."

"That'd be a good way to describe Wyatt Wardell."

"I thought I was fortunate that a great man of business had

agreed to take me under his wing. Wardell paid for my passage and promised to teach me how to become rich in America." Jack scowled. "All I had to do was learn while I worked off my debt. It sounded like the answer to my prayers."

"Well, I be darned," Brandt said. "No wonder he stuck you in them sugar mills. He wanted to teach you to follow in his slave-owning footsteps."

Jack shuddered and strode to the window. He slipped his hands in his pockets and watched the early-morning laborers scurry up and down Fleet Street in preparation for the day of commerce ahead. "I remember the day I boarded the ship with Wardell. My uncle handed him my work contract—that's how he referred to my bind—and said, 'The lad goes by the name Jack. He doesn't have a surname or a family to tie him to anyone, so he's yours free and clear.' Then he slapped me on the back. 'Pick a solid American surname for yourself once you get to Texas, lad.'" Jack mimicked his uncle's stiff voice. "'A few years from now, no one will suspect you were born an Englishman.'" Jack scoffed. "Turned out Wardell didn't care what my name was. He never called me anything but *boy*." Jack began to pace the office. "I can't let him get away with this."

"Don't you worry, he'll get his comeuppance," Brandt said. "We'll make sure, just like we did for Wardell."

"That's not enough anymore. I want justice. He should return what he stole and face exposure as a liar and thief."

"How you gonna make that happen if you ain't got no legal claim?"

"I don't know, but if I can't find a way, it will be too bad for my uncle because my only recourse will be an illegal one."

Brandt lowered his voice. "You mean, kill him?"

"I've killed before," Jack said.

"Wartime is different. You ain't no murderer."

"This is war!" Jack slammed his fist onto the desk. "That man destroyed my life and killed my father with 'is lies."

"Now, you hold your horses 'an keep a clear head about

things, you hear? I won't stay to see you hang."

Fury blurred Jack's thoughts. He inhaled and exhaled slowly, trying to calm his mind.

A timid knock sounded at the door before it creaked open, and Percival's trembling voice sounded. "Did you find the copy satisfactory, sir? You may, of course, take it with you now. It's yours."

"We're not finished here." Jack faced the frightened clerk. "I'll need to see Sir Richard Astyr's will before I leave today."

"Impossible!" Percival blinked. "You ask me to betray a client's trust—a living client, that is."

"What alternative do you have, Mr. Jebkin?"

"But the will in question is currently being revised and is not yet complete. Sir Richard is drafting a new will in light of his impending marriage. It's why my father went to Nottingham-shire."

"What did you say?" Jack strode toward Percival.

"My father is in Nottinghamshire as we speak, drawing up a new will for Sir Richard to be completed before his wedding."

"His wedding?" Jack said. "To whom?"

"Miss Anne Deuxhill, I believe. She's the daughter of a baron-et—a spinster of eight-and-twenty. Her father feared she would never find a suitable match at her age."

"And he thought a man of sixty better than nothing?" Brandt snarled.

"Sir Richard is a distinguished member of society, knighted for his service to Queen and Country. And he is a man of some fortune, who doesn't have any heirs at present, so…" Percival stopped, apparently stupefied by Jack's glare.

"Richard Astyr is a liar and a thief," Jack thundered. "Kindly stop singing his praises like a caged canary and tell me when your father returns from Nottinghamshire."

"I-in two days." Percival stammered. "The wedding is tomor-row, and, as I said, my father went early to prepare the will. Sir Richard wanted it completed before…"

"Go on," Jack said.

"Before his wedding night. He and his bride will be honeymooning in Belgium for a fortnight, and he didn't want to wait until they returned to London to redo his will."

"So, Sir Richard has taken a new bride because he is desperate for an heir and will return to London in a fortnight." Jack glanced at Brandt, who mirrored his smile.

A loud knock echoed through the hallways, making Percival jump. "The other clerks have arrived for work. I'll need to let them inside. You must leave."

"You will make me a copy of Astyr's new will when your father returns, or I will pay your papa a visit and present him with an IOU for fifteen hundred pounds plus interest."

"I will. I will! But please, you must go now."

Jack picked up his grandfather's will. "I am taking the original. You can put the copy back in your archives as a placeholder. It's not as though Edward Knoll will rise out of his grave and come looking for it."

"But—"

"Keep your mouth shut and your eyes open. We'll be in touch," Brandt said.

Jack patted Percival on the back. "Don't worry, old fellow. You needn't hide us from the other clerks. When your father returns, you can tell him that Mr. Jack Bastin, the writer, is impressed by his son and may soon seek council from Jebkin and Jebkin."

A DEWY MIST blanketed the horizon and clouded Ottilie's view from the window seat in the library. She sat with her stockinged legs curled beneath her and Mr. Bastin's novel, *The Renegade*, open on her lap. She'd been enjoying the book more than the first time she'd read it. But now, Ottilie found herself scrutinizing the protagonist—a type of modern-day Odysseus, lost to his family whilst fighting a foreign war in a foreign land—and searching for clues about Bastin.

As she thought, she lifted her head and gazed out into the misty horizon. *Didn't all writers draw on their own lives for material?* Dickens had used his personal struggles to write *David Copperfield*, and it was well known he created his lively characters from those real-life ones he'd met or observed on London's streets.

She ran her hands over the book's blue leather cover. Bastin's universe was one of immeasurable cruelty and deceit, but it also championed justice and celebrated man's strength to endure. Could it be based on what he'd experienced in America?

Ottilie returned to her reading and became so engrossed in the story she failed to hear Benson enter the library; she looked up with a start when the butler alerted her by clearing his throat.

"A letter for you, Miss Hamilton." Benson extended a silver tray, which held a single envelope and a letter opener in the shape of a miniature sword.

"Thank you." Ottilie unfurled her legs, reached for the envelope, and saw the handwriting belonged to her friend Violet Thomas. Her spirits lifted. A friendly voice was exactly what she needed. The atmosphere in her aunt's house had been frosty since the uncomfortable conversation in the drawing room two days earlier. And Ottilie had been grieved to find herself eating her meals alone. Her aunt had taken to her bed and eaten her meals in her room. Each time Ottilie checked on her health, the maid stated that Lady Hudsyn did not wish to be disturbed.

Meanwhile, Henry had disappeared to Kent, apparently to see about an emergency on his estate. But Ottilie knew the sudden "emergency" was a manufactured excuse to aid his escape from his mama. Her remarks had injured him, and he likely needed some time alone. He hated hiding his true self because of his mama's ridiculous notions.

Ottilie picked up the miniature sword and sliced open the envelope.

"Will you be taking tea in the library, Miss Hamilton?" Benson asked when she returned the opener to the tray.

"Tea? Surely, it's not time for tea yet. I only just ate breakfast."

Benson stole a glance at the grandfather clock standing in the corner of the room, and Ottilie turned to look at the time.

"Half-after-two!" she exclaimed. "Have I been sitting here for over four hours?" As if in answer, Ottilie's stomach emitted a low rumble. Benson stiffened and cast his eyes toward the window. She giggled. "I'm sorry, Benson. But you may as well get used to my demanding stomach. I am surprised it took this long to remind me to eat. It's usually far more reliable. I'd like to have tea in the library if it's permissible. Unless my aunt plans to join me in the dining room?"

"I shall inquire on your behalf." Benson gave a sight bow and retreated.

Ottilie repositioned herself on the settee and pulled Violet's letter from the envelope.

My Dearest Ottilie,

We are enjoying a wonderful summer escape at Margate. The twins are thrilled to be outdoors, playing in the sand and running barefoot on the shore. The weather is delightful. Mr. Thomas has been spoiling the children with far too much ice cream and too many sweets. Just yesterday evening, both children complained of stomachache and refused to eat their supper!

We do wish you had joined us here in Margate, but it must be lovely to see your cousin and aunt again. How is the London Season? I have a mental image of you rolling your eyes when you read those words. I remember when my Aunt Prudence, God rest her soul, tried to convince me that I needed a "suitable" husband. I resented her advice at the time, but now I see she only wanted the best for me. Keep that in mind and be gentle with Lady Hudsyn. But don't let her steal you away from us. The young ladies at Canterbury Ladies' College would be lost without their brilliant mathematics instructor—so before some handsome lord casts a spell over you, let him know he will have to move to Canterbury and learn how to keep a house while you tend to the future of women's education.

Ottilie laughed out loud, then she lowered the letter and sighed. She valued her independence above all else, but sometimes her heart ached for want of a family. She longed for what Violet had but understood that a man like Byron Thomas, who treated his wife as his equal, was a rare breed. Even her mama, a dedicated bluestocking, had been betrayed by two husbands.

She recalled the shock and pain she'd felt upon realizing her stepfather's betrayal. His rush to the altar two weeks after her mama's sudden death and six months before the birth of his twin boys made it clear that his new relationship had begun well before his marriage ended. Had her mama known? Did his betrayal contribute to her sudden demise? Ottilie might never know. But her stepfather's current wife did not take kindly to her speculations and so determined her husband had no further obligation to stay in contact with his stepdaughter, who was not even of his blood.

Ottilie wrapped her arms around herself. After two years, the betrayal was still as sharp as a viper's fangs. Would she ever find a man confident enough to allow his wife her dignity and independence while remaining loyal enough to cherish his family over all else? Perhaps if she fell down a rabbit hole like little Alice? Ottilie scoffed at the thought and picked up Violet's letter, reading where she'd left off:

Turning to another matter, I recently read about a scandal involving the author, Jack Bastin. They say a French merchant's wife attacked him during a ball held at her Mayfair townhome. I suppose all of society is in a twitter about it. The newspapers here in Margate declare Mr. Bastin is innocent and condemn the French woman as being deranged. They report that she attacked two innocent bystanders—throwing a glass at one and drawing blood from another with her bare hands! I am certain these are exaggerated claims. Still, it is fascinating to think a famous author like Mr. Bastin is making the rounds during the London Season the same time as you! I do admire his writing, and the thought of you getting a chance to meet him is almost too good to be true. Of course, if you get that chance, you must remember to mention our college to him. Wouldn't it be marvelous for our students if we were to secure a live reading from Mr. Jack Bastin himself? It is worth a try before he becomes too famous and out of our reach.

I am afraid I must end this letter as the twins want their bedtime story. Do write soon and tell us all your news. The children miss you terribly and send kisses to their "Aunt Tillie." I hope you are having a marvelous summer.

Yours forever faithful and affectionate friend,
Violet

A smile formed on Ottilie's lips, and she pressed the letter against her chest. She desperately wanted to write and tell Violet her news, but she couldn't risk disappointing her friend. It was best to secure an agreement from Mr. Bastin, and then she'd have the pleasure of surprising Violet with the good news. But she would have to act quickly and take advantage of her aunt's decision to keep to her bedchamber, which would make it easier for her to venture out unnoticed. Ottilie's insides fluttered despite her refusal to acknowledge her overwhelming desire to see Mr. Bastin again.

CHAPTER SEVEN

Doubt you to whom my Muse these notes intendeth,
Which now my breast, surcharg'd, to music lendeth?
To you, to you all song of praise is due,
Only in you, my song begins and endeth.

—Sir Phillip Sydney, *Astrophel and Stella*

OTTILIE STOOD IN the servant's courtyard of her aunt's residence and adjusted the oversized hood of her cloak. She needed to ensure it hid all her blond tendrils and shadowed a good portion of her face. Gossips inhabited many of the town-homes in Berkeley Square, and if anyone were to recognize her leaving the house unaccompanied, another quarrel with her aunt would certainly ensue. Her adjustments completed, she ascended the outdoor staircase and pushed open the wrought iron gate at the top of the stairs. Taking care to keep her head bowed, she stepped onto the street and scurried across the square, hoping she looked like a humble servant on a rushed errand for her mistress.

It took only a few minutes to arrive at Half Moon Street and locate Mr. Bastin's red-bricked townhome with its contrasting white Palladian windows. Ottilie took a deep breath to steady her nerves before stepping onto the portico. The front door swung open, and she stumbled back in fright.

"Whoa!" A leather-gloved hand gripped her arm. "Watch

where you're walkin, Little Lady. You almost ran me down."

Mr. Bastin's American valet stood before her, looking considerably less disheveled in a three-piece suit and blue cravat than the last time she'd seen him.

"You startled me." Ottilie steadied herself on her feet and put her hand to her chest to still the wild drumming of her heart.

"What are you doin' prowlin' out here like a horse thief?" The valet frowned down at her.

"What? I—I'm here to see Mr. Bastin."

"Course you are. But Bastin's a busy man, an' he don't need no women comin' round here waking snakes."

Ottilie blinked. Was this man speaking English? She could not make any sense of his words. "I think you misunderstand. I'm Miss Hamilton. Lord Hudsyn's cousin. I visited here with him last week."

The cowboy hooked his thumbs in his belt and examined her with steel-gray eyes. Then his countenance relaxed. "I remember you. Miss Favor, right?"

Ottilie frowned.

"Am I right? You're here to ask Mr. Bastin for a favor, ain't you?"

She sucked in her lips. Any hope she'd had of remaining incognito was now certainly lost. She could practically feel every concealed eye directed toward her back, and she could only pray her oversized cape provided her with sufficient protection. She squared her frame and faced the American. "Is Mr. Bastin at home?"

He smiled as if he were privy to a shared secret. "He's here." He stepped aside and allowed her to enter the residence.

Finally, the door closed behind her, shutting out prying eyes on the street, but instead of feeling safe, Ottilie's stomach twisted into a knot as she stood in the silent foyer. Was Mr. Bastin actually home? Or had she just put herself in a dangerous situation with this ungentlemanly valet?

"Come on up." The valet started up the stairs to the first

floor.

Ottilie hesitated, wanting to stay near the front door. "Shouldn't I wait here? I don't wish to disturb his work."

"I can't see how it'll make a difference." He kept walking.

Ottilie swallowed. She could either make her escape now or take her chances and follow this strange American up the stairs. She glanced down the hallway. *Where is that housekeeper Henry mentioned?*

She edged toward the stairs, remaining several paces behind the American. He reached the top of the steps and disappeared onto the first floor. Relief flooded through Ottilie when she heard Mr. Bastin's voice call out in surprise, "Brandt? What are you still doing here? I thought you left."

Ottilie hurried to the top of the stairs then. The sooner she spoke to Mr. Bastin, the sooner she could ask him her favor—and get out of this predicament, hopefully unseen and unscathed.

"I did, but little Miss Favor was waitin' outside, an' she desires to speak with you."

"Who?" Ottilie heard the bewilderment in Mr. Bastin's tone, and she moved forward and stepped into Mr. Bastin's study.

He sat at his desk, the sleeves of his white shirt rolled up and a host of fresh-inked papers spread out before him. Piles of books, crumpled papers, and an open whiskey decanter littered his desk. Ottilie's stomach dropped. She'd arrived at an inopportune time and disturbed his writing.

"Miss Hamilton?" Mr. Bastin put his ink pen down and stood up. "Is Hudsyn with you?"

"I'm afraid not." Ottilie's gaze fell to the sleek ivory handle of the firearm peeking out of the black leather holster attached to his belt.

"Has something happened to him?"

"Henry rushed off to Kent two days ago." She could not force her eyes away from the holster on his hip. "Something about his estate."

Mr. Bastin must have seen her staring because he unclipped

the belt and pulled it from his waist. "I don't know why I wear this thing indoors. Old habit, I suppose." Ottilie widened her eyes upon seeing a row of bullets that studded the back of his belt. "It doesn't scare you, does it?" He placed the belt on top of a pile of books on his desk.

"Do all Americans carry guns on their belts?"

Brandt's laughter sounded behind her, and Mr. Bastin grinned. "Not all, no."

"Then, why do you?"

"Cause he's a cowboy, Darlin'," Brandt said.

Jack cleared his throat. "Cowboys often travel in harsh territories and need guns for self-defense—against venomous snakes, wild animals, and such."

"Horse thieves, too." Brandt chuckled.

Mr. Bastin's brows knitted together in a frown. Then he smiled at Ottilie and shrugged. "The American West is a far cry from Mayfair."

"Of course, it is," Ottilie said sheepishly.

Mr. Bastin remained standing and smiled expectantly at her. His unspoken question—*what on earth are you doing here alone?*—rang clearly in Ottilie's hot ears and left her feeling even more ridiculous. There'd been no emergency and no urgent need for her to rush over and interrupt Mr. Bastin's writing—that much would be as blatant to him as it was to her now.

MISS HAMILTON PUSHED back the hood of her cape, which landed in gentle folds onto her shoulders. Several strands of buttery blond curls, pinned loosely back, hung in tendrils around her face. She met his gaze, her large blue eyes vibrant with intelligence, and smiled. The dimples that kept him awake at night revealed themselves on her cheeks and something deep inside Jack stirred. *God, she's lovely.*

"I reckon she's come to ask that favor," Brandt said.

Jack shot him his best 'get out now' look and said, "Thank you, Brandt. You can leave the door open. We'll talk when you get back this evening."

Brandt grinned and left the room.

"I hope you don't mind my calling without my cousin," Miss Hamilton said.

Jack picked up an ink-stained rag and wiped his hands. "Not at all. I'm glad you came. In fact, I was thinking about you." He noticed the color rise in her cheeks, and it pleased him. "Sit down." He gestured to an empty chair across from his desk.

"Thank you." She moved to the chair and untied her cape. "I feel rather warm after my walk." She slipped the cape from her shoulders to reveal a summery white dress, slim in the waist and full in the skirt. Jack waited for her to sit before he seated himself again.

"Last time you were here, you wanted to ask something of me, but you were interrupted. I'm curious to know how I can help you." He smoothed his hand over his chin. He'd never been apprehensive in a woman's company before, but he felt a tension now that unnerved him.

She folded her red cape in her arm and let it rest on her lap. "That's kind, but I feel rather foolish for disturbing you. I can see you are busy with your writing. I recall you mentioned working on something new."

"It's an epic poem."

"I remember you saying as much. I didn't know you were a poet."

"Neither did I. But we must write what the muses honor us with, and my muse honored me with this poem, so I must write it."

"What's the subject?"

"The huntress Artemis and her flock of maidens. One of her best-loved maidens, a golden-haired beauty, falls desperately in love with a mortal. And they engage in a forbidden and illicit love affair."

"That sounds intriguing. I look forward to reading it."

"I hope to serialize it if I succeed in getting it published."

"Of course, it will be published. The world is waiting for your next work. I am sure whatever you write will be worthy of publication."

"Oh, it is worthy. But society is prudish, and people have convinced themselves they are in full control of their animalistic desires. The affair between Artemis's maiden and the mortal is passionate, illicit, and dangerous. Tempering their ardor to suit society's mores would be false. I'd be betraying myself as an artist. And the result would be a lackluster poem."

Ottilie let out an uncomfortable laugh. "That is why I prefer mathematics. It's free from judgment and scandal."

"Yet, you are a free thinker and live as an independent woman, so I wager you are not afraid of judgment."

"Judgment is one thing, but scandal is quite another. Life is a little easier for me in Canterbury, but I must be more vigilant in London for my aunt's sake. She has tried her best to reform me since my mother's death two years ago."

"Reform you? What do you mean?"

"She'd like to see me married and idle—preferably to some doddering gentleman with a courtesy title."

"Why does it matter so much to her?"

"It's for Henry's sake, I think. My cousin and I are good friends, and my aunt is ambitious for her only son. I believe she wants to rein me in so that I don't tarnish him in any way."

Jack folded his arm. "And Hudsyn allows it?"

"No, in fact, that's the real reason he disappeared to Kent. There was a small disagreement between Henry and his mama after we returned from visiting you last week. My aunt overheard our conversation and discovered he'd brought me to see you 'unaccompanied', as she called it. Things soured rapidly after that. I think Henry needed some time alone. He hates when his mama tries to control him."

"So, you thought it a good idea to leave your aunt's residence and come here alone?"

"I am not used to being caged, and I took pains to conceal myself for my aunt's sake. Besides, I have a purpose for being here, and that is all the reason I need." She lifted her chin as though daring him to challenge her.

He leaned back in his chair and kept his eyes fixed on her. "Tell me."

Ottilie shifted in her seat as though readying herself to deliver a rehearsed speech. "As you know, I teach mathematics at a ladies' college in Canterbury. The number of institutions providing secondary education for women is growing in line with the demand and call for improvement in women's education. Nonetheless, such growth would be impossible without the help of forward-thinking men, who are willing to share their knowledge and education with young women."

Jack rubbed his chin. "Fascinating indeed, but what does it have to do with me?"

"We rely heavily on guest lecturers, and—"

His lips curved into a smile. "You're not suggesting I give a lecture at your ladies' college, are you?"

"It doesn't have to be a lecture. A live reading from your book would be wonderful. Or you could talk about your new poem. Our students are well-versed in Greek mythology and epic poetry."

"I hardly think my presence at your college will enhance its reputation. Haven't you read the papers? I'm a scandalous rake."

"I have read the papers, Mr. Bastin, and it seems your name is clear. They accuse Madame Baudelaire of hysteria and write that homesickness caused her mind to become engulfed in a fantastical infatuation."

Jack raised his eyebrows. "Engulfed in a *fantastical infatuation*? They used those words?"

"They did." Ottilie bit back a smile. "I'll wager those reports are largely nonsense, but it really isn't my business to speculate. Your exoneration is good news to me because it means there's no danger in your giving a reading at the college. We will, of course, ensure the event is heavily chaperoned to calm any persistent fears."

"So, you will add an extra layer of women to the mix—for the younger ladies' protection."

"Married women." The irony must have hit her as she spoke the words because she pressed her lips tightly together.

A smile played on Jack's lips. He could hardly believe his luck. His muse sat across from him, requesting his assistance. He leaned forward on his desk. "Do you know, Miss Hamilton, I think we may be able to help each other."

"What can I possibly do to help you, Mr. Bastin?"

"I saw you the night of the Baudelaires' ball—outside, standing on the stairs of their portico. Imagine my surprise when, as I glanced out my carriage window, I caught sight of you looking as pure and lovely as one of Artemis's maidens." He smiled at the memory. "I thought you a figment of my imagination."

Ottilie lowered her gaze.

"When I returned home, an insatiable urge to write consumed me. I hadn't written anything in months, but after seeing you, the words poured out of me. And I thought, finally, the gods have sent me a muse."

Ottilie laughed. "*I* am your muse?"

"You gifted me this poem. I have no other way of explaining how this work, dormant in my brain, suddenly came alive and started beating on my skull to be let out. It's the best—the *only* writing—I have managed in months."

"Well, it sounds like I have already done my part, and you now owe me a favor."

"But my poem isn't finished."

"What are you proposing I do, Mr. Bastin?"

"I will give a lecture at your ladies' college if you agree to be my muse."

"But how does one be a muse? I'm a mathematician. I don't know how to inspire a writer."

"That's the beauty of it. You don't have to do anything in

particular. You only need to sit with me while I write."

"I couldn't possibly sit with you all day while you write. And my aunt will never stand my coming here unchaperoned—if at all."

"I will engage a chaperone for you. My housekeeper, Mrs. Wilson, will escort you to my residence and back to Berkley Square. And I don't mean you should come every day, only a few hours a week."

"People will assume we are attached."

"Do you care what people think?"

"No, but I do care what my family thinks, so let me talk to Henry first."

"Do you think Hudsyn will object? He's the one who brought you here."

Miss Hamilton fidgeted with her jacket. "He is also the one who told me no woman should trust you."

"I don't believe what you say. Hudsyn knows I am upfront with all the women I—" he paused—"That is, I don't make promises I can't keep."

"I'm sure that's true, Mr. Bastin, and I don't think he meant to imply you are dishonest." She rose from her chair and unfolded her cape.

Jack stood. "Let me help you with that." He approached her and took the cape from her hands. "What do you think Hudsyn meant?" he asked, laying the garment across her shoulders.

She tied the string of her cape and turned to face him. "I think he meant that no woman should trust herself in your company."

Jack leaned forward, taking in her flowery scent. "And what do you think? Can you trust yourself in my company?"

"I don't know." Her lips parted slightly.

Jack's breathing shallowed. If she had been any other woman—anyone other than Hudsyn's cousin—but he could not be disloyal to a friend. "Then, I promise never to give you a reason to distrust yourself. I will treat you as if you truly are one of Artemis's virgins." He straightened and took a step back, increasing the distance between them.

Chapter Eight

Vengeance is in my heart, death in my hand,
Blood and revenge are hammering in my head.

—William Shakespeare, *Titus Andronicus*

JACK BASTIN'S FACE blurred past Ottilie as she stepped, turned, and swirled around the ballroom floor with Lord Towne. She'd accepted his invitation to dance in an effort to placate her aunt, and to make matters worse, he insisted on engaging her in conversation.

"Do you agree, Miss Hamilton?" Lord Towne breathed, rather than spoke, the question.

"Yes, certainly," Ottilie murmured, despite not having heard a word he'd uttered. Her thoughts were entirely on Mr. Bastin, who appeared to be engaged in his own string of fruitless conversations. It seemed the fiasco with Madame Baudelaire had served to increase his popularity.

"I'm glad to hear it. Of course, I haven't read the book myself, but I have it on good authority that it's scandalous."

"What book?" Ottilie asked, the words "book" and "scandalous" having caught her attention.

"Mr. Bastin's novel. I have no idea why society makes such a fuss over him. At least you and I are in agreement."

"Are we?"

He looked down at her as they turned and stepped. "Yes, you agreed his book is scandalous and not worthy of being read."

"I agreed to no such thing. Indeed, I have read Mr. Bastin's novel twice and enjoyed it more the second time."

"Well, I am certain your aunt will not approve."

"My aunt is out-of-touch with the times. She doesn't approve of secondary education for women, either. Yet in a few years, you will see young women attending university and getting jobs instead of getting married."

"Preposterous! First, they will take over our universities, and the next thing you know, they will want the vote."

"They? Do you mean the mothers, sisters, and daughters of this world? You are uncomfortable with the notion of change, I see."

Mr. Towne's light polka step turned into a stomp. "I would have thought you might show a little more gratitude toward me, Miss Hamilton."

"Gratitude?"

"Yes, for offering to marry you. Not many gentlemen of my rank and wealth would consent to marry a six-and-twenty-year-old bluestocking, who—"

"How interesting. I received no offer of marriage from you, Lord Towne."

"That is because I made my offer to your aunt."

"Did you, indeed? And did my aunt accept this offer on my behalf?"

"She thinks it is a splendid match. Although, I am starting to doubt it shall be. I have no desire to acquire a quarrelsome wife."

The music slowed, and with it, their pace. Relief flooded Ottilie when the gentleman released his hold on her.

"Before you go," she said, "let me save you the trouble of retracting your offer of marriage by asserting my right to decline it. I have no desire to acquire a controlling husband."

"Am I correct in assuming you are free for a waltz, then?" Mr. Bastin stepped up beside her then, a wide grin on his handsome face.

"Indeed, I am, Mr. Bastin. Have you met Lord Towne? Only a few minutes ago, he told me how much he enjoyed your book."

Lord Towne's cheeks flamed red, and he bowed curtly to Ottilie before marching off the floor and making his way to Lady Hudsyn.

Mr. Bastin slipped his arm around Ottilie's waist, placed one hand on her back, and intertwined the fingers of his free hand with hers. Together they stretched out their arms and began to glide with the music. He smelled enticingly sweet and spicy, like rum and cinnamon. Ottilie's heart pounded so rapidly that she worried Mr. Bastin might feel its vibrations.

"I can't write without you," he said, pulling her closer. "Have you given any thought to my proposal?"

"You flatter me, Mr. Bastin, but, as I told you, I won't consider it until I've spoken to Henry first. I can't imagine what's keeping him so long in Kent." In truth, she'd thought about little else beyond his proposition, but she wasn't about to let him know that.

"Hudsyn's not in Kent."

"What do you mean? Of course, he is. Where else could he be?"

"He's staying at Albany. It's only a few minutes down Piccadilly from mine."

"I know *that*. But...do you mean to say that my cousin has rented a bachelor set at Albany?"

"He hasn't rented anything. Lord Cavandon is currently out of town, and Hudsyn is staying in his flat. Although, he mentioned something about renting his own set at Albany. He claims it's the only place he can get any writing done."

"You've spoken to Henry? How long have you known he didn't go to Kent?"

"I've always known."

"But you didn't say anything last time we spoke. You let me believe he'd fled to Kent."

"A man is entitled to his privacy, Miss Hamilton. Why do you think he disappeared in the first place?"

Ottilie opened her mouth to protest, but Jack tilted an eyebrow at her and his dark eyes sparkled with mirth.

"Don't admonish me yet. Think about it from Hudsyn's perspective."

Ottilie chewed her lower lip. Jack was right. She'd only been in town a few weeks, and her aunt had already attempted to marry her without her consent. In the two years Henry had been home from Cambridge, Lady Hudsyn must have worn him to a thread with her efforts to control his future. Anger swelled in Ottilie's chest. Her aunt had no right to interfere in their lives on this level. And now she'd chased Henry from his home. Still, it hurt that her cousin had chosen not to tell her the truth.

"He is going to tell you," Mr. Bastin said as if Ottilie wore her thoughts engraved on her face. "He needed some uninterrupted time to himself first, that is all."

"He told you the truth."

"Our situation is different. He values my input on his writing." They glided around in silence for a minute before Jack spoke again. "He admires your independent spirit, you know."

Ottilie grinned. "Oh, you are a clever one, Mr. Bastin. My answer, by the way, is 'yes'," she said as the waltz ended. "You may send Mrs. Wilson for me tomorrow at noon."

The couples surrounding separated and began to move off the ballroom floor. Ottilie shifted her stance in anticipation of Jack's releasing her.

"Not yet," he murmured, tightening his grip on her waist. "Will you stay for another?"

"Are you trying to start a new scandal?" She attempted a lighthearted comment, but her voice quivered and gave her true feelings away.

"I would be content to hang if I were permitted to dance with you all evening."

He locked his eyes on Ottilie's, and she thought they might

have remained frozen in place for all eternity had it not been for the violin's sweet vibrations and the trumpet's short blasts sending them twirling once more in each other's arms across the ballroom floor.

A DISTINCT VOID enveloped Jack as Ottilie slipped from his arms at the end of their second dance. He clasped the fingers of her gloved hand and escorted her off the floor. "Would you care for a refreshment?"

"That sounds lovely, but I had better err on the side of caution and get back to my aunt. I am certain she has developed one of her famous headaches and wants to leave immediately."

Jack's gaze shifted to Lady Hudsyn, who sat stony-faced and rigid on her chair.

"I'd best escort you safely back then."

"I realize it is expected of you, but I think we should make an exception in this case. Let us say goodnight here. I think I can manage to walk the distance of ten feet on my own, despite what society believes."

"I am certain you can," Jack said with a laugh. After witnessing the strength and fortitude women of all ranks exhibited during the war in America, he could neither respect nor understand society's rules. "Until tomorrow," he said and watched as Miss Hamilton made her way back to her aunt.

"Charming, isn't she?"

"Undeniably." Jack turned to see Lady Buntley standing beside him. "I am only sorry she has to leave already." Jack caught Miss Hamilton's eye as she turned to glance at him before leaving the ballroom.

"I'd say she has perfect timing." Lady Buntley smiled slyly at Jack. "It might interest you to know Sir Richard and Lady Astyr arrived while you were preoccupied with Miss Hamilton on the dance floor."

"Did they?" Jack eyed the vivacious, middle-aged viscountess whose passionate liaison with Brandt had proven to be more than convenient. Not only did she pass on the news of Sir Richard's arrival in London, but she agreed to introduce Jack to the new Lady Astyr, giving him the chance to connect with his uncle's wife.

"I think I will steal Mrs. Astyr from her husband and show her my beautiful garden," Lady Buntley said. "Perhaps, you will desire some fresh air in a minute or two."

Jack tugged at his bow tie. "Yes, it's growing rather warm inside."

He watched as Lady Buntley slinked across the room and approached a group of ladies and gentlemen conversing together. He recognized his uncle's rigid posture immediately, and homed in on Sir Richard's hawkish face, taking in the beady eyes and sharp nose that looked as if they'd been created with the express purpose of sniffing out the enemy. His hair had turned gray and was balding in front, and he'd grown mutton chops and a full mustache as if to compensate.

Jack's stomach churned. He'd dreamed of this moment for so long that the reality of it was difficult to comprehend. He clasped his hands behind his back to avoid clenching his fists. *The time of reckoning is approaching.*

Jack watched as Lady Astyr drifted from her husband's side in the company of Lady Buntley and the two made their way onto the patio leading to the garden. He snatched a glass of port from a passing tray and swallowed it before meandering outdoors after them.

"Mr. Bastin." Lady Buntley beckoned to him as soon as he stepped out onto the spacious brick patio.

"Lady Buntley." Jack feigned surprise and approached the two women.

"You must let me introduce you to Lady Astyr. She's recently arrived in London from Nottinghamshire."

"How wonderful." Jack's smile caused his uncle's wife to flush pink. "What brought you to Mayfair?"

"She is newly married," Lady Buntley said.

Jack forced a smile. "Allow me to offer my congratulations."

Lady Astyr looked the picture of misery, like a woman who awakens, after the fuss and flurry of wedding planning, to find herself imprisoned in a lackluster marriage. Jack knew the type well. This was going to be almost too easy.

"Mr. Bastin is also new to Mayfair, yet he's already one of our most famous residents," Lady Buntley said.

"Oh?" Lady Astyr tilted her head like a curious bird.

"He's the author of the wildly popular novel *The Renegade*," Lady Buntley explained. "Have you read it? It's simply fabulous."

"I'm not one for reading novels, I'm afraid."

Jack showed no reaction to her remark. He had long ago mastered the art of keeping a straight face. "What do you enjoy reading, may I ask?"

"I rather like poetry."

"It so happens I'm in the process of working on an epic poem, soon to be serialized."

"Are you, indeed?" Lady Buntley opened her fan and aired her face. "How divine!" She winked at Jack. "Oh! Excuse me, please. I have hostess duties to perform." She floated off to converse with a nearby party of guests.

Jack focused all his attention on Lady Astyr as if she were the most desirable woman in the world.

She lowered her gaze, clearly unused to such flattery and attention from a man. Still, he kept his eyes fixed on her face. "How do you like London, Lady Astyr? You strike me as a little lonely—perhaps homesick?"

"A little," she said. "London is so noisy and different. I miss the peace of the countryside. But Sir Richard says we only need stay in London for the summer. Then we will remove to his estate in Kent."

"Oh, he has an estate in Kent." The muscles beneath Jack's

skin tightened, but he forced himself to relax. "My good friend Lord Hudsyn has an estate in that part of the country too. It's lovely."

"I miss Nottinghamshire, but I suppose I will get used to Kent soon enough."

"Well, do feel free to join me for a stroll in one of London's many parks if you are in need of some greenery before your departure for the country. Hardly a day goes by when I don't spend two or three hours meandering through Kensington Gardens or St. James's. I quite like an early morning ride in Hyde Park too."

"I love to ride." Her brown eyes took on a doleful look. "But I'm not sure it would be proper to accompany you alone. And Sir Richard isn't fond of riding."

"Lady Buntley often joins me with a party of her friends. I am sure she will be happy to accompany us."

"Well, in that case, it sounds lovely."

"Lady Astyr, how wonderful to see you again!" An elderly, ginger-haired man stepped beside Lady Astyr and fixed Jack with a penetrating stare.

"I hope I haven't been gone too long." Lady Buntley flitted between the two men like a colorful butterfly. "Mr. Jebkin, have you been introduced to our famous guest?"

Jack's neck stiffened. *Jebkin. So,* this *is Percival's father.*

The irate expression on Jebkin's face transformed into one of curiosity. "Famous?"

"Mr. Jebkin, may I introduce Mr. Jack Bastin, author of *The Renegade.* I am sure you have heard of the book."

"I have, indeed." Jebkin's voice sweetened as though it tasted money. "All of England is awaiting your next publication, Mr. Bastin. I do hope you have an excellent solicitor to protect your interests."

"As a matter of fact, I am in need of one. I believe I have already spoken with your son. We met at Boise's Gentleman's Club in St. James's. Did he mention me?"

"Boise's? My son? No. He did not."

"Well, he made a good impression, nonetheless."

"Did he?" Jebkin raised his eyebrows. "I am glad to hear it. Do consider our services should you need them in the future."

"Oh, I will, Mr. Jebkin. I am considering them already."

Jebkin smiled obsequiously and turned to Lady Astyr. "How are you finding your new home in Belgrave Square? Do you intend to transfer any furniture from Sir Richard's home on Upper Brook Street before he sells the house?"

"I'm not sure what Sir Richard has planned for the house, but our home in Belgrave is already fully furnished. Sir Richard arranged things before my arrival."

"Upper Brook Street?" Jack interrupted. "Are you referring to the house with the blue door—the one that has been left empty? I think it is rather lovely. I've walked past it several times, and I've thought how wonderful it would be to buy it. I'm on Half Moon Street at the moment."

"Oh no, Mr. Bastin, you mustn't move," Lady Buntley interjected. "Half Moon Street suits you perfectly. I believe Samuel Johnson once resided there."

"Not Johnson, his biographer Boswell," Jack corrected her.

"Oh," Lady Buntley said. "Well, that is still something."

"Are you facilitating the sale for Sir Astyr?" Jack turned his attention back to Mr. Jebkin.

"Yes, as a matter of fact, I am. Are you interested in purchasing it, sir?"

"Perhaps," Jack said. "Why is he selling, may I ask?"

"He shared that home with his deceased wife, and I believe he wants a fresh start. Am I correct, Lady Astyr?"

She nodded.

"Hang on. I see Sir Richard coming our way. You can discuss this with him yourself."

Jack's muscles tightened. He wasn't ready to reveal himself to his uncle. "I am afraid I have another engagement, and I must take my leave now. But rest assured, I will think about it and let you know if I am interested in seeing the house."

"Surely you can spare a moment or two. He is—"

"I am afraid not." Jack bowed to the ladies and turned abruptly. As he did, he brushed shoulders with his uncle; a bitter shiver ran down his spine, but he kept his head down and forced himself to continue walking. The time to confront his uncle had not yet arrived.

⇛⇚

"Mr. Bastin." Lady Buntley's voice sounded behind Jack as he stepped into the hallway.

He stopped and turned.

"A word before you go, if you please."

"Of course. I am sorry to depart in such a rush—"

Lady Buntley leaned toward Jack and spoke in a low voice. "I will forgive you if you promise to tell that divine valet of yours, I'll be waiting for him at our meeting place tomorrow afternoon. Lord Buntley will be spending the day at his club."

"Of course." Jack straightened his shoulders and tried to calm himself, although his mind seethed with violence at the thought of his uncle. "And before I forget, I told Lady Astyr you would accompany us on a ride in Hyde Park. I hope you don't mind."

"Anything for you, my dear. But I must say, I find this whole situation rather mystifying. What prompted this interest in Lady Astyr? I thought you preferred a more mature woman."

Jack forced a smile.

"What is the matter, Mr. Bastin? You seem out of sorts."

"Headache," Jack mumbled. "I need to go home and get some rest. I'll give Brandt your message." He kissed her hand. "Thank you again, my lady."

Jack strode outside, his lungs ready to burst with rage. He may well have stormed back inside and ripped out his uncle's throat had he not glimpsed Brandt waiting for him across the street. Jack blinked at the silhouette of his friend. Brandt leaned casually against a gas lamp with his ankles crossed and the brim of his black cowboy hat tipped low over his forehead. One hand rested in his coat pocket, and the other held a smoldering cigar to his lips.

The image took Jack to his early days in Texas. He was sixteen and indentured to a brute named Wardell, who used a bullwhip to keep cattle and people in line. The month-long journey from England had been tortuous, but it had been luxurious compared to the horror he'd witnessed on Wardell's sugar plantation. When he'd stepped into the fiery sugar mill with its scalding, spitting furnaces and burnt flesh smell, he'd known he'd reached the eighth level of Dante's inferno. Instinct had urged him to run.

And Wardell stopped him with his 10-foot bullwhip. It landed on his back with the full force of the devil's practiced arm, and he went down faster than a tree struck by lightning. When he awoke, dazed and raw with pain, lying face-down and shirtless on a mattress, Brandt was there.

"Hurts like the dickens, doesn't it?"

Jack lifted his head an inch, and every nerve in his body sang.

"There's wire in that blacksnake of his. That's the reason it cuts so deep."

Jack blinked the speaker into focus. He could still see Brandt's tanned face peering at him from where he sat cross-legged on the floor across from him.

"I know 'cause he done it to me too." Brandt ran a finger over a raised welt that snaked from his jaw down his neck.

"He struck you in the face?"

"Nah, he only caught my jaw 'cause I turned as he cracked the whip. See, I'll show you." Brandt swiveled around. Only a year older than Jack, he already had a man's body—powerful and muscular from his work on the ranch. His scar snaked from the bottom of his jaw around his neck and down the length of his back.

"Wardell's too much of a coward to do anything to a man's face." Brandt spun back to face Jack. "He likes to beat folks when their backs are turned or after he ties them up good and helpless." He ran his hand through his mop of sun-streaked hair. "Ain't nobody safe with his back turned on Wardell's land. He's real proud of the scars he leaves on folks. An' that's his mistake."

"What do you mean?"

"I mean, I ain't ever going to forget what he done to me. An' one day, I'm going to do the same to him."

"What are you waiting for?" Jack shifted his body and winced.

"The right time," Brandt said. "Sometimes a man needs to bide his time."

Jack lowered his head and made his own silent vow. He'd get his uncle for selling him to Wardell, no matter how long he had to wait and even if he died trying…

A short, sharp whistle broke into Jack's thoughts and pulled him to the present. He glanced up and crossed the street to join his friend.

"You all right?" Brandt dropped his cigar and killed it with his boot.

"I don't know."

"Did you see him?"

Jack nodded.

"But you didn't let him see you, right?"

"Of course not."

"Good. So, what did you find out?"

"He has bought himself a fancy new home in Belgrave Square and plans to sell his house on Upper Brook Street."

"That ain't the one your grandpa left you, is it?"

"No, that one's in Kent. Still, I'm going to buy his goddam Mayfair mansion and smash it to the ground."

"What for?"

"Because I hate the sight of it."

Brandt wrapped an arm firmly around Jack's shoulder. "Let's go home, Cowboy."

Jack wrenched himself out of Brandt's grip. "I should go back in there and slit his throat."

Brandt caught Jack by both shoulders. "I know you're hoppin' mad right now, but you gotta have a little patience. Dying is too good for that darn fool. Better to make him suffer and leave him writhing in the dirt like we did with that coward Wardell. These things have got to be done right."

Jack nodded and Brandt released his grip.

"Smug bastard!" Jack ripped off his bow tie. "Do you know he intends to occupy my grandfather's estate in Kent after the summer? It's my mother's childhood home!" He clenched his teeth. "It's all I have left of her."

"Buy it from him too. Hell, you got enough money to do it."

"I shouldn't have to buy it." Jack breathed heavily. "It's mine already. I inherited it. He stole it from me. I should not be forced to pay him a handsome sum for it."

"Don't lose your head worrying about what's fair and what ain't. You know as well as I do ain't nothing fair in this world. You get what you take. We'll make him pay one way or another."

Jack breathed evenly and nodded. "I know."

"Come on. You've done enough for one night." Brandt slung his arm around Jack's shoulders and coaxed him down the street. "Now tell me, how'd it go with Astyr's new bride? Did Lady Buntley get you some alone time with her?"

"She'll be an easy enough conquest," Jack said.

"I bet she will. Word is your uncle has an old war wound which makes it difficult for him to perform in the bedroom. So, the chances of an heir from him ain't looking too likely. But I guess he'll die tryin'," Brandt chuckled.

"Humiliating him is not enough." Rage coursed through Jack's veins again. "He deserves to die for selling me to Wardell like a dog. I'd never seen men whipped or chained up in my life before he put me on that ship, and I sure as hell had never been whipped or shackled either. That bastard chose my Jailer carefully. He found the cruelest brute he could because he needed me dead." Jack spat the words. "I still wake up in a sweat sometimes, dreaming about that godforsaken place."

"I understand. I was right there with you, remember?"

They crossed onto Half Moon Street and made their way to the townhouse. "It warn't all bad. We found each other." Brandt fished the door key from his pocket and inserted it into the lock. "And got Wardell's gold, too. You took it and turned it into a fortune. Now here you are in Mayfair, England." The lock clicked, and Brandt pushed the front door open. "We'll take your uncle for all he is worth, just like we did Wardell. It's just a matter of biding our time."

Jack stumbled into the house, and Brandt helped him to the settee in the parlor.

"I could murder the blackguard unseen and make it look like a robbery or an accident. I know how to cover my tracks. We may not have spent long with the Jayhawkers, but they taught us plenty." Jack swirled the whiskey Brandt handed him.

"It ain't wise. Your uncle's a retired general. He must know a thing or two about combat."

"I have youth on my side."

"All right. Let's say you kill him. What happens next? You won't have your inheritance back, and you'll be a cold-blooded murderer."

"So what?" Jack said.

"So, you ain't no cold-blooded killer, Jack. Ain't it why we left Kansas for Nevada after such a short run with the Jayhawkers— too much dang senseless killing? Besides, you'd be letting him die an honorable man. People will mourn the great general, Sir Richard Astyr, knighted for his brave service. No one would know what he did. You'd turn a brute into a legend."

Jack swallowed his whisky. "If I can't murder him in his bed, I'll have to kill him the civilized way."

"What are you talking about?"

"I'll dishonor his wife and force him into a duel. He won't stand a chance against me. There's only one person who's a faster shot than me, and that's you."

"Duels ain't legal here. If you kill him, you'll hang."

"I won't kill him." Jack stretched his body out on the settee. "I only wish to contribute to his war wound and turn him into a real eunuch."

Brandt laughed. "Now you're talking sense."

CHAPTER NINE

...mutual fear brings Peace,
Till the selfish loves increase
Then Cruelty knits a snare,
And spreads his baits with care.

—William Blake, "The Human Abstract"

SUNLIGHT FLOODED THE dining room, but it did little to detract from the frosty silence that hovered between Ottilie and her aunt as they breakfasted together. The silence had begun after Lady Buntley's ball. Lady Hudsyn was indignant and tight-lipped during the carriage ride home and had taken directly to her bed upon entering the house. Now, Ottilie could see her aunt itched to speak her mind, and she wondered how much longer she'd be able to restrain herself from doing so.

Ottilie plunged her silver teaspoon into the white flesh of her boiled egg and scooped out a bite. As soon as she spooned it into her mouth, Lady Hudsyn's voice trilled in her ears.

"Am I to understand the only reason you agreed to attend the ball last night was to consort with that...novelist?" She spat out the word *novelist* as if it was synonymous with *murderer*.

It was not the apology Ottilie hoped to hear. She swallowed her egg and dabbed her mouth with a serviette before replying, "Am I to understand the only reason you enjoined me to attend the ball last night was to further your plan to marry me to Lord Towne without my knowledge?"

Lady Hudsyn rose from her chair like an indignant peacock and strolled to the window. She stood with her back to Ottilie and gazed out at her resplendent garden. Ottilie understood her aunt's behavior as a sign she refused to explain her actions and had reverted to silence once again. She was all too familiar with her aunt's strategy of using silence as a means of attrition. But this time, she refused to be manipulated thus.

Ottilie put down her spoon. "I spend my summers in London because my family is important to me—that means you and Henry." Her aunt kept her body turned to the window, but Ottilie persevered. "To think I didn't even know I had a cousin or an aunt until Mama's death a mere two years ago. It breaks my heart to know you destroyed your friendship with Mama because of silly expectations and traditions. All those years lost, Aunt! Is it really something you wish to repeat?"

Lady Hudsyn turned in slow motion to face her niece. "Therein lies the difference between us. You don't recognize that being part of the peerage comes with responsibilities and sacrifices. In a family like ours, scandal affects generations. Your mama understood only too well how much. Yet, she chose to sacrifice her family. We never abandoned her."

"Whatever happened between you, I don't wish to repeat it," Ottilie said.

"You are loyal in your love for your cousin, and I know he appreciates you," her aunt said. "I want you to remember that I care as much for your happiness as I do for Henry's. But my sister had a responsibility to honor and protect our family name. Instead, she tainted it forever with her scandalous behavior, and I am trying my best to minimize the damage she caused to our family's reputation." She lifted her chin, playing the role of martyr once again. "If you love your cousin, you will do the same."

This argument was new to Ottilie. "In what scandalous behavior did Mama engage? Marrying outside one's rank is hardly a scandal deserving of this much attention."

Her aunt touched her forehead. "I'm afraid there's more to the situation."

"What could be so terrible as to make you break with your family?" She paused to run scenarios through her mind, but only one occurred to her. "Was she with child before she married?"

Lady Hudsyn's body jerked visibly.

So that is it. Mama conceived me out of wedlock. Shocking, to be sure. But shouldn't all have been forgotten and forgiven once she married my papa?

"All I can tell you is that I did what my father instructed me to do—for the good of this family."

"I don't understand your way of thinking, Aunt. But I respect that you did what you thought was right at the time. All I am asking is that you put the past behind you now. Henry and I are a new generation, and we are determined to stay friends, no matter what others say about it."

Lady Hudsyn strode to the table. "When will you learn that reputation is everything, child? One must make sacrifices to keep one's good name intact." She put her hands on her hips. "But I see now, you are too far removed from our world to understand. You aren't committed to being part of this family. You only want to blow in with the wind occasionally and stir up a storm." She flung out her arm as if to illustrate Ottilie's destructiveness. "Well, I'm afraid you cannot have it both ways. Henry is still young and far too much of a romantic thinker. It is my duty to protect his position and reputation in high society, and if you truly love him, you will see it as your duty too. You are either Henry's cousin, and you will behave as such, or you are not. Only you can decide."

Ottilie's heart constricted. Her aunt's words stung. Was there no end to betrayal? She'd felt secure and embraced by a loving family once; now, she realized it had all been an illusion. Her mama's love had been unconditional, but to everyone else, she was disposable and inconvenient.

"Excuse me, my lady." Benson appeared in the doorway. "There is a Mrs. Wilson here to see Miss Hamilton."

Thank the Lord! Mrs. Wilson had arrived to save her like Dante's Beatrice sent from Heaven.

"Who?" Lady Hudsyn snapped. "We don't know a Mrs. Wilson. Tell her to leave her card."

"She's my chaperone"—Ottilie kept her expression stony—"here to protect my reputation." She turned back to Benson. "Please tell Mrs. Wilson to wait while I collect my cape and gloves. I'll be out for the day." She strode toward the dining room exit.

"Where are you going?" Lady Hudsyn demanded.

Ottilie stopped, her fists clenched at her sides. "Instead of asking me where I am going, why don't you ask yourself where your son is and why he has been absent from home for so long?"

Her aunt's face hardened, but Ottilie could see the hurt behind her mask. Her words aimed to sting, and they'd succeeded, but that did nothing to ease Ottilie's pain.

The sugarcane forest grew thick, despite repeated ransacking by starving soldiers and provided a comfortable grassy home for mating cicadas whose satisfied hum filled the muggy night air.

"Listen to 'em." Brandt chuckled as they rode past the fields down the long stretch of dusty road leading to Wardell's plantation. "Ain't they the happy little critters?"

They passed the deserted sugar mill and stopped next to the run-down slave quarters to listen for signs of life. Hearing nothing, they urged their horses to continue their lazy walk down the barren path.

"You think them bags of gold are still in that old well behind the house?" Brandt said as Wardell's once palatial home came into view.

"Only one way to find out." Jack spurred his horse into a trot, eager to get what he came for and get out.

A gunshot cracked through the darkness and shattered the peacefulness of the night. Jack's mustang whinnied and reared on its hind legs.

"Are you hit?" Brandt rode up beside him, revolver in hand.

"Nope." Jack withdrew his pistol from its holster.

"What about your horse?"

"He's okay. Only spooked." Jack patted his gelding's neck.

"See him?" Brandt peered into the darkness.

A shadowy figure stumbled through the overgrown grass toward them.

"I see him."

Brandt pointed his revolver at the figure. "Come any closer an' you're a dead man walking."

"Get the hell off my land, or I'll blow your heads off."

Jack recognized Wardell's guttural voice instantly. "The old fool survived the war," he said.

"Disarm him," Brandt whispered. "I'll get my lasso ready."

Jack leaned forward on his horse and aimed. Next to him, Brandt whirled his lasso in the air.

"You think you can catch me with that there lasso, boy? You don't know who you're dealing with. I'll put a bullet in your head 'afore you can say Billy Yank."

The bullet sped from the barrel of Jack's Colt and hit its target, grazing Wardell's shoulder and causing him to drop his rifle. He barely had time to react before Brandt's lasso caught him around the waist and dragged him through the dust. Wardell screamed and writhed in the dirt, clutching his bleeding shoulder.

Brandt jumped off his horse and stood over him. "Need some help, Wardell?" he asked, stomping on the man's shoulder with his boot.

Wardell's shrieks stretched across the horizon as the blazing Texas sun broke through the darkness and turned the skyline red...

Jack bolted upright. The blood sky and the bloodied ground were gone. Wardell was gone. Texas was gone. Jack ran his hands over his expensive linen.

You're home. In England. In your own bed. In your own house.

He inhaled and exhaled deeply, trying to calm his hammering

heart. He dimly recalled waking up during the early morning hours after falling asleep on the settee in the parlor and hearing Mrs. Wilson going about her duties. He must have dragged himself up the stairs to bed—yes, he recalled having a conversation with the housekeeper—about what? He creased his brow. Then it struck him—Miss Hamilton. He'd instructed her to collect Miss Hamilton from Berkeley Square at noon. He reached for his evening jacket, which lay crumpled on the floor, fished out his pocket watch, and blinked its face into focus. *Hell! That is now! Ottilie is on her way.*

He sprang from the bed, pulled off his shirt, and stumbled to his washroom. The looking glass above the sink showed his face, still heavy with sleep. He plunged his head into a bowl of icy water, allowing the cold to jolt his brain and erase his grogginess. He smoothed his wet palms over his hair before cleaning his teeth and drying himself with a soft towel.

"Did you get a good night's rest, partner?" Brandt appeared in the doorway.

"You're still here?" Jack frowned. "Did I forget to tell you Lady Buntley requests your presence today? The doddering viscount will be at his club all afternoon. She's probably been wondering where you are."

Jack walked past Brandt as he exited the washroom, and his friend followed him to his chambers. "It don't matter. I ain't leaving you alone after last night. I'll send word to her."

"No need." Jack retrieved a fresh shirt from his wardrobe and slipped it on. "I'm not going to be alone today."

"You ain't?"

"Miss Hamilton will be keeping me company. I've asked Mrs. Wilson to act as her chaperone."

"Hudsyn's cousin, again? What are you playing at? How does she fit into your plans to cuckold your uncle?"

"She has nothing to do with it. My agreement with Miss Hamilton has nothing whatsoever to do with romance." Jack turned down the collar on his shirt. "She came here last week to ask me if I would be willing to give a lecture at her ladies' college in Canterbury, and I told her I would if she agreed to do something for me."

"What's that?"

"I asked her to act as my muse."

"Your muse?" Brandt folded his arms.

"Yes, she's the inspiration for my new epic poem. I told you about it, didn't I?" He selected a clean pair of trousers.

"Let me see if I have this straight. Hudsyn's cousin is the inspiration for your new poem about a seduced virgin. Is that right?"

"Not merely a virgin—one of Artemis's maidens…never mind. The point is Miss Hamilton inspired this poem, and I write better in her presence."

"Dang it!" Brandt covered his face with both hands.

"It's not what you think, Brandt. I vowed not to touch her."

"Sakes alive! It gets worse by the second." Brandt hooked his thumbs in his belt and looked up to the ceiling as if an explanation lay there.

"Don't meddle in things you don't understand, Brandt."

"I understand you're a dang fool." Brandt squinted at Jack. "You've turned that girl into the buried treasure. Now, you ain't goin' to be able to stop yourself until she belongs to you."

"Relax, Brandt. This is about work, not romance. I receive what I need to finish my poem, and she receives what she needs to further her ambitions for her ladies' college."

"Are you sayin' you're not attracted to her? Because the woman I saw was real pretty."

"Of course, I'm attracted to her, but I'm also capable of exercising self-restraint. She's Hudsyn's cousin. That's reason enough for me never to lay a finger on her." Jack slipped his feet into his boots. "I thought you'd be happy I have something to focus on besides my bloody uncle. Because if I don't think about something else, I won't be able to stop myself from—"

"You're right." Brandt held up both hands. "You're right." He nodded. "Better a pretty distraction than the hangman's noose."

"I should think so." Jack rolled up the sleeves of his white shirt and smoothed back his hair.

CHAPTER TEN

And the sunlight clasps the earth
And the moonbeams kiss the sea:
What is all this sweet work worth
If thou kiss not me?

—*Percy Bysshe Shelley, "Love's Philosophy"*

"WHAT SHALL I do now that I am here?" Ottilie sat on the buttoned-leather settee in Mr. Bastin's parlor. "Are there any rules to being a muse? Is it like sitting for a portrait?"

"The first rule is that you must stop calling me Mr. Bastin. It's simply too formal, and I see the muse/poet relationship as something more intimate."

"Is that right? What do you prefer I call you?"

"Bastin will do. That's what my friends call me."

"What about Jack?"

"If you prefer it, I have no objection."

Ottilie smiled. She liked the idea of using his Christian name.

"Other than that," Jack continued, "you can do whatever you wish. I suggest reading a book or doing some writing of your own. Perhaps, you'd like to draw or work on some equations. Anything that pleases you."

"Except leave the room."

"You're not my prisoner."

Ottilie stood up and walked to the bookshelf. "I think I'd like to learn more about Artemis. Do you have anything?"

"Ovid's *Metamorphosis*." Jack came up behind Ottilie and peered at the bookshelf. He leaned forward, pressing his chest against her back and sending a delicious shiver down her spine as he reached for the volume.

"I'm afraid I only have the original version." He handed her the text.

"In Latin?" She took the book from him.

"I'm afraid so."

Ottilie shrugged. "I know a little Latin."

"Of course, you teach at a ladies' college," Jack teased, but his eyebrows arched upwards as she returned to the settee still holding the book.

"There's a bowl of chestnuts on the table if you care for something to nibble on, or I can ring for Mrs. Wilson if you want something more substantial."

"Chestnuts will do well, thank you." Ottilie took the bowl, positioned it on her lap, and burrowed down into her seat.

She glanced up at Jack and caught him smiling at her from his writing desk. "What are you smiling about?"

"I am happy to see you making yourself at home. I like that you don't let silly pretenses interfere with your comfort."

"Well, I imagine crafting an epic poem takes a lot of time, so I ought to be here a while."

"It does," Jack said. "It's why I chose to work in the parlor today. I thought it would be more comfortable for you."

"How very kind of you. I'm ashamed to admit comfort is one of my weaknesses, so I am thankful to have it."

"Most people prefer comfort to hardship."

Ottilie lowered her book. "I realize that, but some people— martyrs and soldiers—conduct themselves like heroes, despite horrible discomfort. I doubt I would shine under those circumstances."

"You'd be surprised at the strength of the human spirit. I've known men and women who have not only survived but thrived after enduring unspeakable horrors."

"That's clear from your book. It's what makes the story so remarkable. The characters' emotions and experiences feel genuine, almost as if you'd lived them yourself."

He shifted in his seat. "It's not a good idea to try and read the writer into his work of fiction. My book isn't an autobiography."

"I know, but all writers draw on their own experiences, don't they?"

He picked up his quill. "Maybe."

He seemed reluctant to engage, but Ottilie's curiosity was aroused, so she persisted. "For example, you write about war in your novel."

"What of it?" he said without looking up from his desk.

"Were you involved in any battles during the conflict?"

"The conflict?" He glanced up.

"The American Civil War," she clarified. "You were in America during the war, correct?"

"I was." He returned to his papers.

"Did you fight?"

"For a time, but I wasn't in any particular regiment." Again, he spoke without looking up, which only aroused Ottilie's curiosity more.

"What do you mean? You didn't join the military?'

"Not directly."

"How does one participate in combat indirectly?'

Jack put down his quill and rubbed the back of his neck. "War is complicated, Miss Hamilton, and battle can take many forms. The American Civil War was a particularly complicated and bloody affair."

"I thought it was about ending slavery in America."

"That was part but not the whole of it." He folded his arms on his desk and looked at her in apparent defeat.

Ottilie pressed a finger to her lip, contemplating his words. "Well, I must confess my ignorance. I'm curious to learn more."

"There are books on the subject. I'm sure the library has a few."

"I am certain it does, but I want to hear a firsthand account, not what a history book tells me."

Jack laughed. "Perhaps I will reward your persistence one day, Miss Hamilton. But for now, I must occupy my thoughts with Ancient Greece."

"Of course, you must!" Ottilie covered her mouth with her hand and resolved to be quiet. She returned to her reading but found she could not fully concentrate on the Latin words. Her mind danced with unanswered questions, and her desire to learn more about Jack Bastin grew by the second.

JACK ATTEMPTED TO quiet his mind and settle into the comfortable silence that now filled the room but found he missed the sound of Miss Hamilton's voice. She appeared to be wholly absorbed in Ovid, which intrigued him. Clearly, she knew more than a little Latin. He took in the nuances of her facial expressions as she read. A smile played on the corners of her lips, then her brow creased slightly, and she shook her head as though admonishing or warning someone in the story.

His mind carried him to Ancient Delphi, where his heroine shaded herself from the force of Helios's glory under an olive tree. She sat, wholly absorbed in a book, with her slim, tanned legs and sandaled feet stretched out on the grass before her, and her golden tresses swept back in a loose coil. Her hand moved absentmindedly from a bowl of nuts on her lap to her mouth. It was thus that his hero, a young, mortal poet of humble origins, first encountered the love of his life.

Miss Hamilton glanced up from her reading and met Jack's gaze. His heart jumped, and he half expected to look down and see an arrow lodged in his chest.

She lowered her book. "I see you watching me."

"Does that bother you?"

"Only if I am distracting you from your work. I've done enough to derail you today."

"You haven't distracted me. On the contrary, I was envisioning my heroine sitting under an olive tree, absorbed in the pages of a book, while nibbling absentmindedly on a bowl of nuts."

Her lips curved into a smile, and her cheeks dimpled—a sight Jack always welcomed.

"What type of nut is she eating?"

"Pine nuts."

"I don't believe I've had those before—maybe once in a fruitcake—but I can't recollect the taste. What made you think of pine nuts?"

"They are native to that region. And the Ancient Greeks believed that certain foods, like pine nuts, were blessed by the goddess of love, Aphrodite. They called them 'aphrodisiakos' after the goddess herself."

"Aphrodisiacs." Miss Hamilton nodded. "They have the power of a love potion."

"Something like that." He pushed back his chair and strolled to the settee.

"Is that what makes your heroine fall in love with the poet?" She placed her book and bowl of chestnuts onto the table as he came toward her.

"It intensifies her attraction to him, yes." He settled onto the settee beside her. "Both lovers are playthings of the gods. The young poet rambles through the forest, thinking of his next great work of poetry, when one of Eros's errant arrows strikes him. At that same moment, he sees Artemis's maiden and is overcome with desire. She, being full of pine nuts, is equally drawn to him. Their attraction for one another, powered by Aphrodite and her son, is so strong that they defy Artemis's wrath and risk their lives to satisfy their desires."

"Then your poem isn't about genuine love at all. It's about

the ongoing war between Aphrodite and Artemis—a topic already written about extensively."

"You're right, and I wish to add to the debate. Can chastity withstand the pull of lust?"

"Don't you mean love?"

"No, I don't. Love develops later. Attraction and desire come first. Love may develop, but true, deep love cannot happen without attraction—at least, not in my experience."

She shifted in her seat. "Well, you have an advantage over me as far as that is concerned, but I still think love is more complicated than that. Love comes from mutual respect and like-mindedness."

"And attraction," Jack said. "Without attraction, all you have is friendship. Take your relationship with Hudsyn, for example. You admire and respect one another. You even love each other, I imagine. But if no physical attraction exists, you will never be more than friends."

"Hudsyn's my cousin. It's different."

"Victoria and Albert were cousins but were undoubtedly attracted to one another. That is why they shared a deep love. Everyone could see it wasn't a marriage of convenience." Jack leaned his arm against the settee and rested his head on his hand, gazing intently at Ottilie. "The English like to pretend lust is immoral, but the Greeks and Romans knew better. They understood the struggle. It's perfectly natural, yet women today are made to feel ashamed when they succumb to Aphrodite's whims."

"Perhaps you are right." Ottilie leaned forward as if she willed him to kiss her. She smelled faintly of honeysuckle, and he imagined she tasted like ambrosia. Jack envisioned pressing his lips against hers, and it took all his strength to restrain himself. It wasn't only his friendship with Hudsyn that stopped him. She deserved to be courted by a man who intended to marry her, and he could not promise her fidelity or marriage. But his honorable intentions did him little good. Jack's gaze fell on Ottilie's soft, sweet mouth.

"The maiden is forbidden," he said with a sigh, "which makes her all the more enticing."

Jack's gaze was thick with desire and mirrored Ottilie's own inner struggle. She cleared her throat and forced herself to speak, though she risked revealing too much through her voice. "I imagine your poem will not end happily, considering what I've just read about Artemis's pride and anger."

Jack straightened, easing the tension between them, which left Ottilie both disappointed and relieved. "You are referring to her horrible cruelty after Actaeon stumbles upon her bathing naked in the forest, I assume? Imagine being ripped to shreds by one's own hounds!"

"Cruel indeed, but I hardly think Artemis had a choice," Ottilie said.

"How so? Actaeon is innocent. Ovid makes that clear."

"True, but Artemis must protect herself and her chastity."

"Why so mercilessly? Is it fair to suffer a torturous death for the mere act of strolling through the woods?"

"I believe the situation is more complex than that." Ottilie paused to think how to explain this female predicament to Jack. "Early in life, women are taught to safeguard their reputations and chastity as fiercely as a mother protects her babe. And if she fails to do so, the consequences will be tantamount to death. As the goddess of chastity, Artemis stands as a shining example to women."

"You believe Artemis acted fairly?"

"She acted in the extreme, the way an angry goddess would. But the lesson she teaches resonates with all women—if a woman's reputation is compromised, it is because she wasn't vigilant enough."

Jack's forehead creased. "So, Artemis was wrong for exposing herself by bathing naked in the woods; therefore, Actaeon had to die?"

"She was not wrong for bathing in the woods, but she would

have been wrong to let Actaeon go free."

"I fail to follow your logic. What danger can a mere mortal present to a goddess?"

"He may be a mortal, but he is still a man, and he has the power to damage her reputation."

"Go on," Jack said.

"What if Artemis lets Actaeon walk away unscathed, and a few days later, he drinks a little too much wine and boasts to his friends about how he saw the goddess of chastity bathing in the forest—not an unlikely scenario, is it?"

Jack grinned. "He'd be a fool because Artemis would hunt him down and kill him. And she'd be justified in doing so."

"Exactly," Ottilie said. "She would still have to kill him, but not before he exposed her to the world for failing to protect her chastity. How would she look then? Her reputation would suffer even though her only fault would have been showing mercy. Better to be seen as cruel than unchaste."

Jack edged closer to her, closing the gap between them. "If you follow that logic, you would be wise to kill me."

Ottilie's stomach knotted. He was right, of course. She risked a scandal sitting in Jack's parlor, but she did not care. Everything about Jack made her want to abandon all logic. She craved his touch and doubted she'd be able to tear herself from him if the house suddenly caught on fire. He reached out and caressed her jaw, sending a rush of pleasure surging through her. They gazed at each other as he brushed his thumb lightly over her lips. *Chastity be damned*, she thought, closing her eyes in anticipation of his kiss.

It never came.

She looked at him. Jack's dark gaze had never left her face and expressed the same longing she felt. Ottilie brought her hand to his cheek and leaned forward, aching for the feel of his lips. Their legs pressed together as she touched her lips softly against his. The sensation set her nerves on fire. He let out a soft moan, but instead of returning her kiss, he clasped her wrist and gently removed her hand from his cheek.

The warmth left Ottilie's body. She turned away from him, humiliated. What happened? Had the most notorious rake in all of England declined to kiss her? After she'd offered herself up to him like a dog wanting its belly scratched? She cursed herself. Since when had she become so predictable and pathetically needy? What must he think of her now?

"You're beautiful," Jack said.

She stood abruptly. This was only a game to him, and she refused to continue embarrassing herself. "It's time for me to go."

"Don't." He caught her by the wrist as she turned to retrieve her cape.

He stood up. "Don't leave like this—you're upset with me."

"I'm upset with myself. I have behaved ridiculously."

"No, you haven't. You've behaved like a woman. There's nothing ridiculous about a woman desiring a man."

Humiliation engulfed her. She squirmed to get away, but he pulled her toward him.

"You mustn't think I don't desire you. I have never wanted anyone more. If you weren't Hudsyn's cousin, then—"

Her body went rigid. Henry? Did he restrain himself out of concern for her cousin? Henry had done as he pleased and left her to fend for herself. So had her stepfather, her grandfather, and her own father. She was an independent woman who earned her keep, and she did not need to answer to her cousin.

"Well, I suppose I should be thankful that you harbor such great respect for my cousin."

"It is not only Hudsyn I am concerned about." He let go of her wrist and slipped his arm around her waist. "I wish to treat you with the respect you deserve. Why are you making it so difficult?"

Desire surged through her body; she wanted him to kiss her, and she didn't need him, Henry, or her aunt making decisions for her. "Don't you understand? I want you to—"

A sudden sharp rap sounded at the front door, and Ottilie

jerked in fright.

Jack tightened his hold on her waist. "Keep still. Maybe they'll go away."

"Don't you wish to know who it is?"

"Why would I want to do that when I have all I need here in this room?"

The rapping came again—this time, louder and more aggressive.

Soon a rapid clip-clop of footsteps sounded on the marble floor.

Jack raised his eyebrows. "Why today, of all days, does Mrs. Wilson choose to answer the door?"

Ottilie frowned as she listened to the sound of muffled voices, which grew steadily louder.

"Please wait, sir." Mrs. Wilson pleaded.

"Where is he?" Footsteps sounded in the hallway. "It is most urgent that I speak with him immediately!"

Ottilie sucked in her breath.

"What in tarnation is going on?" Jack said.

"It's Lord Towne. What is *he* doing here?"

"Lord Towne?" Jack narrowed his eyes. "Are you certain?"

Ottilie nodded. "I recognize his voice."

"Sir! If you care to wait, I will inform Mr. Bastin that you are here," Mrs. Wilson's voice rang out.

"Where is he? I demand to speak with him at once." The footsteps grew louder.

Miss Hamilton's body went rigid in Jack's arms. "He's coming to the parlor. I have to hide," she whispered. "He must not see me alone in this room with you."

"Come on. I know the perfect place." Jack pulled her toward a corner of the room.

"Where?" Ottilie said, her voice shaky. "There is no escape. The entrance and exit are one and the same. We are trapped."

"Behind here." Jack directed her toward a sturdy mahogany cabinet, which housed his collection of wines and spirits. Its wide midsection held an array of bottles and in its large wing doors housed neat rows of crystal glasses. The cabinet would easily conceal both their bodies. He put his hand on her back and guided her as they both slipped behind the cabinet just in time to hear Mrs. Wilson and Lord Towne enter the parlor.

"If you will be so kind as to wait here, I will go and find him for you."

"If I must," Lord Towne said gruffly.

Jack's breathing stilled as they ensconced themselves in the snug dark space, their bodies pressed close together. Lord Towne's pacing footsteps sounded in their ears.

"Scoundrel!" Lord Towne muttered to himself.

Miss Hamilton suppressed a giggle, and Jack put a finger to his lips.

"What does he think he is playing at, hey?" Lord Towne's voice drifted toward them. It sounded as if he was approaching the cabinet.

Miss Hamilton tensed in Jack's arms.

The cabinet rattled, and the sound of liquid hitting glass followed.

The cad is helping himself to my alcohol! Jack seethed.

"You will desist wooing Miss Hamilton at once, sir!" Lord Towne mumbled under his breath.

Ottilie covered her mouth with her hand to stifle her laughter.

"Shhh," Jack whispered in her ear. "Try not to move."

They both froze as they listened to Lord Towne gulp down his drink. Seconds later, he slammed the glass onto the cabinet. Ottilie inhaled sharply. Jack slipped an arm around her waist and drew her closer.

The splashing of liquid came again as Lord Towne poured himself a second drink. *Entitled fool!* Jack fumed.

"I mean to have that girl for my wife. And I won't let that rogue take my prize from me," he grumbled.

Laughter rose in Jack's throat. He buried his face in Ottilie's neck. She arched her back as though offering herself up to him. The soft warmth of her skin intoxicated him, and he could no longer resist her pull. He brushed his lips against the base of her neck, and she let out an involuntary groan. Jack placed a hand over her mouth as his lips continued to work their way up her neck. She trembled as he closed his lips around her earlobe.

"I'm afraid Mr. Bastin seems to have stepped out, sir." Mrs. Wilson's voice pulled Jack from the haze of desire, and he lifted his head.

"Confound it! When will he return? I cannot remain sitting in his parlor all day!" Lord Towne barked.

"I'm afraid I don't know, sir. Would you care to leave a card?"

"I will indeed leave a card and this message. Inform Mr. Bastin that I will speak with him regarding one Miss Hamilton, niece to Lady Hudsyn of Berkeley Square."

Jack glanced at Ottilie. Her face was inches from his. *She's so lovely, so perfect, and so very different from the women I've known before.* He inched closer and brushed his lips against hers. His body screamed for more. *What those women desired, I could readily supply. No one got hurt. But this is different. Ottilie would get hurt, and so would I. When she realizes the darkness that lives inside me—the things I've done and still desire to do—no.* He pulled back. *She deserves better.*

"I'm sorry," he said softly. "I shouldn't have put you in this position."

"You have nothing to be sorry for; I came here willingly."

The front door closed with a bang in the distance as Lord Towne exited the house. Ottilie flinched. She peered up at Jack, gripped his arm, and drew him closer.

He closed his eyes and breathed in her sweet scent, savoring the moment and attempting to imprint her smell on his memory. She arched her neck, and her mouth sought his. Jack groaned before steeling himself and forcing his body to withdraw.

"I think it is safe for us to leave now." He took her hand and led her out from behind the cabinet.

"Are you certain Lord Towne is gone?" Ottilie shivered as she scanned the parlor.

He nodded. "I am sorry you were forced to endure such an ordeal." The room's brightness sobered him and helped reinforce the clarity of his thoughts. As long as Ottilie associated herself with him, her reputation would be at risk. He smiled apologetically at her. "It seems that it would be wise for us to end this arrangement. It was foolish and selfish of me to ask so much of you."

"You wish to call off the whole arrangement?" Ottilie's face creased in confusion.

"I wish to free you of your obligation." Jack strode to his desk to avoid looking at her. "I should never have asked you to risk your reputation and become my muse."

"We had an agreement. I agreed to be your muse, and you agreed to speak at the ladies' college."

Jack picked up a pile of papers and shuffled them needlessly. "You needn't worry. I will keep to my end of the agreement and come to your ladies' college as promised if you still desire it."

"That's very kind of you." Ottilie's voice grew stiff, and a pang shot through Jack's chest. "I will inform our headmistress. She will be thrilled." Ottilie paused. "And you no longer need me to inspire your poem?"

"You have given me all the inspiration I need." He plopped the papers back onto his writing desk and turned to face her. "Without you, there would be no poem."

"I will go if that is what you wish, but I hope you are pleasing yourself and not Lord Towne. He has no claim on me."

"I am not acting to placate Lord Towne." He moved toward her. "I don't want you to return because if you do, I won't be able to guarantee your honor will stay intact."

"My honor? Do you mean to say you'd force yourself on me?"

"Of course not. But I am afraid that you would not object, and I would not have the strength to restrain myself."

Ottilie lowered her eyes.

"Am I wrong?" He asked.

She looked up at him. "I am six-and-twenty-years-old and capable of making my own decisions."

"That is true, but I am not making this decision for you. I am making it for myself. I will not be the man who—"

"I think we are talking about two different things. I was only proposing that you kiss me, not that I become your mistress. To that, you can rest assured, I would say no."

Jack smiled. He'd underestimated her. She did not need his protection, after all. "You are correct, Miss Hamilton. It is my heart I wish to protect. And that is the true reason I must send you away." Jack turned and reached for the bell to summon Mrs. Wilson.

CHAPTER ELEVEN

And if I think, my thoughts come fast,
I mix the present with the past,
And each seems uglier than the last.

—Percy Bysshe Shelley, "Song for 'Tasso'"

OTTILIE TAPPED THE metal nib of her goose-feathered quill pen against the writing desk and stared at the crisp, white page before her. She had been trying to write to Violet for two days, but the words would not come. Why? After all, she had good news to deliver. Jack Bastin would be coming to Canterbury Ladies' College to give a live reading of his novel, or perhaps discuss the new epic poem he was writing. Yet, she could not make herself put the words on paper. Violet would read between the lines. She would know that Ottilie was keeping something from her, and she would worry.

Ottilie longed to confide in her friend, but she knew it wasn't advisable to put such private matters in writing. Those were conversations best held in person. Ottilie sighed. She wished Violet were here. Indeed, she would leave for Canterbury immediately if Violet were there. But Violet was in Margate, enjoying a holiday at the seaside with her husband and twins. Of course, Ottilie could go to Margate. Every summer, Violet extended an open invitation for Ottilie to join them at the seaside.

But Ottilie refused to interrupt Violet's much-needed holiday only to burden her with her troubles.

"Is this where you have been hiding?" Lady Hudsyn swept into the library, her emerald-green dress trailing behind her. "I am pleased you have decided to stay home today." Her aunt's voice still carried a sour note.

"Actually, I'm thinking about returning to Canterbury. Henry's not here, and I seem to be causing you nothing but embarrassment, so—"

"There's no need to be dramatic. I never claimed to be embarrassed by you. I realize you enjoy independence in Canterbury, but the rules are different in Mayfair, and I only ask that you follow them."

Ottilie put her quill down and slipped the writing paper into the desk drawer.

"Don't stop writing your letter on my account. I do not wish to disturb you."

"You haven't disturbed me. The letter is not urgent; it can wait."

Her aunt nodded and strolled to the bookshelves.

"Are you looking for something to read?" Ottilie asked, wondering what her aunt wanted.

Lady Hudsyn wiped her gloved finger across several books and inspected for dust. "Mrs. Wilson—your chaperone—she's employed by Mr. Bastin, is she not?"

"She is, but you needn't worry. Mrs. Wilson is a respectable widow."

"She's a housekeeper," Lady Hudsyn snapped.

"Some people need to work to eat, Aunt. There is no shame in that."

Lady Hudsyn swished toward a vacant chair beside the writing desk. "You seem rather enamored with this Mr. Bastin," she said, seating herself next to Ottilie.

"I hardly know him. He is Henry's friend and a talented writer, so I like him for those reasons."

"I wouldn't make too much of his friendship with Henry. My son is young and mistakes Mr. Bastin's notoriety for talent. He needs to be steered in the right direction, and now I see that, despite your age, you require similar guidance."

"I disagree."

"Do you intend to see Mr. Bastin again?"

"There's no need. I only went on the headmistress's behalf to ask if he cared to give a live reading at the college."

"And has he agreed?"

"Yes," Ottilie said.

"That won't do your school's reputation any good."

"On the contrary, it will be fantastic for the college. Mr. Bastin is a well-respected author."

Lady Hudsyn rubbed her thumb across her palm. "Did you ever wonder why your mother waited five years to remarry?"

"Because my father was a rake. He hurt her and made it difficult for her to trust anyone. In fact, she should have waited longer than five years because she was fooled a second time." The sting of her stepfather's betrayal added a trace of bitterness to her voice.

"All true, but that is not the reason she waited." Lady Hudsyn stood up and walked to the window.

Ottilie assessed her aunt, trying to read her motivations. Lady Hudsyn wasn't usually the sort to mince words, so why was she being evasive now?

"Are you going to tell me the reason, Aunt?"

Lady Hudsyn elongated her neck as if she were a martyr about to die for her cause. "Your father didn't die when you were three."

Ottilie stood up and joined her aunt by the window. "What do you mean?"

"I mean that your mother kept the truth from you." Lady Hudsyn retained her martyr's stance.

"Did he go to prison?"

"Not imprisoned, no."

"Aunt!" Ottilie snapped.

"Not imprisoned but locked away." Her aunt said the words slowly as if making time for them to sink in.

"An asylum?" Ottilie's body grew cold as the realization dawned on her. "My father's madness wasn't a figment of Mama's imagination?"

Lady Hudsyn lowered her gaze. "I'm afraid not."

"Are you saying that Mama waited to remarry until I turned eight years old because that is when my father died?"

Her aunt nodded.

"My father lived in an asylum for five years and died after my eighth birthday?" Ottilie repeated.

"Yes," Lady Hudsyn said.

"Where was this asylum located?"

"East Sussex, I believe."

Ottilie's chest tightened. She sank onto the window seat like a deflated sail.

"It was the best institution money could buy," her aunt added as if to soften the blow. "Your grandfather paid for his treatment. He didn't want the gossips saying that his daughter's husband was locked away in a pauper's house for the insane."

"East Sussex? All that time he was so nearby? Why didn't Mama allow me to visit him? Was he so bad that he couldn't recognize his own wife and daughter?"

"Your grandfather laid down stringent conditions for his continued support. Your mother was to have no contact whatsoever with your father. In exchange for her cooperation, Papa paid for her upkeep and those ridiculous tutors she insisted upon for your education."

A numb sensation overcame Ottilie. She turned to the window and blinked at the sunshine and greenery outside. "Did he have a window?" she asked.

"What?"

"A window. Did my father have a window? You said the asylum was a decent place."

"Yes, his room came equipped with a window and a view as lovely as this," her aunt said.

Ottilie pressed her lips together. "All those years, I had a father—only a few miles away—yet nobody told me. It doesn't seem fair."

"There was no choice. You did not have a father. He was insane!"

"No!" Ottilie stood up, her numbness giving way to anger. "What's insane is that you think titles and impressing others is more important than family and happiness."

"Are you saying you didn't enjoy a happy childhood?"

"I was happy, but I would have been happier not to lose my father because of other people's ridiculous snobbery. This grandfather you speak of—a man who sent money but never visited—robbed me of my Papa. And you—who refused to acknowledge my existence while Mama lived—you now think you have the right to tell me how to live my life. At least I understand why you are so desperate for me to marry Lord Towne. You hope it will erase the shame attached to my name— the daughter of your wayward sister and the lunatic she married.

"The decisions your grandfather made were to protect you and this family. My actions, now and then, are all motivated by that same reason."

"Neither of you acted to protect us. You only sought to protect yourselves and your precious reputations. In fact, I wouldn't even be allowed in this house if Henry didn't insist on it."

"That's not true."

"Tell me Aunt, isn't Lord Towne afraid to have children with the offspring of a madman? Mightn't I pass bad blood onto my children?"

"You needn't worry about that."

"Why not? Mama always did. She steered me away from literature and toward mathematics."

"You have no need for either, in my opinion. What your mama did to you with all those silly tutors makes me shudder.

You would have been married years ago if it were not for her ridiculous notions."

A biting retort edged on Ottilie's lips, and she pressed them together to keep it at bay.

"Your father wasn't born with madness in his blood. It was a consequence of his unsavory behavior."

"I don't understand. What caused his madness?"

"Syphilis," Lady Hudsyn said tightly.

"What?" A weight crushed Ottilie's chest.

"Now, do you understand? You can thank your grandfather for getting that devil out of your mother's life before he infected her with his vileness."

Ottilie rubbed her forehead. She couldn't think clearly; this was all too much to bear.

"I didn't want to burden you with any of this," her aunt said. "But I need you to understand why I object to you running out to see that writer. People will start to make comparisons between you and your mother—"

"Don't speak about my mama as though I ought to be ashamed of her."

"Well, now I see that you are getting overly emotional. I will leave you to gather your thoughts and regain control. When you've had sufficient time, you will see sense." Her aunt turned and strode out of the room.

Ottilie pulled her legs up to her chest, rested her head on her knees, and shrank inwards.

JACK RUBBED THE aching muscles in his neck and longed for some distraction. Where was Brandt? He glanced at the pocket watch laying on his desk. Half-after-five. He strode out of his study and crossed the landing.

"Brandt," he called. "Are you in here?" He pushed open his

friend's door and stepped inside his bedchamber. A slim and very naked young woman scuttled from the bed.

Jack turned his back and waited for the woman to gather her clothing and make herself decent. A minute later, she scurried past him, wearing a black and white housekeeper's uniform that looked exactly like the one Wilson wore every day.

Jack spun around and faced Brandt. "Who the hell is that?"

"New housemaid." Brandt threw off his covers and sat up. "Wilson said she needed help, so I hired Lulu to help her."

"Lulu? You hired a harlot to help Wilson with the housekeeping?"

"Relax. She ain't no whore." Brandt stood up and arched his back in a stretch. "She's a trained housemaid. She worked two years in Cavendish Square."

"And?"

"And what?" Brandt reached for his trousers.

"And why doesn't she work there anymore?"

"She was unfairly dismissed." Brandt slipped on his trousers.

"What do you mean?"

"You know. Admiring master, jealous mistress."

"And where did you meet her?" Jack held up his hands in surrender. "Never mind; I'd rather not know."

"Don't be a prig." Brandt poured himself a whiskey. "Want one?"

"No, I'm anxious about the house. When are we meeting Percival?"

"At six o'clock. You ready?" Brandt asked.

"That's in a half-hour."

"Percival will wait if he knows what's good for him." Brandt pushed a whiskey glass into Jack's hand.

"I said I didn't want a drink."

"Well, you're goin' to drink it anyway because if you don't stop acting like you're the sheriff of this town, things are goin' to get ugly real fast."

"Is that a threat?"

"Maybe try an' remember I ain't your valet, but I am your friend, and I don't want to have to hit you."

Jack took the whiskey and downed it. "You're right. I don't know what's gotten into me lately."

"'Course you do." Brandt slipped on his white shirt and fastened the buttons. "Why did you send her away? She makes you happy."

Jack slumped onto Brandt's bed. "She doesn't need to be dragged into my darkness."

"Don't you think that's for her to decide?" Brandt slipped his arms through his waistcoat.

Jack scoffed. "A woman like her could never make sense of the dark thoughts that eat at my heart daily. You remember how it is, don't you? We couldn't rest until we hashed things out with Wardell, and I won't rest until my uncle gets his comeuppance. I intend to break him like he broke me."

"Does that mean you have to give up the girl?"

"You know it does. She's not part of the plan. I don't want to hurt her, and that's bound to happen."

"You can break your uncle without cuckolding him." Brandt clipped on his bowtie.

"I can't. He deserves utter ruin and humiliation, and I mean to serve him the full course."

"Then we best high tail it to Upper Brook Street."

✳

PERCIVAL JEBKIN UNLOCKED the door to the townhome with unsteady hands.

"Sir Richard simply closed these doors and returned to his station in India after Lady Astyr's death three years ago," Percival said as he pushed open the door. "Jebkin and Jebkin assisted him in removing and storing all his valuables from the house, but much of the furniture remains."

Jack strode into the expansive hallway and took in the wide staircase, lush Persian rug, and elegant blue and gold papered walls. *The snake*, he muttered under his breath.

Brandt whistled. "This place is something, ain't it?"

All that time, my uncle and aunt lived like kings, while we—

He shook his head.

No, I would not have wanted to exchange our little cottage for this house. We were free birds on the moors. Free and happy! He thought of his twin sister and smiled. *Frances would have hated this place.* Sixteen years had passed since her death from consumption, and the hole it left in his heart still gaped.

"As I mentioned, the paintings and other valuables were all removed and placed in the care of Jebkin and Jebkin at the time of Lady Astyr's death. Of course, everything remaining in the house will have to be inventoried, cataloged, and sold, which may take a few weeks."

"I don't have a few weeks," Jack snapped.

Percival frowned. "I don't understand—"

"Where are the papers we asked for?" Brandt cut into Percival's sentence.

The law clerk redirected his attention to his work bag and extracted a rolled document secured with a string. "I prepared a copy for you, but I will need to take the original back to the office this evening. If anyone discovers it's missing—"

"Quit yer yammerin'!" Brandt snatched the document and passed it to Jack.

Jack untied the string around his uncle's will and unraveled it. As he did so, another rolled paper fluttered to the floor. Brandt scooped it up and untied the string around it. He unrolled and scanned the document in silence.

Jack saw the color drain from Brandt's face. "What is it?" he asked.

"Nothing. Just some legal talk. Makes no dang sense to me." He rolled up the paper again.

Percival came forward to retrieve the document. "If it's part of the original will, I must return it to the office."

"It ain't," Brandt snapped.

"Let me see."

"It's nothing."

"Don't lie. I saw the expression on your face. You turned as white as a snowdrop. Now, let me have it." Jack held out his hand.

"I ain't gonna do that right now."

"What?" Jack asked, incredulous. Why would Brandt withhold information from him? It made no sense. Something was afoot, and he intended to find out what it was. He tossed his uncle's will aside and put his hand on his holster.

"Give me that paper, Brandt."

Percival whimpered and scrambled on all fours to recover Sir Richard's will.

"Go on," Brandt said without flinching. "I dare you."

"Hand me that damn document," Jack repeated.

"You'd better shoot me, Cowboy, 'cause there ain't no way you're leaving this house alive if you point a gun at me."

Percival cowered in the corner and let out a gurgled sob.

Jack dropped his hand from his holster. "Of course, I'm not going to shoot you."

"Really? Cause I think you know better than to act like you're gonna draw your gun on a man without meaning to shoot or get shot."

"The chamber is empty."

Brandt moved his jacket aside. "Well, mine ain't, so that wasn't too bright of you, was it?"

Jack opened his arms wide. "What's the matter with you? Is this about my mistaking the new housekeeper for a whore?"

"I ain't the one with a problem, pal." Brandt frowned and motioned to Jack's gun. "Give it here."

Jack opened his jacket. "How about you take it in exchange for that document?"

Brandt moved forward and shoved the paper at Jack. "Here,

you dang fool. What do I care?" Jack closed his hand around the document, and Brandt snatched the pistol from Jack's holster with his free hand.

"No bullets," he said, opening the chamber.

Jack smirked and turned his attention to the document. But, before he had time to read a word, the back of Brandt's fist smashed against his cheekbone, and a world of pain exploded on his face. He staggered back. A burning sensation spread across his face, and his vision blurred.

"What the devil?" He glanced at Brandt through his streaming eye.

"Ain't you gonna hit me back?" Brandt stretched out his arms.

"Don't tempt me." Jack clenched his fists, but he knew he'd deserved what Brandt had given him. He would have done the same if Brandt had even hinted at shooting him.

"You gonna read it or what?"

Jack recovered the document and scanned its contents.

Certificate of Death

Name of Deceased:	Sebastian John Greyson
Date of Birth:	March 16, 1840
Father of Deceased:	Rev. Sebastian James Greyson
Date of Death:	September 1856
Time of Death:	Unknown
Manner of Death:	Drowned, Atlantic Ocean
Informant:	Sir Richard Neville Astyr
Relationship:	Uncle

The air left his lungs. He crumpled the paper in his fist, stumbled toward the stairs, and slumped down.

"You happy now?" Brandt sat on the bottom stair next to Jack. "You're one dumb cowboy, you know that?"

"Bastard." Jack unfolded his fist and stared down at the crumpled paper. Rage coiled in his stomach and snaked up his chest. "He had a death certificate issued for me because he needed my death to be official. Without it, he couldn't get his hands on my inheritance."

"I know, but there's no sense in wastin' time getting all fired up over what's been done. You're sitting here alive and well, so that dang paper ain't worth a hill of beans. The only thing to do now is to make sure your uncle gets his comeuppance."

"You're right." Jack stood up and strode across the room toward Percival, who remained cowered in his corner. "You may tell Sir Richard that I will pay ten percent over his asking price for the house as it stands. Nothing is to be removed, do you understand?"

"But—" Percival stammered—"there might be personal items he wants removed."

Jack pointed a finger at Percival, and the man cringed. "He's had three years to remove his items. Anything still here either isn't valuable or important enough for him to worry about. Tell Sir Richard I'll pay ten percent more with nothing removed. Do it, or your dear papa becomes party to your gambling problem."

Percival nodded rapidly.

"I'll make sure he does what needs doing." Brandt came up behind Jack. "Get yourself out of here and go cool your heels."

Jack patted Brandt on the back and strode across the hallway and out the front door.

CHAPTER TWELVE

Drowned, frozen, dead forever!
We look on the past and stare aghast
At the spectres wailing, pale and ghast,
Of hopes which thou and I beguiled
To death on life's dark river.

—*Percy Bysshe Shelley, "Lines"*

THE WALLS SEEMED to be closing in on Ottilie. She no longer knew truth from lie or whom to trust. She'd once thought her life simple, but now she knew that had been an illusion. Since her mama's death, secrets and lies had started to leak from the carefully patched cracks in her past. But her aunt's revelation today had been the biggest shock of all. Was it true? And whom could she ask? Mama had taken all her secrets to the grave, and her stepfather—how much did he know?

Ottilie's chest tightened. She had to get out of her aunt's house. It was suffocating her. She needed time to think—to breathe. But where could she go? Should she risk going to Albany to find Henry? No, that would be foolish. Women were not allowed at Albany, and the doorman would surely order her to leave. Besides, she doubted her cousin knew anything about her father. He'd spent his early childhood in Germany with his mother and only returned to England to attend boarding school.

Now Ottilie understood the reason behind that decision. Her aunt had moved to the continent to escape the shame Ottilie's mama had brought on the family. And she'd waited until her sister was good and buried before she returned home. A bitter resentment settled in Ottilie's stomach when she remembered that her aunt had not even attempted to contact her after her mama's death. If Ottilie's stepmother had not been so eager to get rid of her, she might never have known Henry existed.

She could still recall her stepfather's words when he first told her about Henry. "You know I have always loved you as my own daughter, Ottilie. But you are a grown woman now. You have a job and a life. My boys are infants, and I must consider their futures." Her stepfather ran a hand through his thinning hair. "This tension between you and your new mama must end. She suffered a terrible ordeal giving birth to our sons and cannot tolerate further stress."

Ottilie stared at the man she'd adored since childhood. He'd been the only father she'd ever known. She'd thought he loved her, but now she knew that had been a lie, just like his love for her mama had been a lie.

"She is not my new mama, so please don't call her that again. And you needn't worry about me disrupting your new life. I will return to Canterbury, and you will not hear from me again."

"I did love your mother," he said, "and I do love you. That is why I want to give you this." He handed Ottilie an envelope containing a black-and-white photograph of two young women. Ottilie turned the photograph over. "Alice and Augusta," she read aloud the words penned in her mother's neat script.

"What is this?" Ottilie asked.

"It's a photograph of your mother and her sister, Lady Augusta Hudsyn. She recently returned to England from Germany. Her son, your cousin, is a student at Oxford. I wanted you to know you are not without family."

That was her stepfather's parting gift—a new family to replace the one she'd lost. She'd sought out Henry, and they'd become instant friends. Ottilie supposed Lady Hudsyn had no other choice but to embrace her, with the hope she could reform her or marry her to an aging peer. She'd been trying and failing in this venture for the past two years. Ottilie had viewed her aunt's interference in her life as harmless, but now she understood the gravity behind Lady Hudsyn's efforts. Lady Hudsyn did not merely think of Ottilie as a wayward niece who needed taming but as a canker. The future belonged to Henry, and Ottilie was the remaining link to a sordid past her aunt was determined to bury.

A sudden need for air propelled Ottilie to jump up from her seat and retrieve her cape and gloves. She raced down the stairs and made for the front door.

"Are you going out, Miss?" Benson asked as she scurried past him. "Do you need a carriage?"

"No, thank you. I'm in need of some fresh air," she said without stopping.

"But Miss—" Benson said as Ottilie closed the door on his words.

She left the square, turned onto Mount Street, and hurried toward the Grosvenor Gate entrance at Hyde Park. Her mind churned with questions about her past as she walked to Serpentine Bridge and crossed into Kensington Gardens. Only then did she notice the park was far less crowded than it usually was during the fashionable hours. She glanced up and saw that the sky had turned cloudy. Unwilling to turn back, she continued to Round Pond and rested on a bench next to the water.

Two small boys scampered past her bench and made for the pond.

"Slow down!" their guardian shouted, her yellow dress swishing behind her as she chased after them.

"We want to feed the ducks," one of the boys said.

"Not today. It's time to go home."

"They're hungry." The second child stuck a pudgy hand in a paper bag and threw some breadcrumbs into the water. The ducks immediately descended on the crumbs.

The boys squealed in delight, then cried in protest as their guardian led them away. Ottilie smiled. The ignorance of childhood was blissful indeed. How had her mother kept a smile on her face, carrying all those burdens she'd sheltered Ottilie from?

A sudden wind stirred, and she wrapped her thin cape around herself. The air had grown cooler, and people were leaving the park. It would grow dark within the hour, and it was time to leave. But she loathed the idea of returning to Berkeley Square. She thought briefly about going to Mrs. Briggs, her former headmistress from Westminster Ladies' College, but she often traveled to France during the summer months to visit her daughter, now a French baroness.

Ottilie forced herself to stand. She had no choice but to return to Berkeley Square for the night. But she would go back to Canterbury in the morning. Who knew when Henry would decide to stop sequestering at Albany?

In the meantime, she no longer wished to burden her aunt with her presence. She started for the bridge and realized she must have underestimated the lateness of the day. The sky was darkening, and the park seemed devoid of people. Goosebumps rose on her skin, and she increased her pace. To her relief, she caught sight of a cluster of ladies and gentlemen strolling amongst the trees several feet away. She left her path and started after the group, thinking it would be safer to walk a short distance behind them. After a few minutes, however, she became aware of someone walking behind her. Her neck and scalp prickled. She glanced back and saw a well-dressed gentleman following uncomfortably close to her. He doffed his bowler hat at her and smiled, but Ottilie saw malice in his expression.

"A young lady walking in the park alone so near dusk is bound to find trouble. Allow me to escort you home safely."

"I am not on my own. I am with my friends." She turned to look for the group of men and women, but they were nowhere in sight. Where had they gone? Then she spotted them in the distance. How had they made so much progress? "I must catch up with them." She turned away from the stranger and increased her pace.

He trotted up beside her. "I don't think those are your friends." His breath gave off a whiff of spirits. "I saw you sitting alone. You were not accompanied by a group."

Ottilie lifted her chin and strode forward. But he persisted in following her.

When she refused to acknowledge him, he grabbed her arm. "As a gentleman, I am obliged to see you to safety whether you like it or not."

"Leave now, or I shall scream." Ottilie struggled to remain calm. "We are not alone in this park, and your poor conduct will not go unnoticed."

"My poor conduct? You are a woman walking alone, and I am a gentleman offering his assistance. Yet you stand here being uncivil to me." He cocked his head at her as though an enlightening thought suddenly occurred to him. "Perhaps, you are meeting your lover and don't appreciate my interruption." A sly smile crept on his lips. "I am correct, aren't I? Why else would a so-called lady venture into Hyde Park alone?"

"Let me go." Ottilie's breathing grew heavy, and she struggled to control it. Somehow, the air in her lungs worked to choke rather than restore her, and her head swirled.

WHAT SECRETS DO these waters hold?

Morose thoughts swirled in Jack's brain as he peered into the dark water of the Serpentine from its bridge above. As if in answer to his question, a bloated figure burbled to the water's surface. Jack blinked. Was his mind playing tricks on him? The body sailed toward him. Adrenaline flooded his veins and primed him for action. A young woman, big with child, her skin and lips a deathly blue, floated beneath him on her back and disappeared under the bridge.

Jack raced to the other side of the bridge and gripped the railings as he stared at the Long Water, waiting in vain for the body to reemerge. *It's only the long-suffering wife of Shelley. The wind whispered in his ear. Poor Harriet Westbrook—too late to save her now. She's been dead more than fifty years. And why should she want saving when life treated her so miserably? Twice abandoned and facing disgrace for the crime of carrying a child outside of wedlock— that's why she gave herself to these waters. Is it a mere coincidence Shelley met with a similar fate? Did she pull him under the choppy Italian water, the way you aim to pull Sir Richard down to the depths of hell where he sent you?*

Jack shook the malicious voice from his head and ran his hands through his hair. He gazed at the now serene river and inhaled deeply. His heartbeat slowed as he let his gaze wander to the soothing greenery of Kensington Gardens. A flash of red caught his eye amongst a clump of trees. He squinted. Another flicker of red. Two people—a man and a woman—struggling. Was the lady in trouble, or was his mind playing tricks on him again? He sprinted across the bridge toward the couple. As he got closer, he slowed his pace and kept himself hidden.

The woman wore a red cape. His mind jumped immediately to Ottilie. The man gripped her arm, and she struggled to free herself. Jack moved like a panther, coming up behind the stranger swiftly and silently. He locked an arm around the brute's neck and pressed his pistol against the wretch's temple.

"Let her go." Jack kept his voice low but deadly.

"She is my wife. You have no right to interfere."

Jack tightened his grip on the fiend's throat, cutting off his air. The man gurgled, kicked his legs, and released his grasp on Ottilie. She stared at Jack wide-eyed before dashing behind him.

"Do you know your Bible?" Jack loosened his grip so the scoundrel could answer.

"Y—yes," he stuttered. "I'm a good man. Don't shoot me."

"Excellent. Then you know what happened to Lot's wife when she turned to look at the burning city of Sodom, don't you?"

The man nodded again. "Salt," he croaked. "She turned to salt."

"Correct. Now, when I take my arm from around your neck, you're to walk away without looking back because if you do, I'll use my pistol to blow you away and turn you into a pile of dust, you understand?"

"Yes," he whispered.

Jack slipped his arm from the man's neck and shoved him forward. "Go."

The coward tiptoed away, cautiously at first, and then he broke into a run. Jack grabbed Ottilie's hand and pulled her toward him.

"Did he hurt you?"

"No, he only frightened me a bit." She looked up at him and frowned. "It looks like you are the one who is hurt. What happened to your face?"

"It's nothing."

"It looks awful." She brushed her hand across his bruised cheek.

"I said it's nothing." He closed his fingers gently around her wrist and withdrew her hand from his face.

She winced.

"What's the matter?" He unclasped his fingers. A growing purple bruise marred her skin an inch above her glove, where the fiend had grabbed her.

"Did he do that to you?"

She nodded, and a single tear slid from the corner of her eye.

Overwhelming anger threatened to choke Jack. "I should have killed him."

"Maybe, but what would we have done with the body?" A playful smile appeared on her lips, and Jack's anger melted.

"We could have fed him to the dogs." Jack wiped the tear

from her face with his thumb.

"I might have enjoyed that."

"The wrath of Artemis is making more sense, isn't it?" He shook his head. "What were you doing out here alone?"

"Out here? Do you mean in Kensington Gardens? I was walking, sitting, and enjoying the park."

"But you shouldn't be in the park alone at this hour. It will be dark in thirty minutes. It's dangerous."

"It's only dangerous for women because a few men think it right to put their hands on any unaccompanied female. I would have been out of the park well before dark had that brute not interfered with me. Because of the likes of such men, I should live in a cage?"

"I only want you to be safe." Jack stroked a strand of her hair. The desire to kiss her flared inside him, but it felt more wrong now than ever. She didn't need another man trying to take advantage of her.

"You forget that I am six-and-twenty and have managed to live many years quite safely thus far. I even spent two years in London attending college."

"I haven't forgotten—how could I when you keep reminding me of your age?"

"It feels necessary in Mayfair because the people here seem to place unmarried women in the same category as children who need chaperoning lest they do something foolish. As if women are incapable of rational thinking. It's intolerable, really, and it is not the type of women I am used to associating with."

"Why do you come to Mayfair if you find it so intolerable?"

She dropped her gaze and rubbed at a spot of dirt on her glove. "I've been trying to cling to the little family I have left, but I see now I've been wasting my time. I plan on returning to Canterbury tomorrow."

"So soon?" Jack felt the disappointment in his bones. "Without telling Henry?"

Her blue eyes met his once again. "If you can tell him for me,

I'd be grateful to you. And perhaps you will invite him to accompany you when you come to Canterbury to deliver the reading you promised."

He slipped an arm around her waist and caressed her back. "I did promise a reading, didn't I?"

She arched her body in response to his touch. "You did."

His gaze fell to her mouth. "And you promised to be my muse until I finished my epic."

She tilted her head toward him. "I thought you no longer required my help."

"I lied. I do need you." He caressed her jaw with his free hand and kissed the corner of her mouth. "I don't want you to go," he whispered. He'd never needed a woman before. They'd always seemed to need him. But somehow, Ottilie made his world brighter and better. Without her, anger and vengeance swallowed him whole.

"I will agree to stay and help you on one condition." Her voice was a throaty whisper.

"Tell me?" he breathed.

"That you finish what you started behind the cabinet." She pulled him against her.

All thoughts of Hudsyn, his uncle, and vengeance vanished from Jack's mind. She became the sole object of his wants, needs, and desires. He took her face in his hands, leaned forward, and pressed his parted lips against hers.

CHAPTER THIRTEEN

When fierce conflicting passions urge
The breast, where love is wont to glow,
What mind can stem the stormy surge
Which rolls the tide of human woe?

—Byron, *Translation from the "Medea" Of Euripides*

AS SOON AS he kissed her, Ottilie knew she would not return to her aunt's home that evening. She didn't want to be anywhere else but in Jack's arms. Even if it were only temporary, she would not deny herself the pleasure of his company for a society that had condemned her parents.

"What do you want to do now?" Jack asked when the beginning of a summer shower started to drop from the sky. "I can take you back to Berkeley Square."

"Not yet. I quarreled with my aunt, and I'm not ready to—"

He placed his index finger on her lips. "You don't need to explain. I am happy you want to come with me. That's all you need to say."

The walk home took only five minutes, but seconds before they reached Half Moon Street, the summer sprinkle turned into a summer shower, and Ottilie arrived at Jack's residence soaked through. She had no choice but to strip down to her chemise and drawers and cover herself with one of Jack's long greatcoats. And although it reached to her ankles, she entered the parlor feeling somewhat exposed and rather foolish. But all her awkwardness melted away when she saw that Jack had laid out a makeshift picnic in front of the fireplace. Ottilie laid her wet items by the fire and seated herself on the blanket.

"Did Mrs. Wilson make all of this?" she asked, eyeing the thick meat sandwiches, fresh fruit, and beer.

"No, she has the evening off, so I made the sandwiches myself."

"Did you? Well done." Ottilie smiled. "I will need to send a note to my aunt, or she'll worry."

"What will you tell her?"

"That I'm visiting a friend from my days at Westminster Ladies' College."

"Will she believe you?"

"I don't care. I'm neither her child nor her ward."

He nodded. "The new housemaid can deliver it for you."

"Oh, I didn't know you had a new housekeeper. She shouldn't walk about alone after dark, should she?

"Brandt hired her to help Mrs. Wilson. I didn't know anything about it. Don't worry; I'll send her in the carriage."

Ottilie frowned. She'd never heard of a master of the house allowing his servants to hire help at will.

"Why are you frowning? Do you not like meat sandwiches?"

"I do, and these sandwiches smell delicious."

"Good. Let's eat then."

Ottilie bit into the thickly sliced bread and salty beef. She was hungrier than she realized. They ate in silence for a few minutes, and Jack washed his food down with a long sip of beer. Ottilie hesitated before picking up her cup. She had never drunk beer before.

"Try it," Jack said. "You might find it bitter, but it will quench your thirst."

She took a cautious sip. It tasted strong, but her throat was parched, so she drank until she'd slaked her thirst. She lowered her cup, and blinked, feeling somewhat lightheaded.

"Are you, all right?" Jack asked.

"I've never felt better." She grinned, suddenly feeling light and free of all her worries.

Jack moved his plate aside. "Come here," he said.

Ottilie inched forward.

"Closer." He clutched the greatcoat and drew her toward him.

"That first day I saw you at the Baudelaires' party, you became mine." Jack caressed her face. "I wanted you then, and I want you now more than ever." He rested his nose against hers. The warmth of his breath fluttered on her lips, and her breathing shallowed. She knew she should pull back or do something to break the spell, but she couldn't. She longed to be close to him and feel his body pressed against hers.

He cupped the back of her neck and pulled her mouth to his. He parted her lips with his tongue and kissed her with a passion she never knew existed. Her hands slipped under his shirt and rested on his muscled back. She didn't stop him when he pulled his shirt over his head, nor did she resist when he grasped the buttons on the greatcoat. His hands moved under the coat and encircled her waist, protected only by a cotton chemise. The coat slipped off her shoulders, and Ottilie shrugged free of it.

HE RACED ACROSS the grassy stretch of moorland, colorful and fragrant with the scents of spring, clutching a bouquet of snowdrops. The flowers were Frances's favorite. They would make his sister happy—perhaps even healthy again. One look at these would surely be enough to get her out of bed and back on the moors. The parsonage stood in the distance, beckoning to him, and he yearned to be inside its walls. Mama hung the sheets while Frances ducked between them. What were they doing out of bed?

He ran faster, but not fast enough to stop the flames that burst from the straw rooftop and licked the stone walls. Violet appeared in the window of the burning parsonage, and she banged on the glass. "Sebastian! Help me!"

"I'm coming," he screamed.

"No!" Frances appeared at his side. "Let the flames take her. Mama and I want Violet with us." She turned to the window. "Come to us, Violet. Papa is here too. Leave Sebastian. He's a bad boy."

"I'll be better. I promise! Look, I picked these for you on the moors." He held the bouquet out to her. Frances grinned and stretched out her hand. Her fingertips touched the green stems, but she couldn't grasp them. She coughed, a wild, hacking cough. Blood spewed from her throat and splashed the snow-white flowers with venomous red drops.

"Sebastian. Help me!" Violet banged on the window with both fists.

But he wasn't Sebastian any longer. He was Jack, who lived an ocean away, and he could do nothing to save his sister.

The banging grew louder in Jack's ears. His eyelids flew open. He stared at the ceiling and blinked, trying to get his bearings. The room was dark and somewhat chilly. He struggled to sit up, intent on finding his shirt, but a weight on his arm held him back. He glanced to his right and froze. Ottilie lay beside him, her flaxen hair loose and fanned around her face.

No! Jack's brain screamed. *No!* Ottilie wore a white cotton chemise, and, even in the dark, he could see the pale outline of her shapely body. He pulled his arm gently out from under her, and she stirred slightly. Jack dropped his head in his hands. "Dear God," he whispered. "What have I done?"

A succession of raps sounded and echoed down the hallway. Jack started. He looked around the room in confusion. *Am I still dreaming? Perhaps it is only the wind.*

The knocking grew louder. It was coming from the front

door. *Did Brandt forget his key?*

Jack attempted to rouse Ottilie with a gentle shake, but she did not stir.

"Ottilie," he whispered. "Wake up."

She moved her head from side to side and mumbled as if dreaming.

Another urgent knock sounded.

"Ottilie." He shook her again, a sense of urgency rising inside him.

She blinked and looked up at Jack as if confused. Then she gasped, sat up, and wrapped her arms around herself. "Why is it dark? What time is it? Did I fall asleep?"

"The fire's out; I don't know, and yes. More importantly, someone is at the door. I think Brandt forgot his key. But you'd best grab your clothes and hide lest that lunatic Lord Towne has decided to return. You can wait in my chamber upstairs."

"Oh, dear!" Ottilie scrambled to her feet, grabbing her clothes in haste.

"Wait, let me light some lamps. I don't want you to have to stumble around in the dark." Jack retrieved a paraffin lamp and matches from the fireplace mantle. He knelt to remove the glass cover and light the wick. He replaced the glass, retrieved a second lamp, and repeated the process. Ottilie scooped up clothing, took one of the paraffin lamps, and hurried out of the parlor.

Jack followed and waited for her to disappear up the stairs before he hurried to the door. "Dash it, Brandt, did you forget your key?" He pulled the door open and froze.

"Hudsyn! What are you doing here? It must be past midnight."

"I finished it!" Hudsyn held up a thick bundle of pages. "I've bloody finished my book of poetry."

"Already?" Jack stepped aside to let his friend enter.

"Say, what happened to your face?" Hudsyn squinted at Jack in the dim light of the paraffin lamp. "Did someone thrash you?"

"It's nothing." Jack touched the bruise Brandt had left on his cheek. "I fell, that's all."

"Well, you ought to be more careful." Hudsyn shivered. "Heavens, it's freezing in here. These summer storms are a nuisance. One minute the sun is shining, and the next, we are drenched to the bone. Where's your shirt? Do you wish to die of pneumonia?"

"I fell asleep in the parlor beside the fire," Jack said. "It was warm."

"Well, let's get it started again, shall we? I require a warm fire and a stiff drink to celebrate." Hudsyn marched down the hallway toward the parlor. Jack followed, praying Ottilie would stay upstairs and out of sight.

Hudsyn strode into the parlor and made for the fireplace. "Dash it!" He said as his foot collided with a half-empty glass of beer. He bent to pick up the glass and sniffed it. "Did you fall asleep or pass out in front of the fire?" Jack laughed, but his stomach churned. How could he have been so stupid as to compromise both Ottilie's reputation and his friendship with Hudsyn?

"Got any more of this?" Hudsyn held up the glass.

"Yes, but I thought you wanted something stronger. I can get you a brandy."

"Excellent," Hudsyn said. "I'll restart the fire."

Jack set the lamp next to the fireplace and went to pour Hudsyn's drink. When he returned, a warm orange glow enveloped the room, and Henry stood with a puzzled look. He eyed the two empty glasses, the picnic basket, and the blanket.

"Say, I'm not interrupting anything, am I?"

"No." Jack's muscles tensed. He strode back to the cabinet and poured himself a whiskey. He squeezed his eyes shut. The evening was a blur. He remembered kissing Ottilie in the park and bringing her home. She'd changed out of her wet clothing, and they'd eaten sandwiches by the fire. They'd kissed. He remembered as much. But had he done more than kiss her? His brain couldn't recall.

"Are you all right, Bastin?"

"It's my head." Jack spun around and handed Hudsyn the whiskey glass.

"Drank too much?" Hudsyn suggested. "That's likely what facilitated your fall as well." He sipped his whiskey. "I need to be careful. I haven't had so much as a sniff of alcohol in two weeks."

Hudsyn surveyed the room again. "Are you really alone?"

"Of course, I am. I was writing."

Hudsyn bent down and picked up a gold hair pin dotted with tiny red stones. "What's this then?"

Jack shrugged. "I don't know. Perhaps it belongs to Mrs. Wilson." As soon as the words slipped out of his mouth, he knew he had made a fatal error. "Or someone," he added.

Hudsyn raised his eyebrows. "Does it belong to Mrs. Wilson?"

"How should I know?"

"Well, a man can get lonely."

Jack hit Hudsyn on the shoulder. "Sorry to disappoint you, my friend. But I was alone all evening before I fell asleep."

"All joking aside, I think you're hiding something from me, Bastin. You haven't forgotten about our three-month challenge, have you?"

"Of course not. I've sworn off women to concentrate on my writing, the same as you have done."

"If you are serious, you should get yourself a set at Albany. No women allowed."

"I'm fairly certain prostitutes are allowed."

"Do you have a prostitute hiding somewhere? Because this looks very much like"—Hudsyn stopped—"Ahh, I see. There she is you old dog. Younger than your usual type, I must say."

"What?" Jack grew cold, and he swayed slightly on his feet. He turned slowly to see Brandt's new housekeeper saunter into the parlor completely naked.

Terror, exhilaration, and guilt struck Ottilie in rapid succession as Henry strode into Jack's foyer and announced the completion of his poetry collection. She stifled a cheer and clapped silently upon hearing the pride in her cousin's voice, aching to rejoice with him. But reality rooted her to the spot and weighed her down with a crushing guilt. She clamped her hand over her mouth and squeezed her eyes shut as if that could shield her from her inner shame.

She remained frozen at the top of the stairs long after the men moved into the parlor, straining to hear their muffled voices. How long did Henry plan to stay? Would he remain until morning and then seek her out at Berkley Square to share his news? What would she do? Pretend not to know about his triumph? How could she face him? She hated the idea of lying to him.

The muffled voices grew louder, and Ottilie straightened, listening intently. Footsteps sounded in the hallway.

"I knew you were fibbing." Henry's voice rang clearly in Ottilie's ears. "Why didn't you tell me to leave? I would not have taken offense."

"Don't go yet, Lord Hudsyn," a woman's voice pleaded. "You've just arrived. I wish you would come back and join us in the parlor."

Ottilie held her breath.

Who is that? Not Mrs. Wilson. She has the night off, and she certainly would not speak to her master or his guests in such a casual manner. But who else is in the house?

Ottilie's mind scrambled for an explanation but found none. She placed her clothing on the floor and crept down the stairs. It was a risk she had to take. She jerked to a halt when the petite figure of a naked young woman came into view. Ottilie swallowed her gasp. Gripping the banister, she leaned forward and peeped between the decorative swirls in the iron railing.

Jack's arm hung casually around the woman's waist and came to a rest low on her hip. A river of silky black hair flowed down the woman's back, and she purred like a satisfied kitten as she nuzzled Jack's neck, pressing her pale body and smooth round breasts against his bare chest.

Ottilie's cheeks flamed, and she tightened her grip on the banister. Jack glanced up and met her furious stare. Then he creased his forehead in question as if to ask, *what are you doing?*

He nudged the woman from his side. "That's enough, Lulu!" he barked. "Lord Hudsyn is a busy man and has things to do. Go and get yourself dressed."

The woman—Lulu—Jack had called her—stuck out her bottom lip like a petulant child. Jack glanced at Ottilie, and his frown deepened. She narrowed her eyes at him before retreating up the stairs, her mind a whirling and furious Charybdis.

Lulu! So that is the new housekeeper Brandt hired—the one Jack knew nothing about? Liar! What a little fool I have been.

Ottilie picked up her clothing and pressed them to her chest. What had she done? She'd fallen asleep next to Jack wearing nothing but her chemise and allowed him free access to her body like a common harlot. She clenched her fists around the fabric of her dress. How much touching had occurred? Had he done more than kiss her or caress her? Her memory remained a blur. No doubt the beer had served to muddle her thoughts. Perhaps Jack had given it to her for that very purpose. How could she have allowed something like this to happen? If Henry ever discovered her folly—the thought sent her to her knees. She doubled over on the floor and crouched under the weight of her shame.

Footsteps sounded on the stairs, and Ottilie's head jerked up. Was it Jack? No, the step was too light. It had to be Lulu. Ottilie stood, grabbed the paraffin lamp, and dashed toward Jack's study. *Wait! He'd said to go to his chambers.* She swung around, her mind a whirl of anxiety and confusion, and came face to face with Lulu who stood stark naked and unabashed before her.

Ottilie recoiled.

The naked housemaid placed her hands on her slender hips and assessed Ottilie with a quick sweep of her eyes. "You are pretty, to be sure, but I think you are the frigid type." She smirked. "He doesn't like frigid women. You'll be gone soon enough." Lulu twirled on her heels and sauntered across the landing, swaying her derriere as if proud to display such a fine asset. She stopped and turned to give Ottilie a sardonic smile before disappearing into one of the bedchambers.

Ottilie blinked, too stunned to move.

Had the harlot gone into Jack's bedchamber? She didn't know. But she assumed as much since housekeepers did not sleep on the same floor as their master—unless it was in that master's bed. Ottilie spun around and marched in the opposite direction to Jack's study, anger swirling in her chest. Did Jack employ courtesans and disguise them as housekeepers for his pleasure? Apparently, Henry thought it perfectly normal to see a disrobed strumpet hanging on Jack's arm or strutting freely about his house.

She pushed open the study door and slammed it shut. No matter if Henry heard the commotion, he'd think it was Lulu. How dare Jack ask her to wait in his chambers like one of his harlots? She dropped her clothing at her feet and leaned against the door, clutching the paraffin lamp by its wire handle and dangling it in front of her to better see the room. Tears spilled down her cheeks. She only had herself to blame. She knew what Jack Bastin was, and she'd been foolish to ignore the reality.

Downstairs, she heard the front door open and close. Ottilie lifted the paraffin lamp and moved quickly to the window. Taking care to conceal herself behind the curtain, she peered down at the shadowy street. The gas lamps gave off a dim light, but it was enough to see Henry step outside and turn left toward Piccadilly. She breathed a sigh of relief. He was not intent on going home and would not discover her absence.

An overwhelming sense of despair soon overshadowed her

relief. An only child like herself, Henry had been overjoyed to learn he had a cousin, and they'd formed a close bond in the last two years. And now she had betrayed him, and her betrayal might even cost him his friendship with Jack.

Ottilie wiped her tears. It was time for her to dress and leave this house. She reached for her front-fastening corset and was about to slip it over her chemise when the door opened, and Jack entered.

"I told you to wait in my chamber," he said.

"Did you?" Ottilie bit back. "I think you'll find that it's already occupied."

"What do you mean by that?" Jack asked.

"I mean, I saw your naked harlot enter your bedchamber minutes ago."

"I see." Jack slipped his hands into his trouser pockets and smiled.

Heat spread like a wildfire across Ottilie's chest and neck. "Did you expect me to join her and become part of your harem? In that case, I am sorry to disappoint you."

"You've got it all wrong." He leaned against the door and folded his arms. "That tends to happen when one eavesdrops and makes assumptions."

"Eavesdrops? Is that what worries you? Or is it that I saw you the way your friends are accustomed to seeing you—with a naked strumpet draped on your arm?" She swooped down, snatched her clothing off the floor and moved toward the door, but Jack didn't budge.

"Are you planning to keep me against my will?"

"Of course not," he said evenly. "I'm only asking you to listen. Then you may go wherever you like."

"How gracious of you." She turned her face from his but stayed rooted to the spot, keen to hear his attempt to explain himself.

"As I am sure you heard from your position on the landing," Jack began, "Hudsyn finished his collection of poems and wanted me to have a celebratory drink with him. He was so excited that he marched into the parlor before I could stop him. So, he saw the picnic basket and the empty glasses. After we relit the fire, he picked up one of your decorated hairpins from the floor and accused me of entertaining a woman. I played innocent and tried to shrug it off, but he wasn't convinced. And I was terrified he would recognize the hairpin as one of yours. Then Lulu appeared. She must have overheard our conversation when she came up the basement stairs because she sauntered into the parlor completely disrobed and pretended to be my mystery woman. I panicked and went along with the charade. I think Lulu was trying to help."

"Help?" Ottilie's voice rose with indignation. "What interesting servants you have in this house, Mr. Bastin. Wherever do you find them?"

"I already told you Brandt hired her. She keeps his bed warm, not mine. I don't want anything to do with her."

"You're blaming your valet?" Ottilie said, incredulous. "Do you truly think me such a fool? I saw you embrace her. She stood naked in your arms, and you did not seem the least perturbed. In fact, you stood there conversing with my cousin as though nothing was amiss."

Jack stepped away from the door and ran his hands through his hair. "Believe what you want. I've been honest with you, but if you insist on calling me a liar, so be it. You can sleep in my bedchamber, and I will stay downstairs."

"Your bedchamber! How dare you? I will not stay in this house tonight, and I shall certainly not sleep in your bed. As soon as I am dressed, I'm going back to Berkeley Square. And tomorrow, I plan to catch the first train to Canterbury."

"You can do whatever you like tomorrow, but tonight you shall stay here. It's far too late to venture out alone, and you already sent word to your aunt that you would not be returning to Berkeley Square. It will look mighty suspicious if you bang on her bolted doors, begging to be let in well after midnight."

"None of that is your concern, so I fail to see why you care."

She moved toward the door, but he stepped forward and caught her by the shoulders. "That's precisely my problem. I do care! And I don't think I'm able to stop."

Ottilie stilled, and Jack brushed a strand of hair from her face. "Listen carefully because I'm only going to say this once more. Lulu is waiting for Brandt, not me. She keeps his bed warm, not mine. You can choose to believe me or not, but what I'm saying is the truth."

Ottilie raised her eyebrows. She wanted desperately to believe him but doubt still plagued her thoughts. "And your valet sleeps upstairs, does he?"

Jack dropped his hands from Ottilie's shoulders and exhaled. "Brandt isn't my valet. He's my business partner and my friend. No, that's not correct. He is more than a friend. He's like a brother to me, and he's the only family I have. I wouldn't be alive today if it wasn't for him."

"I don't understand. Why does he pretend to be your valet?"

"It's complicated," Jack said.

Ottilie dropped her clothing on a nearby lounge chair. "I've spent the evening kissing you wearing little more than my undergarments, yet I know nothing about you. You're a complete mystery to me." She covered her face with her hands.

He shrugged. "People get married without knowing much of anything about each other. Title and wealth, that's usually all the information they require before tying themselves to someone for life."

She dropped her hands from her face. "Not me."

He reached for her. "What is it you want to know?"

Still frustrated, she twisted out of his reach. He turned and clasped his hands behind his neck, flexing his back as if trying to release the tension from his body. Ottilie's stared at the scar that marred his otherwise perfect skin. She inched forward and ran a finger along his raised lesion. She wanted to know who hurt him and why. She'd revealed her vulnerability, and she needed him to do the same.

He turned suddenly, and she jerked her hand back in fright.

"That's a long story," he said, and strode to his whiskey decanter.

Ottilie chewed her lip as she watched Jack fill and drain his glass with an unsteady hand.

"I'm sorry," she said. "I didn't mean to—"

He poured a second glass and swallowed another mouthful of whiskey. "Don't be." He cleared his throat and turned to face her. "I want to tell you."

Women always asked about his scar; it was a natural curiosity. And he had told all manner of tales to satisfy their fantasies—he'd received it during his years as a pirate, on a spying mission, rescuing a young lady from a gang of outlaws, and so on. But never had he told anyone the truth. Never had he admitted to being bullwhipped like an animal by a vicious master. That reality wasn't quite so heroic or romantic.

Jack's body tensed as he waited for Ottilie's reaction. He could cope with anything but her pity. He refused to be pitied by anyone, least of all a woman like Ottilie.

Her blue eyes softened, and she rested a hand on his forearm. "Thank you," she said.

"For what?" Jack asked, still looking for signs of pity.

"For trusting me. Henry doesn't know the truth, does he?"

"No one does, except Brandt. And that's because the same thing happened to him."

"You were both indentured to the same man?" she asked.

"Not exactly. Wardell was Brandt's stepfather."

"What?" Ottilie's body jerked visibly. "But how could his mother allow her husband to inflict such cruelty on her son?"

"She was a frail and sickly woman," Jack explained. "Wardell bullied and beat her into submission until Brandt was old enough to step between them and knock Wardell out cold."

"Good for him."

"But men like Wardell don't take kindly to being humiliated, and he didn't let it go unpunished. He waited a few days before surprising Brandt with his bullwhip."

"How awful." Ottilie breathed shakily. "Were you witness to it?"

"No, all that occurred well before I arrived in Texas. By the time I got there, Brandt and Wardell had come to an understanding. Brandt accepted the beating without retaliation and allowed Wardell to recover his bruised pride for his mother's sake. But he made his stepfather understand that he would kill him if he ever laid a hand on him or his mother again."

Ottilie lowered her lashes. "I've misjudged him."

"Yes," Jack said. "He's a good man. If it weren't for him, I probably wouldn't be here."

She looked up. "What do you mean?"

Jack rubbed the forehead. "After I ran from the plantation, nothing could force me back. I didn't care if Wardell beat me to death. I found out later that Brandt convinced him to put me to work on the cattle ranch instead. He offered to train me, and since Wardell wasn't the type to waste what he paid for, he agreed. The ranch was only a short distance from the plantation—but a world of difference existed between the two. Brandt was a talented rancher and a lonely kid, so he took me under his wing, nursed me back to health, and taught me everything I needed to know about ranching." Jack chuckled. "He was a good teacher, and I became a dang good cowboy." He said in the American accent he'd learned to perfect but never adopted permanently.

"But you were only playing at it, weren't you? You're an Englishman at heart."

"True. I never stopped yearning for home, and I never could have made it back without Brandt's help. I knew if I stayed close to him and out of Wardell's way, I would have some protection. Brandt kept his head down, but he never forgot what that monster did to us. He waited for the right time, and when it came, he got revenge. We both did."

"What did you do?" Ottilie asked in a frightened whisper.

Jack's thumb circled the rim of his glass. He could still hear Wardell's screams as Brandt crushed the man's injured shoulder under his boot…

He saw Brandt lean down and unclip the bullwhip from Wardell's belt before using the tip of his boot to roll the wretch onto his belly.

"Move them horses," Brandt instructed Jack. "I don't want those geldings catching any of this."

Jack took both horses by the reins and led them away. He turned to watch Brandt walk several paces back, raise the bullwhip, and bring it down with the full force of his arm across Wardell's back. Wardell's screams echoed in Jack's ears.

"That one's for me." Brandt pulled back his arm and raised the whip again. "An' this one here is for Jack." He cracked the whip, and Wardell's body convulsed in response to the second blow before it went limp.

Jack didn't flinch. As far as he was concerned, Wardell deserved a lashing to the death.

"He still breathing?" Jack asked.

"Hell yes, dying's too good for him. I hope he suffers good an' long." Brandt looked down at Wardell's limp, bloody body. "I told you I'd get you, didn't I?" Brandt spat. "Now, you can stay here an' rot in the dirt or crawl back to your worm hole. Either way, I don't care. Cause as soon as we've helped ourselves to them bags of gold you got stored in that old water well yonder, we're done here." A groan escaped Wardell's lips, and Brandt snorted. "That's right, you old miser. We know your secret." Brandt kicked him in the ribs with the tip of his boot and spat on him for good measure. He clipped Wardell's bullwhip to his belt and strode toward Jack and the horses.

"What are you going to do with that thing?" Jack motioned to the whip.

"Burn it," Brandt said…

"Jack?" Ottilie's voice pulled him back to the present.

He looked down and blinked her into focus.

"Did you kill him?" She whispered the question as if she was afraid to learn the answer.

"We left him breathing. But what happened after that, I can't say."

A sardonic smile pulled at the corners of Jack's mouth as he pictured Wardell sliding on his belly through the grass like a snake. "There were a lot of angry Yankees and wild animals roaming the area at the time."

Ottilie turned her face from his and wrapped her arms around herself.

Jack grimaced. It was just as he thought. His truth was too ugly for her liking. She admired his intellectual personae—Jack the writer and Jack the gentleman, not the man with the dark past and devil's soul. It wasn't her fault she'd been spared life's horrors.

"Perhaps, you should go home," he said. "If the servants can keep a secret, your aunt will likely never know." He moved toward the door. "Get dressed; I'll wait for you downstairs."

"No!" she said. "I want to stay."

Jack turned. "Even after what I just told you?"

"You've told me nothing other than the tale of a young man cruelly abused by the adults he trusted."

"But there's more. You don't know—"

She strode toward him and slipped her arm around his waist. "Why are you trying so hard to chase me away?"

Jack cupped her face in his hands, unable to believe this beautiful woman still wanted him.

"Did Wardell give you this too?" She touched the small scar at the corner of his eye.

He smiled. "No, that's from boyhood wars." He moved to kiss her, but she turned her face and bit her lip.

"What's wrong?" His throaty voice revealed his desire.

She pulled his hands from her face and clasped them between hers. "Earlier this evening—" her skin flushed pink—"before we fell asleep—I don't remember exactly…everything."

"We ate sandwiches, drank ale, and kissed." He leaned toward her, hoping she'd stop talking and let him kiss her again.

"Is that all?" she asked.

"That's all," he said soothingly.

"So, you remember everything?"

He straightened. "It's not altogether clear, and I admit experiencing a moment of panic when Hudsyn woke me up with his incessant banging, and I saw you lying next to me in your chemise, but—"

"What?"

"I fell asleep with my trousers on, so—"

Ottilie's skin turned a deep shade of pink, and she lowered her gaze.

"That is what you were worried about, wasn't it?"

She nodded.

"Well, you can rest assured I would never do anything to dishonor you. Nothing happened. I promise."

Ottilie glanced up at him, her cheeks still flushed. "Good," she said, a shy smile playing on her lips, "because if something had happened, I would at least want to remember it."

CHAPTER FOURTEEN

I am drunk with the honey wine
Of the moon-unfolded eglantine,
Which fairies catch in hyacinth bowls.

—Percy Bysshe Shelley, "Wine of the Fairies"

A SMILE SPREAD across Ottilie's lips even before her she opened her eyes. Jack's musky scent pervaded the air. She buried her face into his pillow and inhaled, thinking about the events the night before and regretting none of them. Jack had kissed her and confided in her. Then he'd escorted her to his bedroom and bade her goodnight. But his hand had lingered on the doorknob for several seconds as though he battled to uphold the strength of his resolve.

Ottilie sat up and stretched before stepping out of bed and onto a plush beige and gold patterned Persian rug.

A washbasin stood ready in the corner of the room, put there, she imagined, for her privacy. She padded across the room to where her clothing sat neatly arranged on a mahogany and beige tufted lounge chair. A small envelope addressed to her sat atop the pile of clothing. Inside, she found a card with the words, *Meet me in the garden*, printed in Jack's neat script.

Ottilie smiled, unsure what to make of Jack's message. Had he planned for them to spend the day together? She readied herself and made her way downstairs and to the garden at the back of the house. As she stepped outside, she saw Jack sitting at a small table onto which an appropriately clad Lulu unloaded a tray of tea, cakes, and fruit. Jack glanced at her and waved. Then he turned to speak to Lulu, who picked up her tray and walked toward the house.

As Lulu neared, Ottilie stiffened. She did not wish for another encounter with the maid. But to her surprise, the girl greeted her politely.

"Good morning, Miss. I hope you had a good night's rest. Mr. Bastin is expecting you in the garden."

"Thank you." Ottilie eyed the maid and wondered at her seemingly miraculous transformation. She approached the table where Jack awaited her.

"Good morning." Jack flashed her a wide grin.

"What's all this?" Ottilie sat beside him and took in the platters containing tea cakes, finger sandwiches, sliced apples, berries, and grapes.

"I thought you might be hungry. It's already past noon."

"Is it? I didn't realize. I must have been more tired than I thought."

"Well, yesterday was a trying day." He reached for the teapot and filled Ottilie's cup.

"Thank you," she said and scanned the table for a sugar bowl.

He picked up a glass honey pot and placed it beside her tea cup. "I don't care for sugar; will you take honey?"

"Of course, what a treat." She spooned a dollop of honey into her tea and stirred.

"Why do we feel the need to mill sugar cane when nature has given us something as perfect as honey? I'll never understand."

Ottilie sipped her tea, conscious of Jack watching her as if waiting for her reaction. "You're right, it's delicious," she said, replacing her cup in its saucer.

"Do you know what else honey pairs well with?"

"Most things, I imagine."

He reached for a slice of apple, dipped it into the honey jar, and held it out to her.

Ottilie eyed the dripping honey that ran from the apple onto his thumb.

"I'm not touching that." She laughed. "It's a sticky mess."

"You don't have to. I'll hold it for you. Taste it."

Ottilie hesitated before leaning forward and biting a piece from the apple. Jack put the rest into his mouth.

"What do you think?" he asked after swallowing his morsel.

She contemplated the mixture of the tart and sweet flavors that lingered in her mouth after she'd swallowed. "You are right. It is delicious."

Jack inched forward and brushed his thumb across her mouth. "Did you know that honey is another food infused with Aphrodite's powers?"

"I believe it," she said, her voice trembling slightly.

He pressed his lips to hers, and she tasted honey. He kissed her and used his tongue to spread the sweetness into her mouth. The yearning she'd endured all night long rose to the surface, and she almost cried out in protest when he pulled his mouth away from hers.

"I'm sorry," he said. "I didn't bring you outside to—"

"If you apologize for kissing me, you will indeed insult me."

Jack grinned. "I only wanted to apologize for my lack of self-control. It seems I find it impossible to be in your company and not touch or kiss you."

"Why did you ask me into the garden if not to feed me honey and kiss me?" she said playfully.

He leaned back in his chair and observed her. "Because I want to sketch you."

"You draw as well?"

"Yes, I am reasonably good at it, and I need something to keep me inspired after you return to Canterbury. I recall you saying that you intended to leave today."

She picked up her cup and eyed him over the rim of her cup.

"I'm not actually required to go back for another month," she said.

He smiled. "I like the sound of that. But you will return eventually, and I want to keep a part of you here with me."

"Very well. I confess I am curious to see what you can do with your sketchpad. Where would you like me to sit?"

"Under that tree where I placed the blanket."

Ottilie rose from her chair and settled under the tree.

"That's perfect."

Jack filled a plate with sandwiches and fruit and set it in front of Ottilie. He positioned himself on the blanket and opened his sketchpad. As he worked, he glanced intermittently at her, and each time her heart grew wings that thrashed against the walls of her chest. She studied his handsome face, furrowed in concentration, and thought about her mother. Had her heart grown wings at the sight of Ottilie's father? Had her father charmed her mama with sweet words, honeyed kisses, and talk of muses? Was she doomed to follow that same path—the one her mama had worked so hard to steer her from? *Yes!* She heard her aunt's resounding caveat in her mind.

Jack looked up from his sketch and caught Ottilie's eye. The purple bruise on his cheek aside, his face revealed no trace of the darkness that made up his past. She saw only tenderness in his expression and kindness in his eyes. He was undoubtedly the most intelligent, charming man she'd ever met, but the things he'd confided in Ottilie had sent chills through her. He'd experienced traumas that could not easily be quieted. She knew in her heart that to be true.

AFTER OTTILIE DEPARTED for Berkeley Square, Jack returned to his writing with her taste lingering on his lips. He touched his mouth and smiled as he entered his study.

"What are you smiling about?"

Jack looked up, startled to see Brandt lounging on the dark brown leather armchair with his legs outstretched and his feet resting on a matching ottoman. "When did you get home?" He asked.

"I've been cooling my heels in here for a while now." Brandt sipped his drink.

"I was in the garden."

"I know," Brandt spoke evenly.

Jack eyed his friend, realizing that Brandt was waiting for him to make some confession regarding Ottilie. When he wasn't forthcoming, Brandt motioned to the sketch in Jack's hand.

"Go on, let me see it?"

Jack handed over the drawing and went to pour himself a whiskey.

"She sure is pretty," Brandt remarked. "Did she stay the night?"

"She did, but only because of the storm." Jack sank into the armchair next to Brandt. "I slept in the parlor," he added.

"Do you love her?"

The question caught Jack by surprise, and it was something he wasn't ready to contemplate. "Hudsyn paid me a visit in the middle of the night." Jack said, changing the subject. "He wanted to celebrate finishing his book of poems. Of all the nights, he chose last night to visit me."

"Yea, I heard all about it from Lulu. I reckon you straightened her out, all right."

"I asked her to keep her clothes on and do her job if that's what you mean."

"You gotta admit she saved your hide, though."

"She embarrassed me."

"Rather you than Miss Hamilton, right?"

Jack angled his body toward Brandt. "Why are you asking me questions about last night if you already know what occurred? Did I do something to lose your trust?"

"A man in love isn't always honest about his feelings." Brandt swirled the whiskey in his glass.

Jack stood up. "I'm not in love. I don't need love." He set his glass, still half full, on the side table. "I need to settle my score with my uncle."

"And once that's done? Then what?"

"Then I reclaim my inheritance and sit back to watch my uncle's life destroyed. What more could I want?"

"A family."

Jack smirked. "Are you suggesting that I get married?"

"If you met the right woman, yeah. What would be so bad about that?"

"Do I strike you as the marrying type?" Jack walked to the window and leaned with his shoulder against the casing.

Brandt swung his legs from the ottoman and sat upright. "That's exactly what you are. An' it ain't a bad thing neither. You've been playing at being a ruffian your whole life, but it ain't who you are. You're a good man. The best man I know. I've seen you risk your life for others."

Bile filled Jack's throat. "Don't fool yourself. I have a devil inside me, same as you."

"That's true, but it don't have to be."

"You think love fixes all?" Jack snorted. "My father once had a wife and five children. Two died within hours of their birth, and a few years later, he had the pleasure of burying his wife and youngest daughter on the same day. Still, he worked hard, prayed harder, and endured. Only to have his heart broken by his son, who left him to die alone."

"He wasn't alone. He had your sister by his side," Brandt reminded him.

"My sister who would still be alive today if I had not left her to fend for herself. I failed at being a son and a brother. What good would I be to a wife?"

Brandt rubbed the back of his neck as if trying to release his tension. "I ain't goin' to be around forever, you know."

"What are you talking about?" Jack straightened his stance.

"This ain't my home. I miss riding across the open plains, where I see nothing but grass, rivers, deserts, and mountains for days at a time."

"There's plenty of countryside in England," Jack said. "We have fields of grass, rivers, even wild ponies."

"I've been to your countryside. An' I didn't see no other cowboys there. I miss the ranching life—herding cattle an' breaking wild horses. Hell, I miss working up a sweat outdoors with the blazing sun on my back, bathing in a cool river, an' sittin' next to a warm fire with the stars above me and a sweet harmonica tune in my ears. I ain't made for life in a three-piece suit, sipping tea."

Jack gave a short laugh. "I've never seen you drink tea."

"Yeah, you got me there." Brandt chuckled.

"I didn't realize you were unhappy here," Jack struggled to keep the disappointment he felt in check.

"It ain't the same for me. This is your home, 'an I get why you love it, but it ain't mine. Besides, someone's got to watch over our investments in America, don't they?"

Jack swallowed. "When do you plan on leaving?"

"I ain't goin' nowhere until you settle your hash with your uncle. I made you a promise, and I intend to stick with it. But I would rest easier if I knew you were happy—if you had someone here to care for you."

"I am not a child. I can take care of myself."

"I know that, but I also know you care more for that little lady than you're willing to admit. We've been talking for ten minutes, and you ain't even asked me about the house. That tells me something."

Jack turned to the window. A pair of gray doves perched on the gas lamp below cooed and nuzzled. Jack closed his eyes. Brandt was right. He'd become distracted again, and he hadn't even given the house a second thought. He turned from the window. "Well," he said, "did we get it?"

"We got it." Brandt drained his glass and pushed himself out of his chair.

"My uncle grabbed the ten percent offer, then. I knew he would, greedy wretch."

"I didn't offer him ten over. You were too dang mad to think clearly when you came up with that sum. I told Percival to offer five percent over asking, and your uncle accepted."

"That's for the house as it stands?" Jack asked. "Nothing will be removed?"

"Yeah, whatever's there now, is all yours." Brandt approached Jack's desk. "Like Percival said, your uncle took the paintings and other valuables out when his wife died. But the furniture ought to be worth a lot. Hell, even his wife's clothes are still there."

"I don't care about the valuables. I wanted the house unmolested because it struck me that my uncle may have been too preoccupied to sort through his personal effects after my aunt died. There's a chance he was careless enough to leave something behind."

"What are you hoping to find?"

Jack shrugged. "Correspondence? Something that confirms his scheme to ship me off to America? Perhaps, he confided in my aunt, and she kept a diary. I don't know."

"You might be onto something. It's worth a try. But first, you gotta sign." Brandt tapped a paper laying on Jack's desk. "The doc is right here waitin' on your John Hancock."

Jack leaned the palms of his hands on his desk and scanned the document. Then he reached for his ink pen and scripted his name at the bottom of the page.

Brandt slapped Jack on the back. "Now, let's hightail this over to Fleet Street and collect them keys. The sooner we start tearing that fine townhouse apart, the better."

CHAPTER FIFTEEN

The flower that smiles today
To-morrow dies
All that we wish to stay
Tempts and then flies.

—Percy Bysshe Shelley, "Mutability"

A LONG SOAK in a warm tub never grew tiresome. Ottilie sank deeper into the soapy water and closed her eyes. She'd been in dire need of a bath, but she was sorry to wash Jack's scent from her body. The taste of his honeyed tongue in her mouth still sent a shiver of pleasure through her. How had she stayed ignorant of such feelings until now? She'd witnessed her best friend's exhilaration and somewhat foolish behavior when she'd fallen in love, but she had not understood it. Was this love? Did she love Jack?

The thought terrified her. How would she cope when the summer came to an end? More to the point, what would Jack do? He'd promised to come to Canterbury for the lecture, but would he stay for an extended time? He had the reputation of a rake—a reputation he did not deny—would he return to his old ways? Her mama had no doubt found herself faced with this same predicament six-and-twenty years ago, and the outcome had not been a happy one for her. Ottilie knew she should save herself and return to Canterbury immediately. Yet, the thought of never kissing Jack again seemed unbearable.

"Excuse me, Miss." Eliza entered the room, carrying a fluffy, white towel. "I've come to see if you're about ready to get out. You've been soaking for a while, and you'll need to get dressed soon. His Lordship is on his way home."

"What?" Ottilie sat up, causing water to slosh onto the floor. "My cousin is coming home? How do you know?"

"I believe he sent a note this morning. Cook received instructions to prepare his favorite dish."

"I'd better make haste, then." Ottilie pushed herself up and elevated her arms while Eliza secured the large towel around her body. She gave Eliza her hand and let the maid assist her as she stepped out of the tub.

"Did someone hurt you, miss?" Eliza focused on the purple bruise that encircled Ottilie's wrist.

"It's nothing." Ottilie clamped her hand over the bruise given to her by the brute in Hyde Park.

"Is it painful? I am sure we can find some salve for it."

"Thank you, Eliza, but that's not necessary. It looks worse than it feels and will disappear in a few days." She smiled reassuringly at the lady's maid.

"We'd best put you in a pair of gloves long enough to cover that until it heals. I expect you don't wish to alarm His Lordship."

Ottilie allowed Eliza to help her dress and arrange her hair in a simple chignon—an extravagance she typically found unnecessary.

"Shall I put one or two of those pretty pins in your hair, miss?"

Ottilie's gaze fell to the sparkling hair pins on her dresser. *Henry found one of your hair pins on the floor.* Jack's voice sounded in her mind. "No thank you, Eliza. I'm not in the mood for anything fancy today." She touched her hair and forced a smile. "This will do."

"Don't forget the gloves, miss." Eliza helped Ottilie slip into a pair of tall white gloves, concealing the bruise on her wrist just as her aunt swept into the bedroom.

"I am pleased to see you are ready for supper." Lady Hudsyn's gaze flitted from Ottilie to Eliza. "Thank you, Eliza. You may leave us."

"Yes, Your Ladyship." Eliza scuttled out of the room.

"I expect you heard Henry will be dining with us tonight." She lifted the sides of her magenta dress and seated herself next to Ottilie.

"Yes, I was glad to hear it."

"I trust you remember what we talked about yesterday before you left the house."

"I do."

"I expect that from now onward, you will stay away from Mr. Bastin and encourage your cousin to do the same."

Ottilie pressed her lips together and paused to control her irritation before speaking. "Mr. Bastin is Henry's friend, and I have no more power to keep him from his friends than you do."

Her aunt fixed her with a penetrating stare. "How do you suppose Henry would feel about Mr. Bastin if he knew he'd enticed his cousin into spending the night with him?"

Ottilie swallowed. "That's not true."

"Isn't it?" Her aunt picked up a hairpin from Ottilie's vanity and turned it over in her fingers.

Ottilie stared at the hairpin. Did her aunt know? Had Lulu betrayed her out of spite or perhaps in the hope of compensation?

"Tell me my dear, what did he say to you? Did he say you were his muse? Did he flatter you with honeyed words and talk of the classics?"

Ottilie felt the color drain from her face. She shifted to face the looking glass and smoothed her hair needlessly, fighting to keep her emotions in check.

Lady Hudsyn's lips curved into a wry smile. "Aah, I see that I am correct. Your father used those same tactics to seduce your mother and get his hands on our papa's money."

Ottilie swallowed the lump of fear in her throat and forced herself to remain calm. "My goodness, Aunt, there is no need to be so cynical. Perhaps my father loved my mother," she said icily.

"Don't fool yourself, child. He was too selfish to love anyone besides himself. What he loved was my father's money."

Ottilie continued to busy herself with needless primping. Lady Hudsyn was doing her best to rattle her, and she would not fall into her trap.

"I don't say these things to hurt you. I never intended for you to know the truth about your father, but you forced my hand when you started skulking around with Mr. Bastin." She plunked the hairpin onto the vanity, and Ottilie's heart jumped in fear. "If you wish to do so in Canterbury, that is your choice. However, you will not do so under this roof." Lady Hudsyn stood abruptly. "Now, let us go down to the parlor and speak no more of this."

Ottilie stood slowly, unable to take her eyes off the sparkling hairpin.

"Are you quite all right, dear? I hope you don't mean to greet your cousin wearing such a sour face."

Ottilie forced a smile and accompanied her aunt to the parlor, but her mind remained plagued by the woman's threat to expose her to Henry if she dared to see Jack again. Henry wouldn't believe his mother—not without confronting Jack and Ottilie first. And therein lay the problem. She could not lie to her cousin. She would try to explain the truth, but he would never understand how she could have hidden away upstairs while he was inside Jack's house and then spent the night under the same roof as that awful naked Lulu, whom he'd seen in Jack's arms! It would end his friendship with both her and Jack. And she could not bear to lose Henry and probably Jack as well.

"Mama! Cousin!" Henry pushed himself out of his armchair and greeted them as they stepped into the parlor.

"Henry! I didn't realize you had arrived," Lady Hudsyn said. "Why didn't Benson send word upstairs?"

"I instructed him not to. I knew you two were getting ready, and I did not wish to rush you."

"Well, what a joy it is to see my son again. How did things turn out with the estate?"

"Excellent," Henry said. "All is well. Now, how about I pour you each a glass of port?"

"Only a drop, dear."

"You look rather pale for someone recently returned from the country," Ottilie remarked as Henry handed her a glass of port. "One would think you spent all your time indoors."

"Yes, well," Henry said evasively and swallowed a gulp of his port.

"Lord Towne," Benson announced from the doorway.

Henry frowned and shot a questioning glance at Ottilie before standing to shake the gentleman's hand. "Lord Towne, what a pleasant surprise."

"It is always a pleasant surprise to receive an invitation from Lady Hudsyn." Lord Towne seated himself and smiled obsequiously at Ottilie.

She forced the remainder of her port down her throat. Would her aunt never give up?

Henry leaned toward her and whispered, "How did you know?"

"Know what?"

"That I never left London."

"You just told me." She smiled.

Henry frowned. "I'm sorry I neglected to tell you, but I became happily entangled in my writing, and I needed not to be disturbed."

"I see."

"I finished my book of poetry." He grinned.

"Oh, how wonderful!" Ottilie clapped her hands together in feigned surprise. "What an accomplishment! May I read it?"

"I left it with Mr. Bastin last night. I want to get his input first."

"What are you two whispering about?" Lady Hudsyn interjected.

"Nothing, Mama, just sharing our news."

"We would like to hear your news too, dear. If you care to share it with us."

"Oh, I fear you and Lord Towne will find it a bore."

Lady Hudsyn glowered at her son and turned to converse with Lord Towne.

"I hope you can forgive me for leaving you alone with Mama."

"As long as you promise not to do it again," Ottilie said.

Henry smiled, reached for her hand, and kissed it.

Out of the corner of her eye, Ottilie glimpsed Lord Towne's bristly brows furrow together, and her aunt's lips press into a hard disapproving line.

⇛⇚

"THERE IS NOTHING of value downstairs," Jack announced as he entered the study on the first floor. "All that remains in the parlor is a settee, two armchairs, and a few dusty novels. I did find a fine porcelain tea set in the dining room, though. And I'd be interested to know if it belonged to my grandmother."

"There ain't nothing of value to us here, neither." Brandt gestured to an ornate mahogany desk. Its four open drawers lay bare, with the exception of a few broken quills and an empty inkwell.

"I see that," Jack said, scanning the room. The bookshelves were empty of books and housed only a spinning globe and a stuffed eagle.

"Let's get out of here and see what's in them other rooms," Brandt said.

They exited the study and crossed the landing into a massive dining room, papered in the same blue and gold floral pattern that decorated the walls outside.

"Ain't this something!" Brandt ran his hand over the soft, blue velvet armchairs. "Your folks sure liked their comforts, didn't they?"

"Don't call them that," Jack snorted and strolled to the window. He pulled open the heavy gold curtains and coughed as a cloud of dust filled his nose and lungs. "I should send Mrs. Wilson round to do some dusting."

"What's the point if you plan on tearing the place apart?"

"I suppose you're right." Jack fanned the dust particles from his face. He turned to see Brandt sitting at a small writing desk, frowning over a weathered notebook.

"Find anything?" Jack walked over to Brandt.

"I ain't sure yet. This is an old account ledger. Your aunt was mighty particular about keeping track of her spending. Seems unusual, most rich folks don't think too much about their spending, I imagine."

"Not my uncle. He has always been a miser."

"I don't know about that. His wife sure did spend a lot at the seamstress, glovers, and milliners." Brandt thumbed through the pages, paused, and scratched his chin while frowning at the figures in front of him. "How many dresses and hats does one person need?"

A trace of bile rose in Jack's throat as he remembered his mother mending the holes in her dresses. "Come on, let's get out of here."

"Wait a minute," Brandt said, and Jack backtracked to the desk. "I think I've found something. See here?" He pointed to a line on the page.

"Five-hundred pounds paid to Canterbury Ladies' College." Brandt ran his finger down the length of the page. "Another five hundred to Canterbury Ladies' College the following month. Here's a note for three hundred paid to the college." Brandt looked at Jack. "There are multiple entries here."

Jack snatched the notebook and studied the entries. "What the hell does this mean?"

"I reckon it means your aunt and Miss Hamilton were close friends. Otherwise, it seems like a mighty big coincidence."

Jack inhaled and exhaled heavily through his nose, trying to calm his thoughts. He snapped the ledger shut. He didn't want to believe this of Ottilie, but he'd be a fool to ignore the evidence staring him in the face. Money had the power to corrupt the best of people, and manipulating a young woman sounded exactly like something Sir Richard would do. "I'm going upstairs and see what else I can find," he said.

Brandt followed as Jack climbed the stairs to the second floor, which housed four large bedrooms, two dressing rooms, and a lavatory.

"I'll check these two rooms, and you take the two across the landing." Jack pushed open one of the doors and strode inside the first room. It contained a bed, stripped of its linen, and wide, empty wardrobes. "Nothing here." He moved into the second bedroom. The pink carpeted floor, white laced curtains, and ornate, standing looking glass told him it had once belonged to a young lady. A silver tray containing a silver-plated hairbrush, comb, and a variety of hair pins lay on the dresser. Jack moved closer to the tray and picked up one of the silver hair pins embedded with sparkling glass stones resembling rubies. The same hair pin was found by Henry on his parlor floor after it had fallen out of Ottilie's hair. "What the hell is going on here?" he muttered.

"Found nothing in them other bedrooms—" Brandt stepped inside the room—"except for your aunt's dresses. They look expensive, so I reckon we can sell them. The furniture should fetch something too."

"I don't care to sell them. We'll give them to charity. London is full of hardworking women who can't afford a decent dress to cover their backs or a good bed to rest their weary bones at night."

"Did your uncle have a ward?" Brandt asked, looking around the room.

"I'm starting to think so." Jack held up the hair pin.

"What's that?"

"A woman's hair pin. Ottilie wore the same one in her hair two nights ago."

"I reckon lots of young ladies wear them things. She can't be the only one."

"Have you seen this particular hair pin in anyone else's hair recently?"

"Hell, I don't know. Even if I had seen it, I wouldn't remember. Lady Buntley always wears them sparkly things in her hair and around her neck. All the ladies do. I'll be darned if I know one from the other, though."

"Well, I remember this particular one because it fell out of Ottilie's hair, and Hudsyn picked it up off the floor. It's how he knew I had a woman with me."

"Did he recognize it as belonging to his cousin?"

"Thankfully not. Although, if she has more of these at home, he might put two and two together. But that's not my concern at the moment."

"You think Miss Hamilton is in cahoots with your uncle?"

Jack bit his bottom lip. "I don't know. But something is afoot, that much is certain."

Brandt shook his head. "If he sent her to spy on you, he must have known you'd returned to England. How could he have known that?"

"Anything is possible. Someone in Dartmoor may have recognized me, or maybe he saw my likeness in the newspaper and recognized me himself. Hell, maybe he's been spying on me all these years. I don't know. But I intend to find out."

"Dang it!" Brandt said.

"What happened to the copy of my uncle's will? I didn't get a chance to read it before you backhanded me."

"It wouldn't have happened if you hadn't been so fast on the draw." Brandt reached into his coat pocket and withdrew a folded paper. "Good thing I had the foresight to pick it up off the floor where you left it."

"Thank you." Jack took the paper, unfolded the will, and scanned through it. "The entirety of my estate and effects shall pass to my eldest living male descendant," he read aloud, "save twenty thousand pounds, bequeathed to my wife, and twenty-five thousand pounds bequeathed to the trustees of Canterbury Ladies' College."

Jack raised his eyes and met Brandt's stare.

"How much did you tell her?" Brandt asked.

Jack closed his eyes. "Nothing about my uncle. But she knows about Wardell."

"God dammit, Bastin! Did you tell her about the gold?"

"I only related his crimes and how we handled his comeuppance, that's all."

"So, your uncle knows you're alive and in town. Changes everything, doesn't it?"

"I don't believe she will tell my uncle anything."

"Then you're a damn fool. Why do you think Sir Richard keeps the money flowing to that ladies' college? It ain't out of the goodness of his heart."

Jack rubbed his forehead as if that could erase the confusion clouding his brain. *This can't be happening; there must be another explanation.* "I'll talk to her," he said.

"You've done enough talking, Romeo. If your uncle finds out about the gold, we could be swinging from the end of a rope. It's time for you to let little Miss Schoolmarm alone an' take care of satisfying Lady Astyr's needs. That way, your uncle will come to you, and then we can take care of things like we planned."

Jack squeezed the bridge of his nose between his fingers. *How could I have been such a fool? Hasn't experience taught me anything? It's been Brandt and me all these years; we knew to trust no one but each other. After a mere few months of Mayfair pampering, I let down my guard.*

A hot shame clawed at his chest. He swung around and cleared the vanity with a swipe of his hand, sending the silver hairbrush, comb, and the array of hair pins crashing to the floor.

"Damn him!" He leaned his palms on the vanity and breathed hard. "Damn that blackguard straight to hell."

CHAPTER SIXTEEN

In secret we met—
In silence I grieve,
That thy heart could forget,
Thy spirit deceive.

—Byron, "When We Two Parted"

OTTILIE VACATED HER four-poster bed as soon as the sun's rays filtered into her room. She padded across the pale blue rug, feeling its softness beneath her feet, and pushed aside the silvery drapes to welcome daylight. Lady Hudsyn's dire warnings had plagued her all night and left her feeling restless. *Did he declare you were his muse? Did he charm you with tender words and poetry?* The accuracy of her aunt's words made her uncomfortable. Yet she could not believe her experiences with Jack had been a lie. She was no child. She knew in her heart he was sincere.

You think him different, an exception to the rule, but I can assure you he is not. Love is a fairytale, my dear. The best thing to do is secure your future by marrying well.

"You're awake, miss?" Ottilie turned to see Eliza enter the room with the morning tea.

"Yes, the day is too lovely to waste time lounging in bed. Is my cousin downstairs yet?"

"His Lordship is breakfasting in the dining room. But he will be leaving shortly for an early morning ride."

"That is exactly what I need." Ottilie's spirits rose. "Can you inform him I wish to accompany him?"

"Certainly, miss." Eliza placed the teacup on a small side table. "I'll go down directly and tell Benson. And I'll be back to help you into your riding habit," Eliza promised as she vacated the bedroom.

Twenty minutes later, Ottilie ventured downstairs wearing a pale blue riding habit, complete with a feathered hat, gloves, and a riding crop. The outfit was one of two Henry had gifted her the previous year.

"Good morning, cousin." Henry looked up from his plate when Ottilie entered the dining room. "I am pleased you will be joining me this morning. I contemplated asking Eliza to wake you, but I thought it unfair. I know how much you enjoy a late morning."

"I'm afraid I did not sleep well last night." Ottilie moved to the table and poured herself a cup of tea. "I seem to be consumed by restless energy."

"A ride will do you good then. It should be interesting to say the least. Bastin sent me an invitation early this morning to join him on Rotten Row."

"Mr. Bastin? I didn't realize—what I mean to say is, I don't want to impose on your outing."

"It wouldn't be an imposition. I understand there will be a party of us."

Ottilie blinked. *A riding party? Why did Jack not extend the invitation to me as well as Henry? Did he not want me to accompany them?*

"Are you going to sit down and eat something?" Henry asked. "We're to meet our party in thirty minutes."

A footman stepped forward and pulled out a chair for Ottilie. She slid into her seat and reached for the sugar bowl, paused mid-air, then redirected her hand to the honey. Perhaps Jack is wise to be cautious, she thought, as she brought the honey jar to rest next to her teacup. *After all, he probably knew Henry would invite me along for the ride, and it is far better to be prudent and avoid arousing suspicion.* She scooped a spoonful of honey from the jar and drizzled it into her cup.

"What on earth are you doing?" Henry asked.

"It's beautiful, isn't it?" she said.

"Are you talking about the honey?"

"It's like a river of sunshine. No wonder it is food fit for the gods."

"A rather poetic sentiment coming from a mathematician."

"Perhaps you underestimate mathematicians." Ottilie stirred the honey into her tea and added a dash of cream.

"Perhaps." Henry gave her a sidelong glance.

Ottilie sipped her tea and smiled. The honey added a sweet, floral hint to her cup, which reminded her of Jack's kiss.

"What are you smiling about?" Henry asked, a curious lilt present in his tone.

"Am I smiling? I didn't realize."

"You're acting rather peculiar this morning."

"Perhaps, I'm happy to have you home. Is that so strange?"

Henry placed his cup in its saucer. "A few minutes ago, you said you were feeling so restless you could not sleep last night, and now you are talking about rivers of sunshine and smiling to yourself. I know something is afoot. Are you going to tell me what?"

"There is something I wish to talk to you about. But it's of a rather serious nature and not what brings a smile to my face."

"Good heavens! Don't tell me you've decided to marry Lord Towne," Henry teased.

"Very funny! You know I'd die before tying myself to that old goat."

"The groom has readied the horses, my lord." Benson appeared in front of them.

"Shall we go?" Ottilie pushed back her chair and stood up.

"Don't you want a bite to eat first?"

"I'll eat later. It's rude to keep our party waiting." Her nerves were alive with anticipation and her appetite obliterated at the idea of seeing Jack again.

"Now, I'm convinced something's afoot." Henry dabbed his mouth with his napkin and stood.

They made their way through the garden to the stables, where the groom handed Henry the reins to his bay thorough-bred and helped Ottilie mount a chestnut mare, side-saddle.

"Shall we?" Henry asked, once they'd settled on their horses.

Ottilie nodded and cued her mare forward. They trotted side by side along Hill Street and crossed into the park several minutes later via Stanhope Gate. Hyde Park sparkled under the cloudless sky and had never looked more lush or green to Ottilie. Perhaps it was the fruit from the rain two nights ago, she thought. As they approached Rotten Row, Ottilie spotted Jack looking regal in a black riding jacket and white breeches. He had on a silk top hat and even his tall, black boots shone in the bright sun. He sat atop a magnificent dappled gray thoroughbred and seemed absorbed in conversation with a lady on a bay mare. His horse stood unnecessarily close to her mare, and Jack angled his body toward the woman, so he almost touched her.

"Did Mr. Bastin say who would be joining his riding party this morning?" Ottilie asked.

"He did not, but I see he brought his cowboy valet along, and there's Lady Buntley on a bay mare. I don't recognize the lady he's conversing with."

As they rode toward the party, Jack turned.

"Good morning," Henry called. "I hope we haven't kept you waiting too long."

"Not at all." Jack smiled at Henry, but his gaze passed over Ottilie, and a whisper of fear brushed her throat.

"Lord Hudsyn, Miss Hamilton, I believe you have already met Lady Buntley, and of course, you know my valet, Brandt."

Aside from a black cowboy hat, which Brandt doffed at them in greeting, his riding costume was identical to Jack's.

"And allow me to introduce Lady Astyr," Jack said.

Lady Astyr? The familiarity of the name struck Ottilie. Could she be a relation of Sir Richard's? Or his new bride? No. Sir Richard has lived in India with his common-law wife for years. And this woman is too young.

"Shall we ride?" Lady Buntley's voice broke through Ottilie's thoughts. "The horses are becoming restless."

"Lead the way," Jack said. "We shall follow."

"Splendid!" Lady Buntley spurred her mare into a gallop. Her horse disappeared down the row with Brandt's black thorough-bred.

Jack remained close to Lady Astyr's side as their horses trotted down Rotten Row, speaking intermittently to Henry and behaving as though Ottilie were invisible.

He is sensible to distance himself from me while in Henry's company, and flirting with Lady Astyr is an excellent ruse. Henry will believe he has returned to his old habits. Ottilie reasoned with herself, but she could not help sensing something was amiss, and it caused a hollow feeling in the pit of her stomach.

JACK WORKED TO keep a smile on his face and his attention on Lady Astyr despite smoldering inside at the thought of Ottilie's betrayal. She stayed close to her cousin and threw cursory glances in his direction as if trying to conceal her devious intentions. When he'd invited Hudsyn to join his riding party, he knew Ottilie would accompany her cousin and take advantage of the opportunity to spy for Sir Richard. And he'd been right. He envisioned her taking mental notes, recording what she saw and heard, so she could report all to the man. Jack smirked. Let the blackguard confront him. He itched to point his pistol at that bastard's head.

Ottilie diverted from the group, leaving her cousin's side and trotting ahead.

Jack watched her. *What is she doing?*

"I'm not racing you!" Hudsyn called after her.

"In that case, I shall win by default." She turned and flashed a dimpled smile at Hudsyn before breaking into a canter.

Jack saw his opportunity. "I'm in the mood for a race. Hudsyn, will you keep Lady Astyr company until I return?"

He spurred his horse into a gallop and raced after Ottilie before Henry had time to respond. Despite himself, he wanted an explanation from her. He wanted to know if it had all been an act. And if it had, he wanted confirmation of her betrayal. He always looked his enemies in the eye, and he'd never shot a man in the back. If she intended to put a bullet through his heart, the least she could do was look him in the eye.

It only took a minute for his gelding to catch up with Ottilie's mare. She slowed her horse when Jack came up beside her.

"Where's Henry? He's supposed to be racing me."

"He doesn't want to race."

"And you do?"

"No," Jack said.

"What prompted you to leave Lady Astyr's side? You seem so terribly fond of her." Her tone was teasing rather than angry, and Jack realized she hadn't taken his courting of Lady Astyr seriously. He would play her game for now, but not for much longer.

"I have something of interest to show you. Will you come with me?"

Ottilie looked over her shoulder. "Henry will be worried if I leave the party."

"No, he won't. He thinks you and I are racing. We aren't going far, and we'll be back before he has time to miss us."

"Very well, then."

Jack directed his horse to West Carriage Drive and across Serpentine Bridge. The waters below glistened, and Jack was reminded of the last time he'd been on the bridge and in the park with Ottilie. The memory soured his mood all the more, and he spurred his horse into a canter across the park, stopping only when he reached the exit at Grosvenor Gate.

"I thought you didn't want to race?" Ottilie brought her mare to rest next to Jack's thoroughbred.

"I didn't," he confirmed.

"And why did you canter across the park as if a band of ruffians chased you?"

"Did you have trouble keeping up?" he asked.

"No—" she lifted her chin—"but a fair warning would have been nice."

"Well, we only have a short distance to go from here, and Park Lane is too crowded for a canter, so you needn't worry about me racing off again."

"You want to leave the park?" Ottilie said.

"Only to go a short distance."

"Where to?"

"You'll see soon enough." He trotted a short way along Park Lane and turned onto Upper Brook Street. A minute later, his horse came to rest in front of his newly purchased townhome.

"Have we arrived?" Ottilie asked.

"We have." He gestured to the white-pillared townhome. "Behold my new home."

Ottilie gaped at the house, too stunned to speak.

"It's been empty for three years, but that doesn't concern me. I intend to tear it down and rebuild."

"Tear it down?" Ottilie looked at the house and back at Jack. "You mustn't! Have you seen the inside? It's a beautiful house."

A thunderstorm settled in Jack's chest. Here was the moment of truth. "You've been inside this house?"

"Yes, many times. My friend—"

"Many times!" Jack snorted. "Just as I thought."

"Lady Astyr was—"

"Don't say another word. I know all about your friendship with Sir Richard."

"My friendship with Sir Richard? I have no friendship with Sir Richard."

"Do you deny knowing him?" Jack demanded.

"I know who he is," she said with a dismissive shrug.

"Have you met him?" Embittered anger rose in Jack's chest.

"Briefly," Ottilie said.

"Yet, he pays you."

"*Pays* me?" Her voice turned sharp. "Have you gone mad?"

"Do you think me naive, Miss Hamilton? Sir Richard has been sending large sums to your ladies' college for years."

"That has nothing to do with me. Lady Astyr was a generous patron of the school and remained one until she died."

"How convenient," he smirked.

Ottilie's face hardened. "There is nothing convenient about it. She believed in our cause. She helped build the school along with—"

"Stop!" Jack refused to listen to more lies. "The charade is over, Miss Hamilton. I know you're colluding with Sir Richard."

"Colluding?" She laughed. "You're not making any sense."

"You've taken me for a fool, haven't you? Throwing yourself in my path and securing a tight grip on my heart two weeks before Sir Richard returned to Mayfair."

"Throwing myself in your path? What do you mean? May I remind you that it was you who begged me to be your muse?"

"You were looking for me the night you appeared on Madame Baudelaire's portico, weren't you?"

Ottilie hesitated, and Jack knew he'd guessed correctly.

"Every interaction between us has been contrived, hasn't it? I see now what a coincidence it is that you were attacked in the park at the exact moment I happened to be walking there." Jack's fury spurred his irrational thoughts.

"How clever you are," Ottilie snapped. "Do you imagine I conjured up the summer rainstorm as well? You really have lost your senses, haven't you?"

"Quite the contrary, I assure you. And you may tell your master, Sir Richard, if he wants his wife, he may look for her in my bed."

His words appeared to have the effect of a sharp slap. Ottilie blinked at him in stunned silence. "I see. You intend to use the new Lady Astyr to settle whatever ridiculous quarrel you have with Sir Richard."

"Precisely. And now *you* may earn your keep by delivering that information to your master."

His words seemed to drain her spirit, and she paled. "My aunt was right about you," she said quietly. "You are mad, and you belong in the likes of Bedlam with Madame Baudelaire." She picked up her reins and made to go.

"Tell me one thing before you depart my company for good, Miss Hamilton. Did you manipulate Hudsyn too, or is he a willing participant in your scheme?"

"How dare you! Henry has done nothing but be a friend to you, as have I." Her bottom lip trembled, and Jack's stomach wrenched in spite of himself. Then he remembered that Miss Hamilton was a consummate actress and hardened his heart against her wiles.

"Good day, Mr. Bastin." She lifted her reins, and Jack watched as her mare trotted down Upper Brook Street with a concoction of fury and sorrow coursing through his veins. He had been foolish to break his rules—rules he'd put in place to protect himself from further betrayal. But no matter, he did not need love. Sweet revenge would soon be his.

⇥⟫⟪⇤

EVEN BEFORE HIS urgent rap sounded at her door, Ottilie heard Henry clamber up the stairs and call out her name.

She debated on whether or not to open the door. She didn't want to speak to anyone, and her tear-stained face would scare Henry and provoke an onslaught of questions.

"Ottilie?" Henry knocked again softly. "Are you in there? May I enter?"

Placing her last pair of gloves into her travel case, she closed the lid and latched it as if sealing off another chapter to her life. Because, she realized, she was. After this moment, everything in her life would change and nothing would be the same again.

Henry's knock and pleading voice sounded again. "Ottilie? I'm not going to leave until you let me in and tell me there's nothing to worry about."

She opened her mouth to say she was fine and would see him later for luncheon or tea. But the urgency in his voice gave her pause. Henry never visited her in her bedroom. Whenever he wanted to speak with her, he would request her presence elsewhere—the drawing room, library, or garden. But this time, concern clearly outweighed decorum in his mind, and she knew that sending him off with platitudes wouldn't suffice.

Ottilie pushed herself to her feet and went to open the door, allowing Henry an unobstructed view of her tear-streaked face.

"What on Earth happened to you?" Henry stepped inside. "Bastin said you were feeling poorly, so he escorted you as far as Upper Brook Street, but then you refused to let him see you home."

"What he said is true. Don't blame Jack. I insisted he return to his friends."

Henry shook his head. "This kind of thing won't do, Cousin. I was worried. Bastin seemed—" His gaze fell to her travel case. He stared at it for a moment before turning to look at her questioningly. "Are you going somewhere?"

"To Oxford. I need to speak to my stepfather."

Henry ran a hand through his wavy blond hair. "I don't understand. Has something happened to him?"

Ottilie shook her head.

"Then please do me the courtesy of explaining what is going on." Henry's tone revealed his frustration. "First you run away from our riding party and now I find you, in tears, with your bags packed, on the verge of departing London. Were you even going to tell me you were leaving?"

"Of course," Ottilie said. "Look, I'm sorry. I just need to speak with my stepfather, and it can't wait."

Henry frowned. "Have you started communicating with him again? Is he expecting you? Why the sudden urgency?"

Ottilie squeezed her hands together. "It's rather a long story. You'd best come and sit down, so I can explain." She walked to the bay window seat and ensconced herself on its silvery-blue velvet cushion. Henry followed and perched on the edge of the cushion beside her. He remained silent as Ottilie gazed out the window at the blooming garden below and collected her thoughts.

"I wish you would tell me what's wrong," Henry said after several minutes. "Bastin seemed agitated when he rejoined the riding party. Did the two of you quarrel?"

Ottilie forced a smile. "Of course not. I hardly know him. What could we possibly have to quarrel about?" She turned back to the window and bit the inside of her lip. She hated lying to Henry about Jack, but at least she would not have to do so anymore.

"I don't believe you. Something happened, and I mean to find out what upset you. If you won't tell me, then Bastin must."

Ottilie turned to Henry. "How much do you know about my father?"

Henry blinked in surprise at the shift in subject. "The same as you, I suppose. He was a rake and a heavy drinker who gambled away his money. And—" Henry snorted—"according to my mother, all these bad attributes stem from his talent for writing poetry."

"I received the same information, but there's a lot more to the story."

"Oh?" Henry raised his eyebrows.

Ottilie took a deep breath before saying, "My father didn't die when I was three. He died of syphilis when I was eight, after spending five years locked away in an asylum in East Sussex."

Henry paled. "What? Who told you this?"

"Your mother."

"To what end? Why would she spring this on you now?"

Ottilie paused. "Because she doesn't want either of us associating with Mr. Bastin. She wanted to warn me against his type, and she insists that I discourage your friendship with him." Ottilie swallowed her guilt for omitting the whole truth.

"Good Lord!" Henry's face blotched red with anger. "Will she never stop trying to control our lives?"

Ottilie reached out and touched his arm. "She loves you, that's all. She believes she is protecting you."

"Don't apologize for her." Henry leapt up and paced several furious steps forward. Then he spun around and paced back again. "Loving me is no excuse for hurting you. Why would she be so cruel as to burden you with this information when there is absolutely nothing you can do about it now?"

"I am pleased someone finally told me. I want to know the truth, no matter how painful. But I need to verify that what your mother told me is, in fact, the whole truth. She asserts my mama sought to protect me by claiming my father was dead, but I have to find out if my stepfather knows more. If anyone does, it will be him."

Henry dropped onto the window seat again. "And do you believe your stepfather will help you?"

"Yes, for the same reason he told me about you two years ago."

"Guilt," Henry said.

"Exactly."

"I'm coming with you."

"That's not necessary. I don't want to cause further strife between you and your mama."

Henry jumped to his feet once more. "Don't argue. I won't change my mind. My mother burdened you with this knowledge, and I won't let you carry it alone. Your stepfather isn't likely to offer you any comfort or support, and I think you will need it. Give me an hour to have my things readied. Then we shall leave for the train station."

"What will you tell Lady Hudsyn?"

"I'll say we're going to Margate for a few days. Didn't you say you have friends holidaying there?"

"Yes, Mr. and Mrs. Thomas are there for the summer. But your mama won't feel satisfied with that explanation."

"Too bad. It's the only explanation she'll receive from me." He kissed Ottilie's cheek and hurried out of the room before she could protest.

Ottilie sighed and turned back to the window. Her eyes burned as she fought to keep back tears. Henry would never know what truly caused her heart to ache. "Oh, Mama," she whispered, gazing up at the clear blue sky. "How you must have suffered. I understand now the agony you must have endured." She'd hardly recognized Jack when he'd turned against her— there was no question some form of madness had taken hold of him, especially when he began raving about contrived meetings and colluding with Sir Richard. None of it made sense. But even if he had gone mad, Ottilie realized—it would not change the fact that she loved him.

CHAPTER SEVENTEEN

Thou unrelenting Past!
Strong are the barriers round thy dark domain,
And fetters, sure and fast,
Hold all that enter thy unbreathing reign.

—*William Cullen Bryant,* "The Past"

S IR RICHARD'S SILENCE unnerved Jack.

With Miss Hamilton acting as his spy, his uncle would have gained full knowledge of Jack's plan to cuckold and humiliate him, yet the man had done nothing to intervene or prevent his growing friendship with Lady Astyr. Sir Richard did not order his wife to stay at home as expected, and his morning rides with the lady continued, unimpeded. Perhaps, Miss Hamilton had failed to report the information to Sir Richard?

It was possible but unlikely. Her ladies' college was far too precious to her. It was more likely that his uncle was devising some trap and biding his time to plot and plan. After all, he'd received a knighthood for his strategic excellence in the Crimean War, and he would approach this personal war no differently. Jack could not allow him that advantage. He needed to play on the man's hubris and provoke him into taking rash action.

Such were his thoughts as he strolled with Lady Astyr in Kensington Gardens during promenade hours on Sunday evening. Sir Richard might have been a brilliant military strategist, but he clearly knew little about women. It had taken only three meetings to cajole Lady Astyr out of her timidity and to win her complete devotion and trust. So, when he'd asked her to meet him in the park in full view of society, she'd readily agreed.

"Your husband doesn't mind you walking out with another gentleman?" he asked.

"I told him Lady Buntley invited me to ride in her carriage." She peeked up at him from beneath a white bonnet and matching parasol, her elfin face overshadowed by a sharp nose.

"How naughty of you," Jack said playfully.

"It wasn't a lie." Her nut-brown eyes widened an inch, expressing her earnestness. "I was indeed riding in Lady Buntley's carriage before stepping out to meet you."

"That's true." Jack tilted his head toward hers. "And it's not as though you need a chaperone. You're a married lady, after all." He waited for her reaction to this last comment, testing her knowledge of his reputation.

"Of course not!" She let out a high-pitched giggle—a habit she seemed to have developed during their last outing. "Lady Buntley assures me you are the utmost gentleman."

"Did she?" Jack murmured and silently thanked Lady Buntley.

The crowd thickened when they reached Hyde Park. They began to stroll east on the busy footpath next to the Serpentine. Jack took advantage of this audience by becoming overt in his flirtations with Lady Astyr. She responded in kind, giggling repeatedly and turning every shade of pink while remaining oblivious to the whispers and disapproving looks cast in her direction. Perhaps she was too green to comprehend the maliciousness of society's gossipmongers, but Jack was not. He understood that news of his latest conquest would be on the lips of every person in Mayfair by day's end.

As they passed the myriad of carriages on Rotten Row, chock full of sharp-eyed high society ladies and gentlemen adorned in the latest fashions, Jack slipped his arm in the crook of Lady Astyr's elbow and murmured, "I've been working on an epic poem. My publisher says it is going to be a sensation."

"I would so love to read it," she said, her voice breathy.

"And I'd love to show it to you. My home is five minutes away on Half Moon Street, and you are welcome to call any time."

"I'd like to see it right now." She gazed up at him, her face earnest and her cheeks devoid of blushes.

"Are you certain?" Jack had not expected her immediate consent, and such an easy conquest gave him pause. If she went with him, he wanted to make sure she harbored no doubts.

"Absolutely," she said, cinching her grip on his arm.

"Well, who am I to deny a lady her wish?" Jack shrugged off his concerns and told himself that being married to a cold gun like Sir Richard had no doubt left the poor woman starved of affection and desperate for a little romance.

Keenly aware of people's open stares, Jack escorted Lady Astyr toward the park's exit. Society would snub Lady Astyr for her indiscretion, but Jack's smoldering hatred for Sir Richard overpowered any pity he felt for her. And thoughts of Ottilie's betrayal cemented his determination to humiliate his uncle in the worst way possible. Sir Richard had sent a beautiful, intelligent young woman to make an utter fool of him, and now he returned that favor by publicly cuckolding the man.

Jack glanced over his shoulder at the horde of promenaders and smiled. There was little doubt in his mind that he would hear from his uncle within twenty-four hours.

"Thank you for coming." Ottilie sat with Henry across from her stepfather inside a small, country tearoom. "I took the liberty of ordering our tea ahead of your arrival. I trust you still like a good pork pie." Ottilie gestured to the meat pie on the table. A bowl of peas, a basket of scones, a large trifle, and an array of tarts accompanied the pie.

"It looks delectable, and I am always delighted to see you, my dear." He glanced at Henry, and Ottilie thought she saw a flash of consternation pass over his face. "And you, Lord Hudsyn. What a pleasant surprise."

"Thank you, sir. I trust you are well."

"Indeed." He nodded, pouring himself a cup of tea.

Ottilie cleared her throat. "How is your—family?" She could not bring herself to say *Mrs. Lewis*—a title that once belonged to her mother.

"Busy as always. Mrs. Lewis has just now embarked on re-decorating the house—again." He flashed a weak smile and ran a hand over his lined forehead.

"And the babies?" she asked, handing him a plate heaped with thick slices of golden-crusted meat pie and a pyramid of sweet peas.

"Rambunctious little fellows," he tittered and took the plate from Ottilie's hands. "The house is a constant buzz. I barely get time to think."

He looked exhausted, and Ottilie noticed he'd aged considerably in the past two years. But she could not bring herself to sympathize with him. He'd chosen that selfish woman over her mama, and now he would have to live with her. "Well, I am pleased to hear they are thriving," she said.

Mr. Lewis shifted in his seat. "I should have liked you to see them, but with Mrs. Lewis's remodeling, things in the house are upside down."

"Of course." Ottilie obliged her stepfather with another stilted smile.

"But, enough about me." He straightened his shoulders as though readying himself for a blow. "What have you come all this way to tell me?" He shot another look at Henry. "You two are not engaged—are you?" The tremor in his voice alarmed

Ottilie. *Why is he afraid?*

"Heavens, no!" Henry exclaimed. "Whatever gave you that idea?"

Mr. Lewis shrugged, and his face relaxed into a sheepish smile.

"I came here to ask you about my father," Ottilie said, anxious to get to the heart of the matter."

"Your father?" Mr. Lewis's shaggy brows knitted together. "What about him?"

"Mama always said he died when I was three, but I know now that is not true."

"You know about the asylum?"

"I do. And I want to understand why my mama never took me to see him. Even if he was gravely ill, it seems harsh to keep a child from knowing her father."

"She did what she thought best." Her stepfather dropped his gaze and stared into his teacup as if contemplating how best to continue. "As I understand it—" he lifted his eyes to Ottilie's face—"your father was a man without morals—one who stopped at nothing to gratify his selfish desires. No woman was safe in his company."

"I know he was a rake, but is that reason enough to keep his only child from him?"

Mr. Lewis's gaze drifted from Ottilie to Henry. "You may not have been his only child."

Ottilie's skin grew cold, and she exchanged a glance with Henry.

"What are you implying?" Henry demanded.

Mr. Lewis shifted in his seat and cleared his throat. "Nature blessed Roger Hamilton with good looks and charm, and he used those gifts to his full advantage." He paused as if reluctant to expel the necessary words from his throat. "As I said, no woman was safe in his company—" Mr. Lewis's tone and expression took on a quiet seriousness—"And your mama's sister proved no exception."

"Now, look here!" Henry stood up.

Heads swiveled. People turned to stare, and Henry straightened his jacket and sat down. A flurry broke out around them.

"I know this may be difficult for you to hear," Mr. Lewis lowered his voice, "but try to remember that you sought me out and begged for the truth, and I am merely complying with your wishes. Remember too that I only know what my wife—Ottilie's mama—told me and nothing more."

"Go on," Ottilie said, "it's time we heard the truth."

Mr. Lewis put down his teacup and straightened his shoulders. "When you were nearing three years old, your mother fell seriously ill with a fever, and Lady Hudsyn came from London to be by her sister's side. She stayed for approximately six weeks—" Mr. Lewis cleared his throat—"and during that time, Mr. Hamilton and Lady Hudsyn engaged in a brief liaison."

"How dare you!" Henry banged his fist on the table, rattling the cups and spoons.

Ottilie touched his arm. "Please, Henry. I only ask that you listen."

Henry clenched his jaw. "What you say makes no sense, sir. My mother wouldn't have deigned to stay in the same house as Mr. Hamilton, let alone..." He pursed his lips and breathed deeply before continuing. "She disliked her sister's husband. They were estranged for that very reason."

"Their relationship had suffered a strain, but they were not yet estranged. Your grandfather vehemently opposed his daughter's marriage and banished Mr. and Mrs. Hamilton to the countryside. But he kept in contact with them and continued to provide his daughter with a comfortable living. For the first two years, the money kept Hamilton satisfied, but with each rejection from a magazine or publisher, his drinking increased, and his behavior worsened. It proved too much for him when his wife fell ill. Then his beautiful and sophisticated sister-in-law arrived on his doorstep and—well..." He glanced at Henry's stony face and paused.

"Go on." Henry's voice sliced the air.

"As I understand it, the situation in the house was stressful. Lady Hudsyn suffered great distress seeing her sister so ill, and Mr. Hamilton took advantage of her fragile state. He used his charms to flatter and seduce her. Six weeks later, when she returned home to London, Lady Hudsyn discovered she was with child."

"Preposterous!" Henry hissed, and Mr. Lewis jumped. "Are you suggesting that Lord Hudsyn is not my father?"

Ottilie pressed her lips together; her heart ached for Henry.

"I don't know for certain—no one does. You may well be Lord Hudsyn's son—or not. No one would have been the wiser, but Augusta wrote to Mr. Hamilton and declared her love for him, saying she was going to give birth to their child."

"I don't believe a word of it!" Henry leaned forward and glared at Mr. Lewis. "My mother would never write such words. She's as stiff and proper as the queen herself."

"He's right," Ottilie said. "This doesn't sound in line with Aunt Augusta's character."

"Not today, no. But three-and-twenty years ago, your aunt was a young woman of two-and-twenty, wed to a man some thirty years her senior."

Ottilie sat in stunned silence.

Did he declare you were his muse? Lady Hudsyn's voice rang in her ears. *Did he flatter you with honeyed words and soft kisses?* She'd thought her aunt's sour attitude stemmed from anger and spite but now realized it served to mask her pain. *Lady Hudsyn didn't hate my father; she loved him. She tried to spare me, but she was too late.* Ottilie's stomach clenched, and pain seared her chest. *Even so, she betrayed my mama. How can I forgive her for that?*

Henry sat beside her. He, too, appeared to be deep in thought.

Her stepfather eyed them fearfully as though waiting for an explosion.

"What happened?" Henry asked, his voice subdued.

"Mr. Hamilton ran off with another woman—she too was married—and the letter Lady Hudsyn sent ended up in her sister's hands."

"So that caused their rift?" Ottilie asked.

"Indeed. Several months later, your papa returned home and declared his undying love for your mama. But she wanted nothing to do with him. He refused to accept her rejection, and his behavior became even more erratic. Your mama feared for your safety, so your grandfather intervened and had him committed."

"My mother's move to Germany wasn't voluntary, was it?" Henry said, his voice flat.

"It wasn't," Mr. Lewis confirmed. "After Lord Hudsyn died, your mother started visiting the asylum—unbeknownst to your grandfather, of course. She took you with her on more than one occasion. And, in doing so, she endangered your title and your future. So, your grandfather intervened again and forced her to move to the continent. As you can see for yourself, the move did her good. Getting out of England sobered her and brought her back to her senses. When I met Ottilie's mother, she'd had no contact with her sister in seven years."

Henry ran his hands through his hair. "My whole life has been a lie."

"Not necessarily," Mr. Lewis said. "There is no proof you are not your father's son. Your mother only spent six weeks in Oxford, and she could have become pregnant soon after she returned home. A babe can come several months early—or late, for that matter." A quivering breath escaped his chest. "You two resemble each other, to be sure, but it's your grandfather's coloring and features you share—not the poet's. Your grandfather had a cleft right here just like yours."

Henry pressed his fingers to his chin.

"On the other hand, your family thought it best to keep the two of you apart. It's not unheard of for cousins to marry, as you know." He dropped his gaze and drummed his fingers on the table before looking up again. "That's why I experienced a moment of panic today when I saw you both sitting here, waiting to tell me some important news."

"But you were the one who told me about Henry and encouraged me to seek him out. Why?"

"I did it to assuage my guilt, I'm afraid. You'd lost your mama, and I'd betrayed you both so terribly. I wanted to give you a new family. The knowledge you were not alone in the world without any familial support comforted me. I acted selfishly."

"No," Ottilie said, "it was the best thing you could have done. Henry and I have been such great friends, and he truly does feel like a brother to me."

Henry turned sharply to look at her, and Ottilie saw the deep shock on his face. He appeared as if he'd only just fully digested the information fed to him.

"I'm sorry," Ottilie said.

"It's not your fault," Henry said in a low voice. Then he pushed back his chair, stood, and strode out of the teashop.

CHAPTER EIGHTEEN

O sin! Oh sorrow! and oh womankind!
How can you do such things and keep your fame,
Unless this world, and t' other too, be blind?

—*Byron, "Don Juan", Canto 1*

LADY ASTYR SOBBED into Jack's linen sheets.

He glanced at her as he slipped on his trousers and cursed under his breath. *Damn, Miss Hamilton. The woman has ruined me.*

He removed a fresh handkerchief from his drawer and handed it to Lady Astyr. "I'm sorry," he said.

She lifted her head, snatched the handkerchief from him, and buried her face in it.

"I'll leave you to get dressed and go arrange for a hansom to take you home." He moved toward the door.

"What is wrong with me?" she heaved between sobs.

Jack paused, his hand hovering above the door handle.

"How am I ever to bear a child if no man can stand to touch me?"

"That's not true," he said.

"It is!" she wailed. "You are no different from my husband. He says he needs an heir but cannot bring himself to lie with me."

Jack's hand fell from the doorknob. "Sir Richard never consummated his marriage to you?"

She shrugged. "He performed his duty on our wedding night but was furious when I failed to do mine and conceive a babe. I don't know what I did wrong. Lady Buntley swears it is his fault because the first Lady Astyr also failed to give him children. So, I thought—hoped—you might—"

"You hoped I would father you a child?" Jack asked incredulously.

"Yes. Why else would I spend time in the company of one of London's most notorious rakes? Lady Buntley says you must have given hundreds of women children, only you don't know it."

"Hundreds?" Jack blinked, taking in the irony of her words. All this time, he'd thought he was seducing his uncle's wife when *she'd* been the one beguiling him. The notion struck him as hilarious. Laughter bubbled up so forcefully inside him that it made him shake.

"What makes you laugh?" Lady Astyr's brows knitted together in angry unison. "Does my predicament amuse you?"

"I'm sorry." Jack tried to steady his breathing. "Truly, I am." But the laughter worked like a storm inside him and spilled forth a fresh wave.

"How dare you?" She wrenched the sheets as if wanting to rip them to shreds.

"Hundreds!" He clutched his chest and wheezed.

Lady Astyr bared her teeth at Jack. "Get out!" she screamed.

He opened his bedroom door and attempted another apology, but laughter choked his words.

The lady picked up a book from a side table and threw it at him. Jack stumbled out of the room, crippled with laughter. He managed to pull the door shut, just in time to hear the book thud against it.

HENRY STARED SILENTLY out the carriage window.

Ottilie glanced at her cousin and worried her bottom lip. Henry's brooding was understandable, but if his thoughts spiraled out of control, he'd enter a dark place that would be difficult to escape. She had to make sure that didn't happen.

"At least we know why your mama worked so hard to see me married," she teased. "Now that I know how desperate she must have been, I'm a little insulted she couldn't find me a better suitor than Lord Towne."

The muscles in Henry's jaw tightened.

"That was meant to make you smile." She nudged him lightly with her elbow, but Henry's body remained rigid. Worry poked at Ottilie's chest. Humor would not solve this problem; she'd have to use logic to shield Henry and prevent him from slipping into darkness.

"There is no proof Lord Hudsyn isn't your father," she said quietly.

Henry turned to face her. "Unfortunately, I may never know the truth."

"I hope you're not thinking of doing anything rash."

"If you mean giving up my title, the answer is no. I will not besmirch my father's memory by airing our family's sordid past in public."

Ottilie sighed a breath of relief. "I'm pleased to hear it, because there is as much chance you'd be giving up your claim to your legitimate title."

"I will never dishonor my father's memory, but how can I hold my head up in society, knowing the title I'm honored with might not be legitimate?"

Ottilie reached for her cousin's hand and squeezed it. "The same way King Edward IV did. His mother engaged in a liaison when his father was away at war, so people claimed he was illegitimate. Do you think it should have been enough to make him relinquish his claim to the throne?"

"Of course not," Henry said. "It's balderdash. People always question the legitimacy of kings and queens. Endless wars have been fought over that very question."

"Exactly," Ottilie said. "No one knows if the man betrothed to their mother truly is their father—and that includes both of us. King Edward's father legitimized him by owning him as his son, and there was no solid proof to suggest otherwise, so Edward kept his claim to the kingdom. We don't know if your father knew about your mother's affair with Mr. Hamilton, but we *do* know that he claimed you as his legitimate heir. I daresay, if that is good enough for a king, then it's good enough for a baron."

Henry squeezed the bridge of his nose. "Look at us. We are practically twins, and where do you suppose I inherited my affinity for writing poetry?"

"A great grandfather or a distant uncle? Who knows? I have often wondered from whom I inherited my affinity for computing sums with a poet for a father and a mother who despised dealing with numbers. Don't you see how foolish it is to play guessing games about something you cannot prove?"

"But how can I look my mother in the eye again after she cuckolded my father?" Henry gripped his knees. "All those years of fake morality! Her endless lectures. It makes me sick to my stomach."

"She's human, and she made a horrible mistake. We should pity rather than despise her for the terrible burden she must live with. I think her moralizing is a reflection of her guilt. She spends her life trying to correct her mistake."

"Do you mean me?" He asked sardonically.

"Of course not. She loves you. You are everything to her. Don't you see that all of her moralizing was aimed at protecting you?"

Anger blazed in Henry's eyes. "How can you defend her when she hurt your mother the way she did? Her own sister, for heaven's sake!"

Ottilie sighed and leaned back on the carriage seat. "It was a heartless betrayal, and I will never forget the hurt she inflicted upon my mama. But to be sure, I blame my father more. He was a rake who thought nothing of a woman's feelings, including those of his wife and daughter. I am at peace now that I understand why my mama kept me from him. It is terrible to feel anger at your own mother. I don't wish it for you. That is why I urge you to look at things from a different angle."

"What are you talking about?"

"You heard what Mr. Lewis said. Your mother suffered enormous stress at seeing her sister near death. My father took advantage of her, and she fell in love with him."

Henry scoffed. "That doesn't excuse her behavior. It only explains her hatred for poets and why she has been so cold and set against love all these years."

"Maybe she's right. Maybe love is a fairytale." Ottilie turned to the window, thinking how Mr. Bastin's web of charming platitudes and lies had almost ensnared her. A shiver ran down her spine as she thought of the night she'd spent in his house. She'd almost given herself to him. Henry's arrival was like a supernatural intervention—as though her mama watched over her and sent him to save her.

The hansom cab rolled to a stop in front of their hotel on Oxford's High Street. Henry stepped out and gave Ottilie his hand as she alighted.

"I've made up my mind to take a flat at Albany. I cannot stay with my mother in Berkeley Square after what I've learned."

"That sounds like a wise choice. And I think it best if I return to Kent tomorrow." She glanced up at the hotel and then back at Henry. "But I would do so with a happier heart if you would accompany me. We can go to Margate and enjoy the benefits of the healthy sea air. You can start work on your second book of poetry."

"I like the idea of going to Margate, but I won't be writing any more poetry."

"What about your book? You'll want to make revisions, won't you? And get it published?"

"No. In fact, I'm going to write to Bastin tonight and tell him to burn it." Henry spun on his heels and strode into the hotel.

Ottilie stared after him, and the brave front she'd been putting on all day started to crumble.

Sir,

It has come to my attention that you gravely dishonored my wife, Lady Astyr, and I demand forthwith that you publicly declare yourself a blackguard by publishing a sincere and humble apology to both the lady and me for the injuries you inflicted upon us. If duels were still fashionable, you would regret having crossed this excellent member of Her Majesty's Armed Forces. You may thank the good Lord that I am a gentleman who, despite enormous temptation, will uphold the laws of his country and refrain from lodging a bullet between your eyes.

Sincerely,
General Sir Richard Astyr

Sir Richard's demand arrived, hand-delivered to Jack's front door within hours of Lady Astyr's furious departure. "Wait where you stand," Jack instructed the messenger. "I wish to send a reply."

Sir,

I shall offer you no apology, public or otherwise. Furthermore, I declare you a coward who hides behind the law's skirts like a frightened child. You are no more than a braggart who received an honorable title for strategizing and issuing orders that sent young soldiers to their deaths. Did you fight, sir? Did you march on the battlefield with those courageous men? Did you look death in the eye? I think not.

If you are indeed the fearless soldier you claim to be, prove your worth by standing up and defending your wife's honor. I

challenge you to a pistol duel at dawn. Name the meeting place.
If England has outlawed duels, let us go to France!
Sincerely,
J. Bastin

Jack smirked as he reread his deliberately outrageous insults, intended to provoke Sir Richard's overblown hubris, challenge his masculinity, and offend his self-righteous demand for unquestioning respect. Surely, no man had ever dared to insult Her Majesty's general in such a manner. Sir Richard, Jack knew, would find it impossible to refuse his challenge. He deposited his reply in an envelope addressed to his uncle and handed it to the waiting messenger. "Tell your master I look forward to his reply." He pressed a weighty silver coin into the messenger's hand. The servant gave a slight bow and retreated.

Sir Richard's reply arrived less than an hour later.

Sir,

I accept your challenge to a pistol duel at dawn. No doubt, your letter shall serve in my defense should my precisely aimed bullet prove fatal to you. No judge would convict a man whose honor has been so hideously maligned as mine, particularly one who has served his country as well as I have done. There will be no need to travel to France. Hampstead Heath will do.

Sincerely,
General Sir Richard Astyr

Jack's heart pumped with renewed energy. He lowered the note and breathed deeply. The moment he'd been waiting for had arrived. It was time to alert Brandt, check his pistols, and ready himself to face his uncle at dawn.

CHAPTER NINETEEN

And drawing from his belt a pistol, he
Replied, 'Your blood be then on your own head.'
Then look'd close at the flint, as if to see
'Twas fresh—for he had lately used the lock—
And next proceeded quietly to cock.

—Byron, "Don Juan", Canto 4

THIRTY MINUTES BEFORE dawn the following day, Jack departed Mayfair for Hampstead Heath in a hired brougham. Brandt stretched beside him, arms crossed and hat over his face. He'd fallen asleep as soon as the carriage rolled away from Half Moon Street, but Jack's body pulsed with energy. He was no longer a vulnerable lad but a man about to meet his uncle on equal footing.

When the darkness outside lightened a shade and the black night transformed into purple dawn, Jack knew they were approaching their destination. He peered out the carriage window as it trundled over the grassy heath toward the dueling spot.

"It's time." Jack lifted the hat from Brandt's face. "Sir Richard's day of reckoning is finally here."

"Already?" Brandt pushed himself upright and rubbed his eyes with his forefinger and thumb. "That sure was fast."

"How would you know? You slept like a babe in a rocker."

Brandt yawned. "Is the big bug here yet?" he asked with a wry smile.

"Let's find out." Jack pushed open the carriage door and stepped onto the field, still wet with early morning dew. A hint of orange filtered across the horizon, adding another layer of color to the sky.

"I reckon that's your man." Brandt pointed to a large, black and gold-trimmed carriage parked under a cluster of trees about fifty feet across the field. A liveried footman alighted from his box seat and opened the door of the stately carriage. Seconds later, Sir Richard emerged and stepped onto the green field. A second, military-looking gentleman followed him, as did his solicitor Jebkin. Finally, a bespectacled man clutching a medical bag stumbled out of the carriage.

"Good thing he brought a doc with him 'cause he's gonna need one." Brandt put his hand on Jack's shoulder. "Remember now, dead men can't talk, so no good will come from killin' him. Keep your head an' do him like we did Wardell. Guaranteed, he'll squeal like a pig."

Jack ran his hand over the smooth handle of the six-shooter ensconced in his holster. Brandt was right. Keeping his head had already worked in his favor. He'd have liked to put a bullet in his uncle the day after discovering his whereabouts, and it had taken a bucketful of discipline to restrain himself from doing so. But this moment made the wait worthwhile. The fool had behaved predictably and walked right into his trap. It hadn't even taken long.

Jack squared his shoulders and strode forward to meet his opponent. The two parties met in the middle of the field, and for the first time in eleven years, Jack came face to face with his nemesis.

Sir Richard stood with his back straight and his body as rigid as a wooden soldier's. Jack hooked his thumbs in his belt and met his uncle's disdainful stare with a wry smile. *You're a fool if you think you can match my quick draw and sharp eye, General. While retirement and luxurious living made you soft, I spent my time watching my back and mastering survival. And now, I'm going to destroy you.*

Sir Richard narrowed his eyes and homed in on Jack, and then shock and recognition registered on his uncle's face.

Acrid bile rose in Jack's throat. Why did the fool look surprised? Hadn't he already gleaned Jack's identity from the information Miss Hamilton passed on to him? *Perhaps my transformation from gullible, skinny boy to hardened gunslinger scares you, Uncle. No doubt, you thought I was good and dead. Little did you know, I've spent the last eleven years planning your demise.*

"Is this gentleman your second?" Jebkin interrupted Jack's mental showdown with his uncle and motioned to Brandt.

"He is," Jack stepped next to Brandt.

"Howdy, y'all." Brandt tipped his cowboy hat at the party of men and smirked at their disdain.

Jebkin pursed his lips in a manner that gave the impression he'd ingested something foul. "Will you state your name for the record, sir?"

"You already know my name. I was in your office last week."

Mr. Jebkin raised his eyebrows. "I still need you to state your full name for the record."

"Most folks back home call me Brandt. So, I reckon Brandt will do you fine."

Jack suppressed a smile, knowing Brandt deliberately played the fool to irk the snobbish solicitor and inject a false sense of security and superiority in their opponent.

"I mean, I wish you to state your full name for the record. As it is stated on your birth certificate."

"Well—" Brandt hooked his thumbs into his trousers— "sometimes, when I made her hoppin' mad, my grandma used to holler, 'Owen Grant Jedediah Brandt, now you stop that and git over here before I tan yer hide!'" He shrugged. "So, I reckon that's my birthed name."

"Mr. Owen Grant Jedediah Brandt," Jebkin muttered as he

scribbled the name in his notebook. "Second to Mr. Jack Bastin?" Jebkin looked questioningly at Jack.

"That's it," Jack said. "My uncle assigned the name to me. He wanted something commonplace—something forgettable." He fixed his eyes on Sir Richard's stony face.

"Right," Jebkin said, looking up at Sir Richard's second. "Would you be so kind as to state your full name for the record, sir?"

The second, a sharped-faced gentleman sporting silver mutton chops, squared his shoulders and lifted his chin as though answering a military command. "Robert Edmund Chelmsford, retired Lieutenant General of Her Majesty's Armed Forces."

"Thank you, sir." Jebkin gave the man a servile nod before logging his name into his notebook. "Now, gentlemen, may we see your weapons, please?"

Mr. Chelmsford produced a silver box, which he opened to display a brass pistol encased in red velvet.

"Excellent." Jebkin nodded. "A fine piece of weaponry."

"It served me well during two wars and will serve me well today. Mark my words." Sir Richard glared at Jack.

"I am certain it shall, Sir Richard." Jebkin bowed as though he was in the presence of the queen. He turned to Jack. "Mr. Bastin, your weapon, if you please."

Jack put his hands on his hips, opening his coat wide enough to reveal the two six-shooters resting in their holsters on either side of his belt.

Jebkin paled. He glanced at Sir Richard, who narrowed his eyes into two furious slits.

"This isn't the Wild West, sir. Only one pistol per man is permitted."

"Fair enough." Jack snatched the revolver from his left holster, twirled it on his trigger finger, and handed it to Brandt.

Jebkin's large Adam's apple bobbed in his throat as he swallowed. "Gentlemen," he said, "you will turn and walk fifteen paces. Once you are in place, you must wait for my command.

Then, and only then, may you fire a single shot each. Is that clear?"

"Crystal," Jack said, flinging off his coat and tossing it to Brandt.

"Not so fast." Jebkin eyed Jack nervously. "You must walk first, and I haven't started counting yet."

"Well, what are you waitin' for?" Brandt said. "We ain't got all day. Get this showdown started."

Jebkin lifted his chin and cleared his throat. "You may turn and begin your march."

Jack spun around and marched the fifteen paces as Jebkin counted them. He stopped on command then turned to face his uncle.

Sir Richard angled his body sideways and lifted his pistol.

Jack kept his forward-facing stance and stood with his legs slightly parted. His hand rested next to his holster, and his fingers danced as if they itched to draw the gun.

"Ready?" Jebkin called.

Both men nodded.

Jack cleared his mind as he homed in on his target.

"On the count of three—one, two, fire!"

Jack whipped the revolver from its holster, cocked the hammer, and fired in one swift motion. Smoke clouded the air as the bullet from Jack's six-shooter sped toward its target. It collided with Sir Richard's pistol before the man had time to pull the trigger. Metal, blood, flesh, and bone sprayed into the air. Sir Richard shrieked and dropped to his knees, clutching his hand.

"My God! I think he's lost a finger." The doctor scrambled toward his patient.

"Back off." Brandt strode forward and aimed his revolver at the doctor. "We ain't done with him yet."

"You don't understand. He needs medical attention!" The doctor gesticulated wildly at Sir Richard, who'd collapsed onto his back.

"Don't panic. He's only lost his thumb. He'll be right as rain so long as he does what he's told." Brandt lifted his boot and brought it down on Sir Richard's mangled hand. The man shrieked.

"Now, look here," Chelmsford roared. "What is going on?"

"Stay out of it." Brandt swung his revolver at Chelmsford.

"Stop this at once! Do you hear?" Jebkin bellowed. "This is highly illegal."

"I'll tell you what's illegal—" Jack strode forward, revolver in hand—"Stealing another man's inheritance, that's what."

Brandt lifted his foot off Sir Richard's open wound and moved it to the center of the man's palm.

"Hello, Uncle." Jack looked down at Sir Richard. "Why don't you introduce me to your friends?"

"Will somebody please explain what all this madness is about?" Jebkin pleaded.

"The fine general is about to confess his sins and tell you who I am and what he stole from me." He smiled down at Sir Richard. "Aren't you, Uncle?"

"Help me!" Sir Richard looked wildly between Chelmsford, Jebkin, and the doctor. "Please! He's mad!"

Mr. Chelmsford dashed toward the carriage.

"Hold your horses!" Brandt fired a round near the man's feet.

Chelmsford leapt in the air and held up his hands in surrender. "Don't shoot!" he said, getting down on his knees.

"You two"—Brandt gestured toward the carriage and motioned to Sir Richard's footman and driver—"get down from that carriage."

The terrified servants scuttled to join Chelmsford, who kneeled, helpless, in the eye of Brandt's revolver.

"Now," Jack pointed his revolver at his uncle, "speak."

"You're mad!" His uncle babbled. "You'll hang for this!"

Jack cocked his revolver and fired a shot, narrowly missing Sir Richard's kneecap. The bullet plowed into the ground in between his legs.

Sir Richard screamed.

"I won't miss next time." Jack aimed his pistol at his uncle's foot.

"Don't shoot!" Sweat beaded Sir Richard's forehead as he looked wildly between Jack and the onlookers. "I'll tell them."

Jack gestured to Jebkin. "Come closer and ready your notebook. I don't want you missing a word of this. Tell your friends who I am," Jack said quietly.

"Sebastian—" Sir Richard gasped—"His name is Sebastian John Greyson." He wheezed. "My deceased wife's nephew. The grandson of Edward Knoll."

"The dead boy?" Jebkin paused his scribbling.

"Except he ain't dead, as you can see for yourself," Brandt said.

Jack stepped away from Sir Richard, and the doctor rushed to tend the man's injured hand.

"I have here the will of my grandfather, Edward Knoll." Jack reached into his jacket, extracted a rolled paper, and handed it to Jebkin. "I think you will find that the estate now in Sir Richard's possession legally belongs to me."

Jebkin frowned and snatched the document Jack held out to him. Jack watched as he untied the string with trembling hands and scanned the document. "Where did you get this?" he asked, looking up at Jack.

"Never mind where I got it. The only thing that matters is what it says. I am my grandfather's rightful heir, and his property needs to be returned to me immediately."

"Well," Jebkin sputtered, "it's not that simple. Your identity will have to be verified, and you will need to appear before a judge."

"My uncle has already verified my identity, so all he has to do is sign over to me what is rightfully mine."

"That won't do. You and your American brute tortured Sir Richard. A man will say anything when he suffers great pain. One cannot—"

Jack took a step closer to Jebkin. "My name is Sebastian John

Greyson. And eleven years ago, that vermin on the ground indentured me to a Texan named Wyatt Wardell and faked my death so he could steal my inheritance."

"I'm not suggesting you are lying, Mr. Bastin, but the court will want some sort of verification—a birth record or a relative."

"I need to get this man to a hospital at once." The doctor said as Mr. Chelmsford draped Sir Richard's arm across his shoulders, helped him to his feet, and dragged him toward the carriage.

Jebkin moved to follow, but Jack stood in his path.

"I have no other living relatives." He glared down at the man. "So, either advise Sir Richard to do what is right, or you can answer to a judge."

"What do you mean?" Jebkin heightened his stance.

"I think you know. You prepared my grandfather Sir Edward's will, yet you never advised his daughter that the birth of her son made her child heir to her father's estate, did you?"

Jebkin swallowed. "It wasn't necessary at the time. The estate was to stay in a trust until the boy came of age."

"But you never informed my parents because Sir Richard asked you to keep it from them, didn't he?"

Jebkin paused in thought and then nodded as if conferring with himself. "If you truly are the grandson of Edward Knoll, then you have a sister, and she will be able to verify your identity."

Jack stiffened. "What did you say?"

"Sir Richard returned to India in 1857 to help quell the rebellion, and he was required to stay there for some years after, but he thought it too unsafe for his wife. She must have grown bored or lonely because, in 1861, she brought a young woman up from the country to live with her."

"Miss Hamilton?" Jack frowned. Was this idiot confusing Miss Hamilton for his sister?

"I believe the girl was her niece, a Miss Greyson."

"What?" Jack's voice was a ghostly whisper even to his own ears, as his mouth dried and his throat closed.

"About a year later, the young lady married and moved to Canterbury, where she opened a ladies' school. I know this because your uncle has left her school a most generous sum in his will. I questioned him about it when I redrafted his will for him a few weeks before his recent marriage."

"What did he say?"

"He said something about the former Lady Astyr forcing his hand from the grave."

"Mr. Jebkin!" the doctor shrieked. "We will be forced to ride without you."

"That is all I know. If you find this sister of yours and she vouches for you, you will have a valid claim. Now, if you will excuse me, I must get to the hospital before Sir Richard loses more blood."

Jebkin huffed and pushed past him. He hesitated, and when Jack offered no resistance, he made a mad dash for Sir Richard's carriage.

Jack stood motionless in the open field. Putting one foot in front of the other suddenly seemed like an impossible task, as if the soles of his feet had sprouted roots and anchored him to the ground as firmly as the trees enclosing the heath. He envisioned Violet as she was the last time he'd seen her, sitting on the moor with a book resting on her knees. She'd glanced up at him as he'd crept away from their home during the early morning hours. He'd frowned in response to his sister's wave—angry she'd caught him fleeing. *What is Violet doing up at this hour? Was there no escaping his family?*

She'd motioned to him, but he'd ignored her, and started down the path that would lead him away from their stone cottage. He'd glanced over his shoulder once more before descending the slope. Violet'd blown him a kiss. But, he'd turned his back on her again, and carried on down the hill, disappearing from her view forever.

He'd spent years regretting that day and praying for a second chance to connect with his sister, only to learn she was dead. But now, that second chance had come.

"Violet is alive," he whispered. "She lives," he repeated, trying to expel the darkness from his mind.

The sun moved from behind a cloud, spreading its rays across the horizon and warming the earth below. Jack opened his arms. Helios had chosen to smile upon him once again.

CHAPTER TWENTY

Sebastian was my father
Such a Sebastian was my brother too,
So went he suited to his watery tomb:
If spirits can assume both form and suit
You come to fright us.

—Shakespeare, *Twelfth Night, Act V*

T HE SALTY BREEZE awakened Ottilie's senses and imbued her with calm as she strolled above Margate's chalky cliffs with Violet.

"I'm so glad you decided to join us, Ottilie darling." Violet pressed her cheek against her friend's shoulder. "You've been through such an ordeal these past weeks, and the sea air does wonders for health. It's sure to restore you in no time."

"It already has, but nothing compares to the generosity and support you have shown me." They ambled past the Clifton Public Baths leaving behind the crowds of holiday makers and entered the developing area of Cliftonville.

Violet inhaled deeply. "I think we shall stay in this area next year. It's so peaceful, and they plan to build an elegant hotel on the edge of the cliffs, which will boast exquisite ocean views."

"That sounds lovely," Ottilie said, gazing at the sparkling ocean. "I feel awful about imposing on your holiday."

"Don't you dare say such a thing. You are part of our family. The children are thrilled to see you, and Mr. Thomas is pleased to have the company of Lord Hudsyn. He's such a fine young man."

"I only mean that I'm sorry for the circumstances clouding my visit. I loathe to burden you with my woes during your time of rest."

"You know very well I would be furious if you had not done so. Learning what you have about your father is shocking, and what kind of friend would I be if you couldn't turn to me for support?" She paused. "But I can't help feeling there's more to your melancholy."

They stepped onto a small iron bridge that joined two chalky cliffs, cleaved to make a pathway to the shoreline, and admired the view. Parasol clutching women and straw-hatted men strolled on the sands below while children with hiked skirts and rolled pants ventured barefooted into the waves. Ottilie watched two excited young women skip toward the designated bathing area and climb into one of several bathing machines perched in the water.

She sighed. "It seems no one has a care, doesn't it? Our troubles consume us, but they're insignificant to the rest of the world."

Violet pressed her lips together. "I wish you would tell me what else is troubling you," she said.

Ottilie swallowed. She'd kept her problems with Jack to herself, partly because she didn't want to cause Henry further suffering and partly because it pained her too much to think about him.

"I know there's something," Violet pressed. "You're not typically one for philosophic meanderings. What are you not telling me?"

"Do you remember what it felt like when you thought you'd lost Mr. Thomas to Amelia Farthington?" Ottilie sighed.

"Of course. It felt as if he'd shredded my heart and trampled it into the ground. If it weren't for your support, I don't know how

I would have survived the pain." Violet reached for her friend's hand. "Wait a minute, are you saying what I think you're saying?"

She nodded, blinking to stave off impending tears.

"But you've never mentioned any man in your letters except Mr. Bastin." Violet's hands flew to her mouth.

"I am sorry." Ottilie inhaled in a shaky breath. "I ruined everything for you. I know how badly you wanted him to give a lecture at the college." A tear rolled down her cheek. "I still cannot comprehend why he changed so suddenly. He went from professing his love for me one day to shunning me the next. I was such a fool to have trusted him."

"It's what rakes do, isn't it? They charm a woman and make her fall in love with them, only to abandon her to pursue a new conquest. I suppose it makes them feel powerful to have such command over women."

Ottilie shook her head in protest. "He wasn't like that at all. He shared things with me about his past—deeply personal things. He is sensitive and caring." She chewed her bottom lip. "Admittedly, there is something very dark about him too."

"Are you sure nothing happened that can explain why he shunned you? Could it have been because of some misunderstanding?"

Ottilie frowned as she thought about her last encounter with Mr. Bastin. She gasped. "Yes! With everything that happened, I neglected to tell you. The last day I saw him, he informed me that he'd purchased your aunt's house on Upper Brook Street."

Violet's forehead creased. "How strange. But I suppose it's about time Sir Richard sold the house. If he intends to spend the rest of his days in India, he hardly needs to maintain a mansion in Mayfair."

"Oh, but he's no longer in India. He has remarried and purchased a new home in Belgrave Square. The strange thing is that Mr. Bastin told me he intended to tear the house down and rebuild. I begged him not to, and when he discovered that I was well-acquainted with the first Lady Astyr and that she was a patron of the college, he grew furious and accused me of colluding with Sir Richard."

"It sounds like Sir Richard behaved unfairly in his dealings with Mr. Bastin and made an enemy of him. If it were anyone else, I'd think your story rather strange, but not Sir Richard. It's not unusual for Sir Richard to enrage people with his offensive behavior."

"Yes, but to take it out on me in the manner he did makes no sense whatsoever. It has led me to believe that my aunt was right. He *is* mad."

"I imagine he's probably embarrassed by his outburst, and if he's a worthy gentleman, then he will send you a letter apologizing. I dare say there is an envelope with your name on it at the college now."

Ottilie forced a smile.

"Oh look," Violet said, pointing to a group on the beach. "I think I see the children with Mrs. Cole." She snapped open her reticule and extracted a small pair of brass binoculars. She held the glasses to her eyes and waved excitedly as if the children could see her. "It is them. Here, take a look," Violet handed the binoculars to Ottilie.

Ottilie peered through the magnified lenses and searched for the children. "I don't see them," she said.

"They're to the left by the water."

"Ottilie looked to her left and scanned the beach.

"Shall we go down and surprise them?" Violet asked.

"Only if you allow their auntie to buy them an ice cream." Ottilie continued to scan the shoreline and then she saw something that made her body turn cold. Two gentlemen stood side by side facing the ocean. Both wore cowboy hats seated low on their foreheads.

PARASOLS DOTTED THE shoreline. Jack eyed the women who sheltered beneath them surreptitiously in the hope of spotting Violet amongst them.

"Someone's gonna challenge you to another gunfight if you keep eyeballing every lady like that," Brandt warned.

Jack sighed irritably and folded his arms. "I can't help feeling like this is all some cruel trick masterminded by Jebkin."

His quest to find his sister had turned into an odyssey, souring Jack's initial excitement and turning it to doubt. He'd departed London for Canterbury the day he'd learned Violet was alive, traveling by steam train from Victoria Station to Canterbury West and then by carriage a mile north of Westgate to the Ladies' College, only to find the expansive college grounds empty and the three-winged stone building locked.

"There must be a groundskeeper or caretaker here," Jack had rapped on the door of the main building multiple times.

"Hold your horses! You ain't given it enough time. It's a big place, an' they most likely ain't expectin' visitors this time of year."

Brandt had been right. Minutes later, an elderly housekeeper had answered Jack's knock, and she'd confirmed that the school was closed for the summer, saying that Mr. and Mrs. Thomas were on holiday in Margate. He'd explained that finding Mrs. Thomas was a matter of great urgency, but the woman had hesitated when he'd asked for their address in Margate.

"I am a friend of Miss Hamilton," Jack had added in desperation.

The housekeeper's face had brightened at first, and then her brows had creased in apparent concern. "Has something happened to our Miss Hamilton?"

"Miss Hamilton is quite well," Jack had assured the woman. "She sent me to speak with Mrs. Thomas about giving a lecture on my new book. Forgive me for not introducing myself," he'd said. "I am Mr. Jack Bastin."

The housekeeper had tilted her head and frowned as if inspecting his features. "You're the one the newspapers are always writing about, aren't you?"

"That's correct, but nothing they say is true." He'd flashed her a winning smile, and she'd chuckled.

"Mr. Thomas has a copy of your book on his shelf, and I heard Mrs. Thomas call it a masterpiece." Her cheeks had flushed pink, and she'd given Jack the address without further hesitation.

An hour later, he'd boarded a train from Canterbury West to Margate Station, where an open carriage had dropped him off in front of his sister's holiday residence in Fort Crescent. Once again, he'd faced disappointment when his knock went unanswered.

"If that scoundrel lied to me…" Jack seethed.

Brandt put a hand on Jack's shoulder. "She's out for the day with her family, is all. Come on. Let's get ourselves a room in a hotel, take a walk an' check back later."

Childish chatter and shrieks of delight drew Jack from his thoughts, and he looked ahead at two children crouching on the rocks of a shallow tide pool and pointing to whatever sea creature they'd spotted in the water. A woman of petite stature, dressed in a plain brown skirt, white shirt, and a straw hat hovered over them.

Jack stepped off the walking path onto the sand.

"Where are you going?" Brandt asked, but Jack failed to answer. Some familiarity with the woman drew him forward. He stopped a few feet away and watched the children dunk their small buckets into the water.

"Caught it!" The little girl shouted and sprang to her feet.

"No, you haven't." The boy jumped up and reached for her bucket. "Let me see."

"Stop it!" The girl sped forward and leapt onto the sand.

"Do be careful." The woman spun around, and Jack's heart sank. Her face revealed her youth, and he estimated her to be no older than nineteen—a full ten years younger than his sister would be today.

"Look, it's a star."

Jack dropped his gaze and saw the little girl holding her bucket up for him to see. Her dark brown eyes looked earnestly at him from behind strands of black curls. She reminded him of Frances, his twin, and his heart clenched.

Jack blinked. Was this another of his dreams?

The child jiggled the bucket. Inside, the starfish curled one of its tentacles. Jack dropped to his knees. "Frances?"

She cocked her head. "How do you know my name? Are you Mama's friend?"

"Yes." Jack smiled, certain now that this was another of his dreams. During the day, he found it hard to recall the details of Frances's features, but, in his sleep, she appeared as clearly as if she stood directly before him. Just like now.

"I want to see." The little boy came up next to the girl and squinted at her bucket. He wore a sailor suit and on top of his honey-colored hair perched a matching sailor hat.

"Here, but don't touch!" The girl swung the bucket in the boy's direction.

"Frances, what have I told you about running off like that? You must remember to stay with me." The young woman, who had not been far behind, came to a rest beside them.

"I had to get away fast," Frances wailed. "Sebastian tried to grab my bucket!"

Jack's head jerked toward the boy. "Frances and Sebastian?" Dream or not, these children belonged to Violet. He squeezed his eyes shut and opened them again. The children remained standing before him.

"Come along," the woman stretched out her hands for the children to take. "You mustn't waste any more of this gentleman's time."

"But he's Mama's friend, and I want to show him my starfish," Frances said.

"There's Mama now." Sebastian pointed.

Jack turned and saw two female figures striding toward them. He blinked. One of the women was Ottilie. The other was Violet.

The two children squealed and waved. Frances bolted forward, and Sebastian followed. Their governess threw her hands in the air, lifted her skirt, and went after them.

Jack watched Violet rush forward, open her arms, and smother their faces in kisses. Ottilie stood behind the trio. His heart contracted as he met her perplexed gaze. A yearning flared within him and his desire to take her in his arms and comfort her was conquered by the army of emotions that stormed him upon seeing Violet.

He tore his eyes from Ottilie and focused on his sister. She was older than he remembered her, of course, but she was still his Violet—the same blond hair, the same porcelain skin…Jack blinked back unexpected tears.

"Mama, that man says he's your friend. I showed him my starfish." Frances pointed at Jack. Violet glanced up. Her light blue eyes, that he remembered so well, met his gaze.

"Violet?" He inched forward, his heart racing ahead of his cautious steps.

She stepped back, shaking her head.

"Violet, it's me." He pulled off his hat and held it to his chest. "It's Sebastian."

"No," she whispered as she took another step back. The children hampered her steps as they clung to her skirt. She continued to shake her head and mouth the word *no*, and the children stared at him with eyes now wide with fright. *I'm a stranger to her. She doesn't know me anymore. She has a good life now, and who am I but a dark shadow from her past coming back to haunt her?*

"Mr. Bastin," Ottilie stepped forward, breaking tension. "What are you doing in Margate?"

Violet blinked and turned her head as if Ottilie's voice awakened her from a dream. "Jack Bastin?" she said.

Ottilie nodded. "Yes, may I introduce—"

"Sebastian John…" she said, looking back at Jack.

"Greyson." He furnished his true last name for her, his voice a mere whisper as tears choked him.

Violet's bottom lip trembled, and a sob escaped her throat.

Jack threw down his hat and ran to embrace her.

CHAPTER TWENTY-ONE

Nothing in the world is single;
All things by a law divine
In one spirit meet and mingle.
Why not I with thine?

—Percy Bysshe Shelley, "Love's Philosophy"

FRANCES AND SEBASTIAN raced on the grassy area of Fort Green, squealing with delight as Jack chased them. He caught a child in each of his arms, swung them around, and planted a kiss on each of their cheeks before standing them back on their feet.

"Again! Again!" they shouted, bouncing on the tips of their toes.

"Your uncle needs a rest from this game," Violet said with a laugh. "And I'm afraid it's time for your morning lessons." She waved at Miss Cole, who strolled toward them.

"No!" They cried in unison, but a stern look from Violet stilled them. "Yes, Mama," they said and ran to clasp Miss Cole's outstretched hands.

"I do believe that is the same look you used to give me when I was their age." Jack laughed.

"Yes, and to think I was only seven at the time," Violet teased.

Frances turned and waved before she crossed the street with Miss Cole, and Jack blew her a kiss. "Frances is so like her namesake; it's uncanny."

"She's the image of our dear sister and has the same lively spirit. Her energy is boundless. I'm afraid she tires out Sebastian sometimes."

"Don't concern yourself. Twins share a soul and understand each other's needs. They will always take care of one another."

"The way you and Frances always did." Violet smiled.

"I still dream about her," Jack said.

"I do too. But mostly, I dreamt you were alive. And now you are here." She clutched her brother's arm and rested her head on his shoulder. "I still cannot believe this isn't a dream."

He kissed her forehead. "It's no dream, sister. I fought long and hard to find my way back to you, and tomorrow, we will travel to London and meet with Sir Richard's solicitor. Then Mama's childhood home will be ours."

"That is wonderful to hear, but I will forever be furious with you for risking your life by engaging in an illegal duel." Violet linked arms with her brother as they strolled west along the promenade toward the Nelson Pier. "Sir Richard is a military man; he could have killed you."

"Believe it or not, I learned something about war and self-preservation during my years in America."

Violet pressed her lips together. "I don't condone violence, but I must say that brute must be held accountable. When I think what you have suffered because of him—"

"I wasn't without fault," Jack cut her off. "In many ways, I needed a taste of life's harsh reality. It pains me to think of the trouble and heartache I caused Papa." He touched the scarred corner of his eye, reminding himself of the times he'd come home bruised and bleeding in his youth.

"Don't be so hard on yourself," Violet said as they stepped onto the iron pier. "That was a long time ago. But if it's any comfort to you, people learn from their mistakes, and they can and do change. Aunt Prudence proved that much to me."

"Perhaps she simply returned to her old self after shedding that blackguard, Sir Richard."

"I think that is a fair assumption." They veered right and walked along the jetty, which jutted over the ocean. "Aunt Prudence grew wiser when Sir Richard discarded her for another woman, and she realized what he was capable of doing. At some point, she must have discovered he stole your inheritance. I am certain that is how she forced him to leave twenty-five thousand pounds to the ladies' college—bless her."

"If that's true, then someone still has that evidence in their possession."

They stopped to enjoy the view from the jetty, watching the rowboats and bathers bobbing about in the water.

"I'm just now remembering something Aunt Prudence told me before she died." Violet gazed at the ocean as if it was the keeper of her drowned memories. "It didn't make much sense at the time, but it speaks to me now."

"Yes?" Jack raised his eyebrows.

"She remarked, 'If your uncle doesn't do right by you in his will, go see Mrs. Briggs, and she'll have something for you.' I didn't press her for more information because I was too preoccupied with her health."

"Who is this Mrs. Briggs?"

"She's my former headmistress, dear friend, and mentor."

"Was she also close friends with Aunt Prudence?"

"She was. They came to know each other through me. When Mr. Thomas and I opened Canterbury Ladies' College, Aunt Prudence became our patron and an avid campaigner for women's education. Headmistress Briggs shared her passion, so they grew close."

"That's the answer then. Aunt Prudence must have gathered whatever incriminating evidence she had against Sir Richard and given it to this Mrs. Briggs whom you both trusted. If Sir Richard tries to fight us, we may have need of it. As for the twenty-five thousand, it hardly matters now. When I get my inheritance, your school will be well-funded."

"I'm glad to hear it, but the money is yours. You have earned it, and your future should be filled with nothing but joy."

"You have no idea how much joy it gives me to help you in your endeavors, Sister."

"Excellent!" She nudged him playfully. "I shall enjoy having the great Jack Bastin at my disposal, readily available to the college for lectures on writing and literature."

Jack took off his hat and bowed low. "At your service, Madam. Your interests are mine as well."

Violet put an arm around his waist and gave him an affectionate squeeze. "Your brotherly devotion gladdens my heart. But in all seriousness, I want you to focus on fulfilling your own needs and desires. When the world treats you harshly, people put up shields that block happiness and deny love. They're in too much pain to understand how wonderful life can be, especially when it involves love."

Jack stiffened. "If you're referring to Ottilie, she's been avoiding me. I doubt she wants to talk to me."

"She does—more than anything—trust me. She's only kept her distance these past three days because she wanted to give us the space and privacy we needed. Now that the initial shock has worn off, we have a lifetime to rebuild and reconnect, and you have your future happiness to think about."

"In truth, I'm ashamed of how I treated her and afraid of how she feels about me now. I will not blame her if she never trusts me again."

"If you love her, you must talk to her, or doubt will take hold and erode the connection you share."

Jack exhaled heavily. Violet was right, but why did a conversation with Ottilie frighten him more than facing the barrel of his uncle's pistol?

"But enough lecturing from me. It's time to get down to important business." She retrieved binoculars from her skirt pocket. "Last summer, a lady claimed to have seen a whale through her spyglass."

"I doubt you will see very far through those opera glasses."

Violet giggled. "I'm not really looking for whales. I like to watch the swimmers. There is something about the ocean that sets people free."

Jack took the binoculars from Violet and pressed them to his eyes. "Yes, it seems men and women mingle freely together in the water."

"It's become a bit of a scandal, but I have no objection. Margate isn't London, and many break protocol here. I think it's healthy for hard-working people to relax and escape society's burdens."

"I quite agree." Jack lowered the glasses and leaned his arms over the jetty fence. "That's why Brandt likes it here so much. He's even agreed to stay in England until the end of summer."

"What will he do in America?"

"Our investments there have earned us plenty of money, so he has more than enough to start his own ranch. It's what he has always wanted."

"You'll miss him."

Jack nodded. "A great deal."

"Does he have someone waiting for him over there? Family or a fiancée?"

Jack shook his head. "Brandt's a lone star. All he needs are his horses, cattle, and plenty of open space."

"But you're not like him, are you?" Violet placed her hand over her brother's.

Jack's thoughts turned to Ottilie, and a weight settled in his chest. "No." He lowered his gaze and looked at his sister's loving hand, covering his own. "I used to think I was, and I tried hard to live my life unattached, but it never served me. I was living a lie."

HOW CAREFREE EVERYONE looks.

Ottilie sighed as she gazed at the holidaymakers strolling along Fort Promenade. She and Henry sat on a bench near the Paragon Hotel, unable to muster the energy to partake in the strolling, swimming, boating, donkey riding, or other enticements Margate offered its visitors. Both had spent the last three days concealing their misery while rejoicing in Jack and Violet's happy reunion. And the turmoil of changing emotions had left them exhausted.

"Why don't you join Mr. Thomas at the public baths? He so enjoys your company." Ottilie turned to Henry and forced her voice to a cheerful lilt.

"I'm not in the mood for the baths today." Henry's voice weighed heavy with gloom. "Would you mind terribly if I went back to London tomorrow? I'm hoping Bastin will let me stay at his Half Moon Street residence until a flat becomes available at Albany."

"If that will make you happy, then, of course, I don't mind. But I am worried about you. How long do you intend to punish yourself for something over which you had no control?"

"I don't blame myself for my mother's sins. I feel lost, that's all. Perhaps my life would have been better were I not born a baron. Being a member of the peerage feels rather pointless. There's nothing more to a gentleman's life than attending balls, drinking, gambling, and talking politics."

"That's not true. You have a seat in the House of Lords. And I'm counting on you to help women obtain the vote one day."

Henry crossed his arms and exhaled a puff of air. "I don't care for politics anymore."

Ottilie eyed her cousin's slumped shoulders. "You sound like a man who has lost his passion. Why not pick up your pen and make yourself happy by reaffirming your love for poetry?"

Henry shifted, angled his body away from Ottilie, and said nothing.

Ottilie inhaled deeply and cast her eyes toward the ocean,

taking in its serenity.

The world is vast, and your problems small. She inhaled and exhaled through her nose. *All will be well in time—Violet and Jack are proof of that.* She closed her eyes then, trying to be content with the feel of the warmth of the sun and the salt-scented air.

"Hello, you two." Jack's voice sounded nearby.

Ottilie opened her eyes then, startled to see Jack standing in front of her. She opened her mouth to greet him, but Henry cut her off.

"Bastin!" Henry leapt to his feet. "I've been meaning to speak with you."

Ottilie stood up, not wanting to be left looking up at the men. Jack glanced at her and gave her a tight smile. Her heart shriveled. Every time they encountered one another, the rift between them seemed to widen.

"I plan on traveling to London with you and Violet tomorrow," Henry said, drawing Jack's attention away from Ottilie, "And I need a place to stay while I wait for a flat to become available at Albany. Would it be all right if I stayed at your residence?"

"You have an aversion to Berkeley Square all of a sudden?" Jack raised his eyebrows, oblivious to Lady Hudsyn's betrayal and the question of Henry's legitimacy.

"Something like that." Henry lifted his chin.

Jack's forehead creased. "Of course, you're welcome to stay at Half Moon Street as long as you like. Brandt wishes to stay in Margate until the end of summer, and then he'll return to America."

"Thank you." The relief in Henry's voice was palpable, and Ottilie's heart ached for him.

"As a matter of fact, I'm pleased you're coming with us to London tomorrow. We can meet with my publisher before I return to Kent."

"Why should I need to meet with your publisher?" Henry asked.

"Didn't I tell you? I gave him your book of poems, and I am sure he will have finished reading it by now."

Ottilie gasped.

"You *what*?"

"I read your work, and I was impressed. So, I gave it to my publisher, and after glancing through a few poems, he asked me to leave it with him."

"Why?" Henry looked aghast.

"I assume he's considering publishing it."

"Henry, that's wonderful!" Ottilie clasped her hands together.

"Didn't you get my letter?" Henry frowned.

"The one where you asked me to burn your poems?"

"Yes, why didn't you do as I asked?"

"Because you're a *writer*, Henry. And there isn't a writer in this world who hasn't wanted to burn his manuscript at some point, only to rescue it from the embers, minutes later."

"Do you really think he'll publish Henry's poems?" Ottilie had to restrain herself from hugging Jack.

"I cannot say for certain, but at the very least, he is considering it, so he must think Hudsyn's work has promise."

"I don't know what to say—I can hardly believe this." Henry removed his straw hat and ran a hand through his hair.

"There's nothing for you to say." Jack slapped Bastin on the back. "All you need do for now is meet with the publisher."

Henry rubbed his forehead. "I need time to think on this." He took a step forward and then stepped back again as if he could not decide what to do with himself. "If you'll excuse me, I'm feeling rather warm. I have a sudden urge to free myself of these clothes and dive into the ocean." He pushed his hat back on his head and strode down the promenade toward the beach.

Ottilie's chest constricted as she watched Henry march away. "I hope he will be all right," she said.

"He's feeling a little nervous, that's all. Perhaps I should have consulted him before giving his work to my publisher. I acted too hastily."

"No, you didn't." Ottilie turned to him. "You acted out of friendship and with great generosity. Thank you for that."

A sheepish smile appeared on Jack's lips, giving his face the appearance of boyish innocence. "He has talent and would have met with success without my help."

"Still, that was kind of you, and I know Henry appreciates the gesture."

Jack lowered his gaze, giving Ottilie a view of his long, black lashes. "I'm afraid I wasn't very kind to you the last time we talked," Jack said, lifting his dark eyes back to meet hers.

Heat prickled Ottilie's neck. "No, you weren't."

He clasped his hands behind his back and squared his shoulders. "I owe you an apology," he said. "There is no excuse for accusing you of—"

"*Colluding* with Sir Richard, I believe you called it," Ottilie concluded for him.

He nodded and hung his head like a shamed puppy.

"Thank you. I accept your apology."

Jack nodded, and Ottilie had the distinct feeling he wanted to get away and only just restrained himself from running after Henry.

"I must get back to the house—" Ottilie's throat closed. An impenetrable wall stood between them; it pained her to look at him.

"I hear they serve refreshments at Flagstaff, and Palm Bay is said to be beautiful."

Ottilie blinked. Awkward seconds crawled by as she processed his words. "Are you inviting me to walk with you?"

"Would you?" he asked softly.

Ottilie's breathing shallowed under his gaze, and she nodded her consent.

They walked in silence for several minutes, allowing the soft ocean breeze and rippling waves to act as a balm for their past hurts.

"Can you ever truly forgive me?" Jack said, breaking the

silence.

Ottilie paused, trying to decide how best to express herself. She'd already forgiven Jack—how could she not after all that had happened? He was Violet's long-lost brother, and he'd just saved Henry from utter despair.

"I'm sorry," Jack interrupted her thoughts. "I don't wish to press you. You should take your time, and if you find you cannot—" he broke off as though he preferred not to finish the thought.

"When members of your own family betray and injure you," Ottilie said, "it becomes difficult to trust anyone. This week, I had the displeasure of experiencing that myself." She pressed her lips together. "So, I understand that your lack of trust was not personal. That's not to say it didn't hurt me, but it makes it easier for me to forgive you."

Jack swallowed hard as if digesting the bitter parts of her speech. "I know I hurt you, and if it's any consolation, I despise myself for it."

"It doesn't console me to know you punish yourself. We must put the past behind us and be friends."

"Friends?" A note of surprise colored Jack's voice.

Fear quickened Ottilie's pulse. "Promise me you will try—for Violet's sake."

He nodded. "Of course," he said.

"Thank you," Ottilie flashed him a weak smile and fell silent as they squeezed across the crowded Newgate Bridge. They continued their walk along the cliffs in silence, the only sounds to be heard were the whistle of the wind, the gulls, and the ocean far below. Once or twice, Ottilie glanced sideways at Jack, but he appeared to be swallowed in thought. She focused instead on the ocean, inhaling deeply, and clearing her mind of troubling thoughts.

The landscape grew rugged as they crossed a second bridge into Flagstaff. Ottilie stopped to admire the stretch of white cliffs fringed with green grass and dotted with white wildflowers.

"It's beautiful here," she said and stepped forward for a closer look.

Jack caught her arm, and she turned. A crease settled between his brows, and she thought he might be angry.

"I don't want to be your friend, Ottilie." He stepped toward her. "I want to be your husband."

The air left her lungs. "Don't say things you don't mean." She edged away from him.

"I do mean it." He clasped her other arm and turned her body toward his. "I love you." His voice sounded as gentle as the ocean breeze.

Ottilie furrowed her brows. The sound of her heartbeat filled her ears. "You've experienced a tremendous shock discovering the sister you thought dead is alive. You aren't thinking clearly."

"I've never been clearer about anything in my life." He gazed at her as if awestruck by her very presence. "For the first time in years, I am free to think with a clear mind. I am free of guilt, free of pain, and free of anger. For the first time, I am free to choose love. And I choose to love you."

Tears pooled in Ottilie's eyes. Fear tightened its grip on her heart. "I just—I can't—"

"Do you love me?" He asked.

She nodded. "I do," she said, wiping away a tear. "You know I do, but—"

He moved toward her and enveloped her face in his hands. "If I kiss you in public, you may be forced to repeat those words in front of a clergyman."

She smiled through her tears, unable to deny him any longer. "You had better hurry up then."

He ran his hands down the length of her back and clasped her around the waist.

"Am I to be called Mrs. Bastin or Mrs. Greyson?" she asked, looking up at him. But before he could answer, she added playfully, "or would you consider showing your support for women's rights by taking my surname?"

"Whichever name we use," Jack murmured, pulling her closer, "the one I will call you is 'My Wife.'" He pressed his lips to hers, and Ottilie welcomed his mouth, letting it become one with her own.

Author's Note

Like many readers, I am a lover of literature, and part of what makes writing enjoyable for me is drawing inspiration from and alluding to literature and literary figures. That said, all characters in this book are fictional, and none represent actual people.

Lord Byron's real-life tumultuous affair with Lady Caroline Lamb inspired the incident between Jack Bastin and Madame Baudelaire in chapter one. Lady Caroline famously experienced a breakdown after her relationship with the poet ended. In 1813, she grew hysterical after an encounter with Byron at Lady Heathcote's party and caused a scandal when she slashed her arms using either a knife or a broken piece of glass (the story varies due to gossip).[*]

Jack's residence on Half Moon Street is legendary for its list of literary occupants. Albany in Piccadilly is another famous residence frequented by bachelors and artists (Byron rented a bachelor pad there 1814). In *The Importance of Being Earnest*, Oscar Wilde makes Half Moon Street Algernon Moncrieff's home and places Ernest (Jack) Worthing in Albany.

In chapter ten, Jack imagines seeing Harriet Westbrook's body in the Serpentine. Westbrook was the first wife of Percy Bysshe Shelley and the mother of his two children. She drowned herself in Hyde Park's Serpentine two years after Shelley left her

---

[*] Douglass, Paul. Lady Caroline Lamb: A Biography, Palgrave Macmillan, 2004.

for Mary Wollstonecraft Godwin (author of *Frankenstein*). Harriet, said to be pregnant at the time of her suicide, may have been abandoned a second time by her unborn baby's unknown father. Six years after her death, Shelley drowned in Italy when a storm capsized his boat, the Don Juan. Jack's thoughts about Harriett pulling Shelly under the "choppy Italian waters" illustrate his dark state of mind and are not intended to hint at Shelley's guilt.

About the Author

Aviva holds a master's degree in English and has a keen interest in British literature. She is an anglophile and Brontë enthusiast who is happiest when traveling to or writing about England. Inspiration for her first book, The Mist on Brontë Moor, came after she visited the Brontë Parsonage in Haworth.

Born and raised in Cape Town, South Africa, Aviva now lives in Southern California with her husband, two daughters, and rambunctious Yorkshire terrier—named for the oft-forgotten Brontë brother Branwell.

Website: www.avivaorrauthor.com
Twitter: twitter.com/aviva_orr
Facebook: facebook.com/AuthorAvivaOrr/
Goodreads: goodreads.com/author/show/6464067.Aviva_Orr
Bookbub: bookbub.com/profile/aviva-orr

www.ingramcontent.com/pod-product-compliance
Lightning Source LLC
Chambersburg PA
CBHW061241210726
48293CB00003B/860